Death Whispers

Death Whispers

⁊⁊

Jim Malloy

To order additional copies of this book, contact:
Xlibris
844-714-8691
www.Xlibris.com
Orders@Xlibris.com
828789

To my friend James "Bob" Murphy—honorable hustler

When I was at the very lowest, darkest point in my life questioning whether I should go on living, my friend, a decorated Vietnam veteran, asked me this question, "Jim, no one's shooting at you, are they?"

"No," I answered.

"Well then, fuck 'em. Their trash."

It's all a matter of perspective. Thanks for the revelation, Bob.

Although the actions of law enforcement in this book are fictional, at some level, I'm sure, those not in law enforcement believe that is the way it is and to those in law enforcement, at some level, I'm sure, wish that it was.

BOOKS BY JIM MALLOY

Historical Adventure

Raptor's Revenge

Hard-Boiled Detective

Lollipop Murders
Death Whispers
Die, Mother Goose, Die
The Twister
Snake Bite

Jimmalloy-author.com

A special thanks to the technical and content editors Paul and Martha Strifler, my aunt and uncle. Their contribution was the missing link.

Odin, the master of light, peered from the heavens at man's wickedness and awakened his Valkyrie to balance and redeem mankind through the destruction of black souls. She, the maiden of just death was the instrument fashioned from his hand to cleanse the earth from what it had become.

Flight of the Valkyrie

The beautiful maiden started to tremble. Her resting wing tips twitched and then quivered as she desperately tried to remain dormant, reluctant to stir.

But control of her awakening was not hers as the beckoning voice drummed from the heavens. Her birth again was at hand, the command sure. The angel of death would soar for justice once more.

As she stirred from her sanctuary, she wondered how many sunsets this time? How many eras have passed? How many civilizations have come and gone before this summons?

Resigned, she stretched and flexed her wings preparing for her spirit flight. Her death whisper wings thrust slowly at first and then with a thunderous roar, beat the air in perfect rhythm matching every pounding heartbeat at the center of her divine and deadly core.

So, into the shadowed blackness of night the angel of death rode with her fiery sword to wreak her justice for she was fashioned without mercy, knew no mercy, and would show no mercy on her destruction of evil once again.

All hail, mighty Valkyrie

By friend, Robert Smith

CHAPTER 1

THE JUNGLE SUN was wet, hot, and the stench of dung coated the air. Only inches away, the Ghost was invisible to any eye wearing green and black camo grease and bush suit blending him as one in the gnarled growth. even his eyes, cold black, watched natural as any wild thing as the villagers moved about, unknowing, in the distance.

Crouched with the patience of a lone wolf, he let his eyes drop to his watch. He had exactly forty- six minutes to make the rendezvous with the chopper. His eyes raised again to his target. The slipping time did not faze him, waiting without emotion like he was born to it. Sweat bled from his body like a sieve just like the bayou, but he paid no mind as he watched the village elder step from his hooch.

Ghost's mind clicked cold in the zone. His every muscle,

his every nerve, his every thought centered on the target. He watched the old man smile greeting the VC commander with a bow of respect as he handed over the leather pouch.

Not a leaf moved as Ghost raised, nocked his needle-barbed arrow, pulling it smoothly to his chin. Sighting down its shaft, he let his breath out slow and easy as his three fingers, ever so gently, slipped from the bowstring.

The arrow whispered through the still air like the spirit of death.

Ghost quick twisted and collapsed the bow, calmly turned, and disappeared, not waiting for the result.

The arrow pierced the back of the VC commander's skull, punching out his left eye and into the forehead of the elder. The two stood, hanging in death, joined like Siamese twins stuck together by the aluminum shaft.

Finally, their legs crumpled as they slumped slow to their knees and stopped, seemingly at prayer. As the two kneeled in death, the villagers started screaming and babbling, "Le revenant, le revenant." (the ghost, the ghost.)

The Ghost melted into the jungle, allowing himself the smallest smile.

Headshots were his favorite.

Forty-one minutes later, he left the safety of the bush and jumped aboard the chopper for the last time. This was his final mission.

The copilot turned, saying, "Welcome back, Ghost. Good hunting?"

He grunted, pushing himself back against the flak jackets

strapped to the bulkhead of the Huey and closed his eyes. The whoop of the chopper blades beat a dulling rhythm as he laid his head back and fell asleep.

The two pilots glanced at each other and shrugged. It was the same every time.

Gabriel Dupre, nicknamed the "Ghost", was small and light, about five feet six, one hundred forty-five pounds. His bones were rock hard, and every muscle cat strong with zero body fat. His skin, the color of pale dirt, confused those trying to guess his lineage, and his eyes, shale black, seemed born of ice. His primal law, *survival of the fittest*, matched his cold good looks, spelling danger to men and the surrender of women.

No man of any size was stronger, faster, or more wily.

He was pure Cajun, raised in the bayous of Louisiana, who hunted wild things for food since age eight. Except for his family, he disliked people and avoided them as often as possible. Although he understood English, his language, Patois, was foreign to those around him, which suited him fine.

The copilot glanced back again, wondering what made him tick.

CHAPTER 2

MARION LEANED HIS forehead against the cool bars. Two tears rolled down his cheeks and his hands blanched white squeezing the round steel in frustration. His decision was made.

He would take revenge and die tonight.

CHAPTER 3

MONDAY MORNING AND Micky was feeling pretty good. He was surprised. In the interest of good fellowship, he already insulted five of his comrades on the way to his office. He was on a roll. He absently listened to the click of his steps moving down the hall toward the squad room. The smell of Mabel's coffee already permeated the air and his eyes blinked from the fumes.

"Mornin', Mabel. Good weekend?"

The words slipped out and he groaned, immediately regretting it.

"Well, I didn't get lucky," she grumped.

Micky kept moving, taking the topped coffee cup from her outstretched hand and pushed through the squad room door. A fast glance to the ceiling showed the gathering of the usual

Lucky Strike fogbank being sliced by the single sick ceiling fan. His guys were bitching already about the mountain of paperwork that grew over their two days off.

They wore their usual uniform of cheap suits, loose ties, and skinny snap-brim hats trying to imitate Old Blue Eyes. Their fags bobbed wild talking from dry lips while eyes squinted from the curling smoke. The joint reeked from the sour mist coating the ceiling puke yellow.

Micky hustled forward, holding his breath, trying to grunt his good mornings, weaving past the desks. He didn't smoke and was trying to make it to his office before taking a breath, but he knew these assholes knew what he was doing and always held him up for some bullshit reason.

"Hey, sarge, take a look at this, wouldja?"

Micky turned with a groan to the shit-eating grin of Dago, grabbing the report.

"You, asshole," he mumbled.

He scanned the report. It was bullshit and he tossed it on the desk, continuing on, feeling lucky he narrowed it down to just two breaths before slamming his office door and plopping in his swivel. Sucking a deep breath of good air, he twisted, facing the squad room, resting his size twelves, one hooked over the other, on the edge of his desktop. His cubby hole space in the corner with glass walls chair height up allowed him to keep an eye on everyone.

Scanning, he noticed the ceiling fan was still sick. If it went any slower, it would be going backward, plus, this irritating click every third revolution absolutely drove you nuts. Last week, when the needle hit ninety-eight degrees, Cheeks threatened to put it out of its misery with his thirty-eight.

The team still rode high from the last series they solved. the grand experiment was, so far, a roaring success. Micky's team, christened the "Doom" squad, had the best dicks assigned and handled the cases that were too time-consuming or weird. the latest victory was a couple of three-time losers pulling a string of liquor store robberies leaving two people dead. But Micky knew, they all knew, the powers that be could pull the plug tomorrow if they stumbled or created too much heat. Micky, with a low snort, knew that pansy mayor would flinch if somebody struck a match.

He uncurled the *Post-Dispatch* and without thinking, took a gulp of coffee.

"Shit."

He winced, taking his breath away. He cursed himself, eyes watering, for forgetting.

Mabel, their secretary, kept everything shipshape. A retired WWII supply officer, was twice widowed, and tough as bark. After being assigned to the Doom team, she spent a month in the squad room before declaring they were unbearable human beings and shoved her desk out in the hall. She quickly found a long phone cord, lamp, file cabinets, a throw rug, and even a picture.

Micky didn't ask any questions.

She was in charge of the coffee and seemed hell bent on killing them all, probably for revenge. Micky imagined her at home in the kitchen, experimenting with Bunsen burners, beakers, and flasks, creating the perfect concoction to finish them off. Of course, these macho assholes were determined to show her they could drink anything she could brew.

Last week though, he got a little worried when Cheeks said he used a batch of her coffee to strip the paint off an old dresser. Everybody snickered at the comment but pulled up tight, realizing he was serious for it was a well-known fact it ate through paper cups. Kraut swore last month he watched his porcelain cup crack as it sat on his desk.

Micky took a careful sniff. One thing sure, he thought, if you got it down your gullet, the caffeine buzz damn near lasted a full day.

He looked up and counted noses, noticing Pop wasn't in yet. Glancing at the calendar on the wall, he spotted the notation "New Guy".

That's right, he recalled, Pop's training the new kid today, Shamy's replacement. Micky's thoughts mellowed remembering his best friend was killed in the line of duty saving Micky's sorry ass. Six months had slipped by already and he put off getting a replacement too long. He just didn't want to face it, to be reminded. Damn, he missed him, missed him bad. They were inseparable, best friends since eight, through school, summers, first piece of ass, the war, and the police department.

Two peas in a pod.

Micky shook himself, pulling out the transfer papers to check him out.

Joseph O'Brien, great, he thought, a fellow Irishman, twenty-seven, cop for six years. A little young for the Doom squad, he thought. transferring in from the eighth, a solid wasp area, and the opposite side of the world. Micky wondered if the kid ever saw a Negro. the report said he took down three bank robbers off duty.

He was making a deposit when they took it over. Two with shotguns and the other, a forty-five semi, army issue.

Officer O'Brien, like a good cop, followed the rules, which interpreted, said, "When off duty, don't be a hero unless lives are in danger. Be a good witness. It's only their money."

But this heist was a Bonnie and Clyde, a complete takeover. One asshole put a twelve-gauge blast into the ceiling to get everyone's attention as the other two side-hopped over the counter stripping the cash drawers. Officer O'Brien, being a good boy, laid face down with the others memorizing, height, weight, clothing, etc.

The bad guys screamed and hollered as a few customers whimpered. O'Brien lay there, getting pissed.

All of a sudden, a robber screamed at a teller, "Don't look at my face, cunt," and smacked her in the teeth with the butt of his shotgun. the poor gal fell like a box of rocks and good cop O'Brien could take no more.

He sprang to the nearest bad guy, whipping out his four-inch Cobra and smacked him across the mouth. He quick jumped behind him and wrapped his forearm across his throat, bending him back for a shield. Bad guy, shocked. Yanked his trigger, cutting loose a burst of double-O buckshot, shattering the glass partitions at the teller's windows. The other two robbers twisted to the blast as O'Brian, who must have seen it in a movie, ordered the two to drop their guns, *yeah, right.*

They answered by filling their buddy with lead.

As O'Brien's shield slumped to the floor, he took a dive to the side, rolled to a crouch, and dumped three rounds in the ten-ring on bad guy number two. As two gurgled his last, slipping to the floor, O'Brien hot-footed it across the lobby a step ahead of the twelve-gauge, trying to catch him. He launched himself over the courtesy counter headfirst and settled behind the president's desk. Bad guy three, cursing at the top of his lungs, racked his shotgun, blasting away. Papers, wood, and glass flew everywhere as O'Brien, jumped clear, rolled prone, and deposited two rounds in the guy's chest. The third round missed.

Well, nobody's perfect, Micky thought.

Officer Joseph O'Brien was a hero, got a medal and his wish to be assigned to the Doom squad. Dumb shit.

Micky grabbed the phone, punched two, watching through the glass as Dago picked up.

"Pop's bringing the new guy. Is it your turn?"

"Yeah, sarge, what's his name."

"Joseph O'Brien."

"Shit, another Mick. Don't we ever learn."

Hanging up, he turned, grinning, and Micky gave him the finger.

Micky's real name was Jack Delaney, Irish down to his circumcised dick. He earned the handle "Micky" from his days pounding a beat in the old neighborhood and it followed him.

A dash over six feet, he was ordinary looking, except for bullet eyes of steel blue that saw deep and suspected all. He tiptoed the high wire, better than any other, that separated the thin line between cop and crook. His hunches rivaled female intuition and sworn by his fellows to border on witchcraft.

Dago, real name Anthony "Tony" Angelo was one of the few wops on the department because most piss and vinegar-wise guys got recruited into the mob. It wasn't kosher for a wop to be a cop. Hey, Micky snickered, that rhymed.

He smiled, watching him through the glass. Dago was a damn good cop that earned every notch.

Just then, the squad room door opened and Pop walked in with Officer Joseph O'Brien. The whole squad room hushed as Micky started rooting for the transfer papers. There was no way this guy's Irish. He stared through the glass at a tall guy on the thin side with a double black hair crew cut straight as needles with eyes that couldn't decide if they were black or blue. They looked kinda spooky. The guy was Indian red with a beak an eagle would love. Shit, Micky thought, he looks like Geronimo. No way this guy's Irish, no way.

Pop, taking a seat behind his desk, directed O'Brien to the chair on the side usually reserved for suspects. The surprised hush in the room ended, and everyone picked up the pace.

"Let me see your piece," Pop said.

O'Brien looked at him, puzzled. "What for?"

Pop held out his hand with a bored look.

"New assignment, gotta check to make sure you're using issued weapon and ammo."

O'Brien shrugged thinking it was weird but pulled his Colt from his shoulder holster, unloaded it, and handed it over.

"Your hideout too."

O'Brien gave a half snarl and pulled a Smith and Wesson from his ankle holster.

Dago, glanced at Micky, who gave him the nod. With a snicker and a thumbs up, he ambled over to Pop's desk.

"What the fuck we got here? Your name ain't Joe O'Brien."

Joseph looked up slow at Dago. "Yes, it is."

"You're not a fuckin' Irishman. You look like Tonto for Chrissake. You're straight off the reservation. Where you from, redskin?"

Joseph flushed redder than his skin. He was pissed, wondering what kinda welcome was this? Maybe this transfer wasn't a good idea.

"My dad was Irish. My mom's Apache."

He straightened, returning Dago's glare with ghost eyes.

Nothing shook Dago.

"Jezus H Christ, you're a fucking half-breed."

Dago stood stiff straight, showing the flat of his hand.

"How, Big Chief. Ya gottum any scalps?"

At the insult, O'Brien started to rise from his chair, when, on cue, the squad room door slammed open. Kraut was hauling Grezer, acting like a scumbag, by the collar and shoved him in a chair across from O'Brien. As planned, Kraut turned his back, exposing his two-inch, and started talking to Cheeks.

Grezer caught O'Brien's eyes and smirked, looking at Kraut's gun. The next choreographed move was to grab Kraut's gun, which was empty, jump up, and take a prisoner. They made sure O'Brien was the closest, without a gun, to test how he would handle the situation.

Just as Grezer started to make his move to grab the gun, O'Brien casually reached up behind his back and pulled a ten-inch Bowie knife tucked between his shoulder blades. Leaning forward, elbows on knees, his ghost eyes locked on Grezer's as he spun the Bowie, flipping it to his other hand. Giving the slightest cop smirk, he started cleaning his fingernails.

Grezer's eyes popped wide.

"Shit. Shows over guys. Look at that pig sticker."

It was the biggest knife he'd ever seen, and he was Puerto Rican.

Everybody stared quiet.

O'Brien caught their eyes and smiled, "Now about those scalps."

He figured out what they were doing.

"Fuck me, you passed," Dago declared.

They all laughed and introduced themselves, welcoming him aboard.

Micky took a breath of relief. One of these days those assholes are gonna go too far and figured he better tone down their initiations. He hated too though. The initiation built a strong bond and esprit de corps for the whole unit. They worked as one, stood as one, and watched each other's back. Micky smiled, thinking the half-breed would probably say, "We are all blood brothers."

"Eureka", Micky mumbled. He had the answer he was tryin'

to figure. He dialed Pop and gave him the word. Micky had a moniker for everybody on the squad to be used only by the squad. It made them more of a team, like family.

Officer Joseph O'Brien, the resident half-breed, would now affectionately be called "Breed" from this day.

Enough fun and games, he thought, gathering up his reports for the morning briefing. When he pushed away from his chair, the phone rang.

"Sergeant Delaney."

Micky listened close as homicide filled him in.

"Be there in twenty," he said, hanging up, moving to the squad room, banging on the door frame for attention.

"Head's up, homicides got a messy one at Fourteenth and Madison. twelve cold ones at some church, let's hit it."

The room emptied like it had a bomb.

CHAPTER 4

MARION WATCHED THE sun dim from the window in his cell with a sinking heart. Resigned to his fate, he listened to the guttural grunt of his cellmate rolling over on his bunk.

He whispered a prayer as a shiver of fear crawled up his back. He wished his brother was here. His brother would help him, protect him. He wouldn't be in this mess if Gabriel was home. God, please help me.

"Come here, ya little gimp."

Marion turned slow, resigned, shuffling forward. He was hurt, in pain. His rectum was still bleeding from last night. Marion's shame burned his soul. He would rather be dead than submit to that black buck's cock. He limped forward, all hundred and twenty-five pounds of him. His left foot, withered and toed inward unnatural, seemed to drag as he looked at the blubbered hulk standing before him, naked and smelly black.

Marion's stomach turned from the man's stink, his eyes watering with tears. He must be brave. He must be strong like his brother.

The black hulk smirked.

"Come o'here, little lady, on your knees. You be good to old Bubba."

He smiled, excited.

"You be good an' I won't hurt ya."

Marion's eyes locked on the black's cock, fat and standing hard.

"On yer knees, little lady. You lick it first."

Marion froze, realizing what the hulk wanted him to do. Suddenly, his fear turned to a burning rage as he decided how he would die. He raised his eyes from the black cock to the black's eyes and smiled.

"That's it, little lady. You suck it deep. You love it."

Marion went to his knees between the big fat black legs and leaned slowly forward. He felt his bile rise, forcing his head down, holding his breath against the shit smell. He felt the black's meaty hand on the back of his head guiding his mouth down.

Marion opened his mouth wide, taking the cock deep in his throat, cradling the black's testicles in his hands. The salty-sour taste gagged him, listening to the black's sigh of pleasure, pumping his hips up.

Marion's heart smiled as he suddenly snapped his jaws shut

like a gator His teeth chopped through the hard meat, feeling blood spurt in his mouth. At the same time, he squeezed and yanked the black's nuts down with all his strength.

The big black screamed. His bellow of pain echoed through the cellblock as he beat his fists frantically against Marion's head and ears.

Marion bit harder, chomping, gnawing as sticky blood choked him. Sagging dizzy from the blows, he yanked up and down on the testicles, snapping down as hard as he could. He felt the cock meat tear as he was whipped around like a pit bull with a death grip. The fists pounded against his head and ears like a hammer, the big black thrashing around, wild, wailing and cursing.

Marion turned to the side and gnawed the cock with his molars. The stringy meat finally ripped free as the final yank ripped off the scrotum sack.

Marion rolled away on his back, spitting the chunk of cock on the cell floor. His ears, running blood from his cracked skull, blurred his eyes looking up at the horror in the black buck's eyes.

Smiling with a last effort, Marion threw the sack of balls in his face.

Then, his eyes drooped, his world became gray and then dark.

As Marion felt his death, he knew his brother would be proud of him.

CHAPTER 5

T HE DOOM TEAM arrived at the crime scene in convoy and gathered at the barricades while the homicide lieutenant briefed Micky. Uniforms were stationed at the right places, keeping everybody back. The press was acting like jerks. Micky took a quick look to see if Cynthia was there. She was. He couldn't tell if there was a panty line from this distance.

The big barn of a house was Victorian with a garish neon sign, hanging cockeyed, buzzing, blinked red over the front door declaring "Seek Your Salvation." It was in a bad neighborhood and needed more than a coat of paint. Yellowing shades covered the dirt-streaked windows as a flock of pigeons gawked from the roof gutters, wondering who had the food. Two mangy mutts, tied with a clothesline, apparently decided to quit as watchdogs, cowered by the lattice skirting around the bottom of the porch.

It was Monday morning, the sun was up, and the joint looked haunted.

Micky could only imagine what it looked like at night.

Just then, a black cat screeched, hopping from the porch swing. Everybody jumped, thinking the same thing.

Micky, calling the team over, entered the foyer single file. They turned left into the large living room, shadowed gray with stuffy air, hanging with a blood taste. Standing silent, they stared at the death scene before them. The sun, squeezed around the shades, shooting narrow beams of light, letting dust motes show off with twirls and spins.

Attached to the far wall was a crucifix with a young boy nailed like Jesus. Hanging naked but for a loincloth, the kid even had the slice in his side and a crown of thorns. Very realistic, Micky thought. The kid's blood, already coagulating, hosted a swarm of flies that thought they died and gone to heaven, no pun intended. Micky noticed the smell wasn't too bad yet and dropped his eyes to the straw baskets at the kid's feet filled with apples soaked in dripping blood. Micky thought they looked like the caramel apples sold at the fair.

No one said a word, taking it all in. On the floor, placed perfect in a half-circle around the crucifix, twelve male bodies lay on their back, evenly spaced, facing the cross. Their crimson gowns, with pressed pleats, draped perfectly as each lay with hands crossed over their chests. They showed no visible cause of death. Their heads were propped on gold-printed chair pillows and a small teacup sat in a matching saucer at their feet. All appeared between twenty-five and thirty-five, and one body, in the middle of the arch, wore a heavy gold chain with a cross. Probably the leader, high priest, and crazy shit, Micky thought. There was no furniture, rugs, or curtains in the room. Micky gave his guys a nod, and they filed out as the lab team moved in.

Huddling at the cars, Micky told them homicide asked for their help because they were buried with other cases. He quickly made crime scene assignments and the team fanned out to investigate by the numbers. He figured the lab report would take a while.

Walking over to the press pool, Micky did his usual good job of not answering any questions, using his tried-and-true standard statements.

"We are investigating a multiple death crime scene. We have no leads at this time. I will hold a press conference when we have something to report. Thank you."

They groaned and started yelling questions all at once. Micky spotted Cynthia, the only female reporter, knew she was hungry. She wanted to show these macho police beat reporters a woman was as good or better. Sure enough, Micky glanced down, no panty line. His eyes raised to hers and she smiled. She knew he noticed. Her smile said, *You, give me what I want and I'll give you what you want.* Micky thought that another time, another place, he might've done her, but he had absolutely no interest.

He smiled back with that *sorry-can't-do* look, and she huffed away.

CHAPTER 6

ARMY CAPTAIN J. Sanders arrived in country in the muggy evening and was at his desk at 0800 the next morning trying to get up to speed. He shuffled through the stack of reports looking for one in particular. Finally, after some impatient grumbles, it was in his hand. He quickly scanned through it and called his aide, ordering him to find Lieutenant Singer and have him report ASAP.

"Lieutenant Singer reporting, sir."

"At ease, lieutenant, have a seat. What's the story on this Gabriel Dupre?"

As they both sat, Singer gave the smallest smile.

"He's our secret weapon, Captain, a one-man killing machine. One hundred fourteen confirmed kills as of yesterday."

"I noticed his tour's up in two weeks. What's his background?"

"Sir, army intel gave me part of it. He's a Cajun from Louisiana. His mother and father are dead. He was a kid at the time and raised his younger brother and sister alone in the bayou. Later, he got pinched for driving a load of bootleg booze and the judge gave him a choice of us or prison."

The lieutenant sat back, relaxed with a breath, relieved he or his men weren't on the carpet for some bullshit.

"He's a real loner and talks a little strange, but he's smart as a whip, always got his nose in a book. Don't smoke or drink. Sarge and I tried to draw him out but he don't share much."

"How old is he?"

"Paperwork says he's twenty-one, but intel winked when they delivered him. Looks like a kid. He's small and wiry but strong as any man I know, bar none. He pulls a hundred-pound bow like a rubber band. He's an OK Joe, but there's somethin' hiding under that cool manner. His eyes are cold as a snake's. I'd hate to have him pissed at me."

"What's this bow and arrow crap?"

"Well, seems his drill sergeant in basic heard him make a comment on the range. Dupre was hitting two bits at any distance with his AK and said somethin' about a bow and arrow being better. Word worked its way up the ladder, and the CIA swept him up. Next thing ya know, he shows up here."

"Do we want to keep him?"

"Yes, sir. He's saved a shitload of our people. We loan him to intel when they have a hit in Saigon or wherever. He's also the only good tunnel rat in the platoon. The gooks call him the

"Ghost". They're not too far off. the guy's spooky, but he's worth his weight in gold . . . Anything you can do, sir."

After the lieutenant left, Captain Sanders decided to put in a call to his good friend, Stan Levy at the CIA. He wanted to make sure this kid wasn't going to be more of a liability than an asset. He might like killing too much.

An hour later, Stan was on the horn.

"Stan, this Gabriel Dupre kid. I need more info to decide if we should keep him. I haven't met him yet but he sounds a little weird."

"Well, Jack, he was assigned to me for evaluation. I observed and interviewed him for two weeks. He's an interesting character. Never seen anything like it, not even in textbooks."

Stan Levy held a doctor's degree in psychology, charged with signing off on the mental stability of their people.

"Anyway, the kid raised his younger sister and brother since age eleven deep in bayou country north of New Orleans. A family friend, an old Indian, hung around and taught him Indian ways. When he turned sixteen, he drove a truck of bootleg booze north and was arrested in St. Louis, Missouri.

Now get this, there's no record of his birth so his attorney informs him that if he tells the judge he's only sixteen, they'll send him to some camp till he's twenty-one, and his sister and brother wouldn't get any money. But if the kid swears, he's eighteen, the attorney was sure he could get him sentenced to the army for only three years, and they'd pay him so he could send money home.

"The kid took the army deal, and when they discovered his

special talent, they called us. We brought in archery experts and they all said they'd never seen anyone as talented. They said he was what they call an instinct shooter. His depth perception is phenomenal. To give you an idea, if you throw an apple as far as you can, without warning and in any direction, the kid would have an arrow in it before it hit the ground."

"What about his mental health and moral compass?"

"Another weird story. After a bunch of interviews, he said his favorite book was Lafitte, savior of New Orleans because he had the same French blood and fought for right. I read the book that night and found out what his standard for killing was. The next day, a half-hour into the interview, he said, and I quote, 'What's right is right, what's wrong is wrong. I would kill an evil man to set things right but never a woman or child.'

"His moral code is a little twisted, more black-and white, somewhat animalistic. So, in a week, we designed a training program tailored to his beliefs and taught him about the evil of communism, the evil of the North Vietnamese army with emphasis on the evil officers. We convinced him for every one of the evil men he killed, he would be saving the life of hundreds of brave young men fighting for his country and the safety of his sister and brother. We kept pounding the word evil and flashing pictures and telling stories. A little brainwashing goes a long way."

"Stan, you telling me we took a kid knowing he was only sixteen and made an assassin out of him?"

"Now don't get on your high horse. You have to look at the bigger picture. We kept the kid out of jail, and his brother and sister are being taken care of. When he still hesitated to come on board, we made a deal to send the brother and sister five hundred bucks a month until he got out. Bill, the kid had a talent we needed and still do, now more than ever. That's the bottom line."

The captain sat quiet a long moment, silently cursing the evil of war. A lousy five hundred a month for your own private assassin, not a bad deal.

"Stan, thanks for filling me in. I'll let you know what happens."

"Jack, I know it sounds heartless, but sometimes ya gotta do what ya gotta do. One more thing, I studied him and learned what makes him tick. The day he left; I knew he was resigned to his calling. When we shook hands, he told me that when he was young his mother told him that Gabriel was one of God's archangels, who was the messenger of death.

When I looked in his eyes, I felt a hell of a shiver."

* * *

Back at his quarters, Gabriel scooted comfortable against the headboard with his three letters from home. He finished his report to the lieutenant, soaked in a cool shower, and slipped on a cotton tee shirt and cargo shorts. With a sigh, he popped the cap on an orange soda and picked up the first letter, careful to open them in order of their posting. All three, as usual, were from his sister, Angel. He missed her.

He was sixteen when he got in trouble and sent to the army, leaving Angel and his brother alone in the bayou.

She was only twelve. That was three years ago, a long three years that seemed forever.

The first two letters were the usual, hoped he was well; everybody was okay at home; she got the money, thanks, can't wait till he came home, missed him.

Slowly opening the last letter, he thought of old Palo, the Indian that taught him what he needed to know to survive and provide for his brother and sister. Palo, a Choctaw Indian, helped his papa run the still. He didn't talk much and worked for free liquor. Gabriel smiled, remembering his papa saying as much as that old Indian could drink, it'd be cheaper to pay him hard money.

Gabriel was eleven when his papa was killed. His mama, two years back, died in childbirth and his sister, Angelica, took over her job. She was only eight. His brother Marion, six, was a handful and always hungry. Thank the good Lord for Palo. His papa took the rifle with him. They didn't have money for another so Palo taught him to hunt with bow and arrow. So, between hunting, fishing, and planting the small field, they got by.

Palo stopped drinking during that time and taught Gabriel how to hit a deer on the run, a bird on the fly, or a fish in a stream.

As he took a long swig of the orange soda, Gabriel's thoughts came back as he smoothed out the last letter.

Dear Gabriel,

I have bad news. Marion is dead. They killed him when he was in jail in Missouri . . .

Gabriel's eyes never blinked; his blood flushed like a torrent through his body.

> *He made me promise not to tell you he was in jail.*
> *I'm sorry.*
> *I guess I did wrong. I'm scared. Please hurry home.*
>
> *Love,*
>
> *Angel*

Gabriel settled back, cold and numb. His eyes, glint cold, stared at the one sentence. *Marion is dead.* Little Marion, the one with the biggest smile paying no mind to his withered foot. Always clowning, he limped along, doing fine, hating people feeling sorry for him. He always stood tall in his little body with the courage of a lion. He was his papa's favorite as he should have been.

Now his brother was dead.

Gabriel was the oldest, the quiet one, and the strongest. He was the one that helped his papa and shouldered any chore thrown his way.

When Papa was killed, Gabriel was in charge, and Marion tried to follow him everywhere. Marion idolized his brother, wanting to be just like him, but his leg prevented that. Gabriel could see past Marion's joking and goofing around, knowing the hurt and frustration he felt from his handicap.

Gabriel sat straight, pushing himself off the bed. He was head of the family, responsible for their care, and see to it they were treated fairly. If not, it was his job to see that things were set right.

Gabriel rooted in the drawer, grabbed some paper and pencil, and sat at his small desk. After wetting the tip of the lead with his tongue, he started.

Dear Angel,

    I will be home in two weeks. Do not worry. Please find out the information listed below before I arrive . . .

He made a list of the information he wanted waiting for him when he got home. It was a long list.

    I have enclosed some money. Stay strong.

                     Love,
                     Gabriel

Nobody had better not killed his brother for no good reason, he thought. If they did, he, for sure, would set things right.

Gabriel reported to Captain Sanders as ordered but refused the ten thousand re-up-bonus. He also refused when it was raised to twenty. He had business to take care of at home.

CHAPTER 7

MICKY WAS SITTING in his office waiting for the squad to return from the haunted house. With everyone gone, it was nice and quiet except for that fucking fan. Well, at least there were no Lucky Strike thunderclouds.

Reaching for the phone, he dialed the FBI in Quantico. While waiting for his pal, Tommy, to pick up, he remembered when they first met. Micky, in blues, working a beat, got a disturbance call at a so-so hotel. When he arrived, he noticed a guy raising hell with the front desk clerk. As he walked over, he sized the guy up with one word, *big and nasty*. Well, two words.

Micky walked up to his side with his best smile.

"Hey, Mack, what's the problem here?"

Big-and-Nasty turned and cold-cocked him. Micky didn't see it coming. As he was sliding backward on his ass on the freshly waxed Tarrasa, he spotted this guy through blurry eyes, half-back Big-and-Nasty, taking him down to the floor. By that time, Micky was back on his feet and dove in. Between the two, they twisted Big-and-Nasty's arms behind and slapped the cuffs on. Micky squeezed them extra tight, a little payback.

They both stood, sucking for breath. Micky remembered Tommy's shit-eatin' grin and swollen eye with necktie crooked and three buttons missing. He had just stepped off the elevator when Micky took the first fist.

Anyway, after hauling the asshole away, Micky bought him a cold one and they'd been friends since.

It seems ol' Tommy was F.B.I. in town for a seminar and the last time they talked was over the "Lollipop series". He was overdue to rag his ass for old time's sake.

"Hey, Tommy, thought I'd give you a break from staring at your navel."

Tommy groaned. "Man, haven't they fired your ass yet?"

"They can't. I got pictures. Tommy, old pal, I need info on cults, religious ones. Do you guys have any profile stuff or info of any kind?"

"Whatta ya workin'?"

"Looks like some Jesus freak crucified one of his own and committed mass suicide with all twelve of his apostles...I mean followers."

"No shit. Man, we haven't had one of those for a while. I'll put some stuff in the mail today. Also, check with the local diocese and the library. You can read, can't you?"

"Just not big words . . . Thanks, Tommy."

Mabel heard the clatter and looked up to see the seven members of the Doom team shuffling down the hall, hot and sweaty. Shit, she thought, all they need is tiny picks and shovels.

As they passed by, she said, "Where's Snow White?"

Without missing a beat, Kraut shot back, "Home, in bed, exhausted, sore, but very happy."

The others, on cue, marched by, singing, "Hi hole, hi hole, she likes my eight-inch pole."

Mabel just looked at them, shaking her head.

When they pushed through the squad room door, Micky told them to get something cold and form up in the briefing room. Ten minutes later, they lounged, facing the blackboard.

"Who wants to start?"

Spook stood.

"Lab said they'd have a prelim late afternoon. This doesn't seem like your run-of-the-mill cult mass murder. Somethin's not adding up. The Jesus kid died from wounds, and the others probably by some kind of poison. We found a small oriental teacup by each body, smelled like peach pits. Rigor was just startin'. We guess they been dead about four hours. So, one of the questions is, why get up at four in the morning to do yourself in?"

Dago piped in.

"No ID, no money, no cars, no jewelry. They were naked under the robes. Although the outside looked like hell, the inside was very clean. There's a huge calendar on the wall in the dining room with certain dates circled and numbered in no particular order."

Cheeks stood with Spook. He was the resident Viking, pale as chalk with baby-pink cheeks and hair the color of anemic wheat. He stood six foot three with a voice deep as Odin and shoulders to match. He earned his seat on the Doom squad by winning a John Wayne fast draw with a rape suspect.

"They were all males between twenty-five and thirty-five. No evidence of any females anywhere in the joint . . . I mean church. We found a large bedroom on the second-floor empty except for wall-to-wall mattresses covering the floor.

"The overhead fixture had a red bulb. In an adjoining bedroom, we found some queer magazines and pictures in a double-locked closet.

"Get this, there was a one-way mirror with a clear view of the mattress room. The same closet had an eight-millimeter projector and spools of film. Looks like queer stuff."

The new guy Breed wanted to contribute.

"The fridge was well stocked with expensive food along with the pantry, no dirty dishes, no garbage, no trash. Also, we didn't find any clothes they were wearing before changing to the robes, they arrived wearin' 'em."

It was Kraut's turn.

"Did a neighborhood check, not much. The people hangin' there are not near the top of the IQ ladder. They all kinda ignore each other. They never saw anyone comin' or goin' during the day, just evening. It started with just a few at first about three months ago. They didn't see anybody wearing a robe, just regular clothes. The paperboy is the one that found 'em. He was tryin' to collect and when they didn't answer, he peeked through the window."

"Okay. Spook, Cheeks. You contact somebody in the Catholic hierarchy about different religious cults. Figure out how they think. Kraut, Pop, you two go to the library. See what they got on cults."

"The library, you mean the place where they got books?"

Micky gave him a *don't-fuck-around* look.

"Breed, Grezer, I want every stiff ID'd. Cross-check with missing persons, fingerprints, whatever. Dago, contact the city, find out the owner of the house. Get me a profile. Also, copy that calendar and show it to a priest to see if there is any religious connection to the dates.

"Meet up at Greasy's tomorrow, zero seven-hundred."

* * *

That evening, the headline on the front page of the *Post-Dispatch* blasted.

Mass Murders Stump Police

The Infamous Doom squad led by Sgt. Jack Delaney have no clues . . .

CHAPTER 8

ANGELICA READ HER brother's letter for the fifth time and looked at the calendar. He'll be home in eight days; she couldn't wait. She hadn't seen him in three years. After he got arrested, two men in suits visited her and said he was on a special assignment for the government and would be away for some time. They handed her an envelope with five hundred dollars and said she would receive one every month while he was away.

She had never seen so much money. They were rich but she got an uneasy feeling. She didn't like the way they stared at her body, smiling at each other when they left. They refused to answer any questions, telling her not to worry. But she did, every day.

She remembered when Papa died. Gabriel took charge and she minded the cabin and Marion.

She was only eight years old.

When she turned thirteen, their life had become pretty regular living on a low knoll in the bayou away from the rest of the world. Their clapboard shack had a kitchen and two small bedrooms. Gabriel was like the papa and she was the mama. The cabin was very small with only two beds for everybody.

One evening, near dark, Gabriel came home with a ripped cut to the bone on his arm. After killing a boar, he bent to gut it and before its last breath, it snapped around and gored him. She cleaned the wound as best she could, but it laid open deep and needed stitches. He told her to get a needle and thread and started drinking some of Papa's old whiskey. He gulped from the jug till his eyes glazed and told her to sew him up. She stood there, terrified, shaking like a leaf.

"Angel, calm yerself now. Jus' do it like yer sewin' a dress."

"I canna do it. I canna."

"Cheri, here, take a couple of swallows of *Pére's* stuff."

She took a gulp. Her eyes watered and she couldn't catch her breath. the whiskey first burned her throat like fire, but then she felt a warm feeling rush through her veins. She took another swallow, settled down, and went to work sewing the gash tight and neat.

After she finished, she washed and covered the wound with a clean cotton shirt. then, they both took a relieved breath, looked at each other, and started giggling from relief. They tried to stop but started again every time they glanced at the other.

A half-hour later, Gabriel was fast asleep as she started to sober up. She was exhausted as the adrenaline started to wane, but she was also still excited, her blood still pumping from fear and worry. She slipped in the bed next to him, thanking God he was all right. She depended on him for everything. She would be lost without him.

Angel cuddled up, putting her arm over his chest and dozed. Soon, crazy dreams from the stress flitted through her mind. She dreamed her brother was her husband, and Marion was their child. It was wonderful. They were happy and safe, needing no one.

She rolled, half-asleep, feeling hot and flustered as a thrilling feeling started pulsing between her legs. She unconsciously spread herself, wanting more, dreaming of making love with her brother-husband like she watched her mother and father in the middle of the night. She moaned, dreaming, her hand circling his hardness.

Felling the weight of him, she whimpered her pleasure and lifted her hips, wanting his love. She raised and spread wider, feeling his shaft slip into her wetness, filling her with thrilling waves. She squirmed against him, matching his every pumping groan. Reaching her peak, she felt like crying out as both spasmed together, again and again.

Angel shook herself back to the present, thinking she should be ashamed. Brother and sister were not supposed to mate. It was a sin against God. But she wasn't ashamed. She loved him more than a brother. She loved him as a husband.

They continued sleeping together from that night, comforting each other, and she wasn't ashamed, sin or not.

* * *

Gabriel pocketed his discharge papers, walked out the barbed wire gate and jumped in a cab to the airport. There were no friends to say goodbye or wish him well. Operating alone those years, he kept to himself. It was as he wanted it. *"Moi laisser tranquille."*

He traveled light, a duffle bag slung over his shoulder and a long-padded case similar to the ones for pool cues.

Stuffing his gear in the overhead compartment, he slipped into his window seat. As the plane leveled out at twenty thousand feet, he listened to the drumming roar of the turboprop engines knowing he would be home in five hours. Settling back against a pillow, his mind wandered back home to his brother and sister when he was eleven, helping his papa run the still. His mama had passed on two years before while giving birth, leaving him, his sister Angelica, and his brother Marion.

They lived on an acre mound of dirt in the bayou swamp on the border of the Choctaw reservation. they shied away from the rest of the world, including their own kind. Their Cajun blood ran deep with chunks of French, Spanish, Indian, and Negro blood, and their language, patois, was as foreign in the city as they were.

The death of his mama was terrible hard on all of them. After burying her and the baby, his papa went off drunk for a week while the rest cried, hugging each other like abandoned puppies. Finally, papa came home clear-eyed and got everybody up and going, taking care of life. But they all missed her poorly and prayed specially for her before each evening meal.

With mama gone, the care of the men and the cabin fell to Angelica. Papa called her his little angel, so that became her name. She washed, cooked, and tended the cabin while they minded the still, farmed the small patch of ground, and hunted meat for the table. As time settled, their life became passably routine.

One day, he was helping his papa load the skiff with whiskey.

"No, sir, they canna stop me. I gotta right jus' as much."

"What, papa?"

"The big city boys. They's want it all fer them, no sharin'. But we got rights same as them."

In Gabriel's dreams, he remembered like it was yesterday. His papa left that morning for New Orleans with a load of white lightning saying he would be gone his usual five days and put Gabriel in charge. Papa picked up Angel, hugged her tight, gave Gabriel a grown-up handshake, and Marion a fast tussle of the hair.

"It's on you, Gabriel, till I get's back."

Small Marion started crying, running after him, dragging his bad foot, but Gabriel pulled him back, promising to read him a story that night.

It was always scary and lonely with their papa away, but Gabriel put on a brave face. He was in charge. That evening, settling in under a coal oil lantern, he pulled out one of the well-worn books. He learned to read from his mama. It came easy for him and he loved to show off as he taught his sister. His mama had some old school books on geography, history, english, and arithmetic. She also had a thick dictionary and a thicker Bible tucked next to her bed.

Gabriel and Angel liked the parts about angels and the archangels the best and read them over and over. Marion was upset his name was not in the Bible, so they told him he was named after a saint, Saint Marion. He smiled wide and couldn't wait to tell his papa when he got home.

But Gabriel's favorites were ragged copies of *Tom Sawyer*, *Huckleberry Finn*, and the *Cry of the Wild*. He had never seen snow but thought he'd like to. His very favorite though was *Lafitte*, *Savior of New Orleans* because he was a French pirate that helped Gen. Andrew Jackson defeat the British in the Battle of New Orleans.

He would read to them, huddled around the lantern before bed, no matter how tired.

His papa never returned so after ten days Gabriel went looking for him, leaving Palo to watch after Angel and Marion. He didn't know where to start but headed off in the flat bottom for the small Cajun settlement five miles down. He poled along natural, passing alligators, birds, snakes, and even a feral-pig or two rustling in the brush.

When the shadows started getting scary, he reached the village, and they told him his papa passed through but didn't come back this way, which they agreed was mighty unusual.

Gabriel was worried, confused, hungry, and didn't know

what to do. He was just eleven, skinny as a rail, and scared. Kindly Mrs. Jantot, with a brood of her own, took him in, stuffed him with her stew, and told her husband to ask around on his next trip to Black Creek and Garyville.

The next morning Gabriel headed back home with a sack of food. Mrs. Jantot told him to come back in five days.

Hopefully they'd have word on his papa.

Five days later he returned.

Mrs. Jantot hugged him and sat him down with a long look. With tears in her eyes, she told him his papa was shot dead. They said there was a fight with some city boys over territory, and they killed his papa and stole his load saying it was a warning to the rest.

Gabriel just stared off, numb. He couldn't even cry.

"I gotta get home," he mumbled.

"Well, I fixed a little bundle for your ma and the kids. You tell her to come by if she needs anything, ya hear?"

"Yes, ma'am."

Gabriel realized she didn't know his mama was dead. Papa, for some reason, never told anyone. Gabriel kept his mouth shut thinking it would just make matters worse if they knew.

Around the bend, he finally let his tears fall.

He didn't know what they were going to do. He cried for a long while until he got mad, crazy mad at his papa, the whiskey men, his mama for leaving them, and the mess they were all in. Then, his spirit fell low as a shiver of stark fear struck. He cowered in the bottom of the skiff, huddled, whimpering, afraid of any shadow.

Sudden terror of the unknown filled him.

When his despair was the deepest, for some reason, he heard his mama's spirit voice float across the still waters.

"Take heed my son, be strong. Evil is born in the minds of men. Protect your brother and sister."

Her whispering voice surrounded the air, engulfing him, chilling and thrilling him to the bone.

Time slipped by and finally, he stood hard and started poling toward home, numb and resigned, to battle on for his brother and sister. Rounding the last bend, he spotted the cabin, mopped his tears with his sleeve, and bucked up. He stood straight. He had to be strong. He was now head of the family.

It was God-awful tough for a while. Angel and Marion cried their eyes out until he hollered at them. He thought about leaving and moving to the settlement but figured they would split them up. Finally, he gave it some deep thought and realized he knew how to run the still, could hunt and fish, and Angel could still mind the cabin.

Palo, when he heard about papa, set the whiskey jug aside and grunted his sorrow. every morning Gabriel would watch by the edge of the swamp waiting for him to wander out of the misty bayou like a friendly spirit.

As the years wore on, Palo taught him Indian ways with his longbow. Gabriel learned to hit any deer on the run, any bird on the fly, and any fish wiggling away. Palo told him to search his heart for the hunter's spirit. Gabriel didn't know what he meant until a couple years later, tracking a wild boar. Facing the snorting animal, pawing the ground like a bull, Gabriel felt the spirit flow over him and the oneness shared with his quarry. As his arrow flew, he felt the animal's spirit and thanked it for its sacrifice.

When Gabriel turned sixteen, Palo took him aside, saying with a toothless smile, he never saw any brave hunt better. Palo taught him how to fade invisible in the bush and wait forever still as an alligator. His papa's skinning knife felt good in either hand and on the run; he chased whitetail deer for sport, learning to zig and zag just as quick.

Then one day, Palo took him by the shoulders, smiled into his eyes and grunted his approval, telling him he was grown. That evening, with a serious smile, he wished the three a spirit life and disappeared into the mist of the bayou with his jug of whiskey.

He never returned.

Gabriel, now sixteen, felt a full man, strong and clever as any bayou animal. He knew his books forward and backward. He studied the Bible over and over and burnt his father's words in his heart.

"What's right is right, what's wrong is wrong. Damn the wrong and set things right."

That fall, Gabriel decided to ferry his own load to New Orleans instead of selling and trading it for less in the settlement. Angel argued with him not to go, afraid he would be killed. He said he was teaming up with the other men and they were going as one. It was safe and the money would be three times better.

Angel argued and begged, but in the end, he poled away in the flat bottom filled to the gunwales with moonshine.

Angel and Marion stood on the bank, crying.

Five days later, he returned fat with money, supplies, and a dress with a big hat for his sister. The three laughed and danced relieved at their good fortune, even taking sips of whiskey from the jug. Later, with Marion asleep, he told Angel one of the big bosses offered him a job driving a load up north. It would only take three days and he could make four times the money. Beneath the lantern light, with excited eyes, he explained seriously.

"So, with a day down, three days driving, and a day back, in five days we can buy our own mule, or even a horse, a wagon, a rifle, and everything else we need."

Angel suddenly quieted, worried. It sounded too good. She didn't want him to leave again.

They were fine the way they were. She loved her new dress though. It was her first. Maybe with the money, he would buy her another.

Gabriel saw her hesitation.

"Don't worry, it's not right away. We'll talk about it some more."

Two days later, his arm was gored by the wild boar.

The plane hit an air bump and he grunted, shuffling in his seat, allowing thoughts of his dear Angel, his sister, his love. He had never taken another woman and had no desire to. He knew others would condemn them for what they did, but he did not care. theirs was a special bond born out of circumstance and need. After all, Lott took his daughters, to hell with the rest of the world.

He missed the feel of her body against his. The hum of the turboprop engines lulled him deeper as he remembered the hot wetness between her legs and her wanton thrashing, begging for more of him, always more. He craved the sweet taste of her sex as she enjoyed his. They would play and tease until each begged for release. then he would turn and enter her deep, letting her spasms suck him dry.

At that special moment, both felt *la petite mort.*

The jet lurched from an air pocket, shaking him awake. He blinked, remembering his dream and realized he was hard. His watch showed four more hours, he smiled and pulled a book from his pouch.

The male passenger sitting next to him seemed surprised when he spied the title, *The Descent of Man* by Charles Darwin.

CHAPTER 9

JULIE GLANCED AT her watch. It was five to eight. Any minute now, she thought.

She slid the Tuesday morning special in front of Dan, the current beat cop, at the same time her left hand refilled his cup with her famous back wrist pour. She was an expert. She also never used order pads and mastered the foreign language between waitress and cook.

Glancing at the front door, she noticed it was pretty tame today. Cops going on or getting off, sucking on a cup, muttering about their day.

"Just in time, Julie," Dan mumbled through a mouth full of flapjacks.

She smiled, turning to the tinkling bell on the front door.

They were here.

The Doom squad sauntered in cocky, raring for the morning bullshit.

Pop started it off. "Hey, Gill, nice catch yesterday."

"I got one with your name on it, asshole."

Walking his beat, Patrolman Gil was peppered with raw eggs on his clean uniform.

"Didja get bacon with that?" Pop shot back.

"Hey, Kraut, Juicy said to meet here at eight."

Another cop in blue giggled.

Juicy Lucy was the local pro who'd been working the area for the last twenty years.

"At least I'm getting some, Quasimodo."

"Ooh, a big word, I'm impressed."

"Harry, my boy," Cheeks jumped in. "My sympathies. Those hydrants are always jumping in front of cars."

"Fuck you, Viking."

"Damn," Grezer said. "Ya mean he finally took a shower."

Harry, in hot pursuit, missed the corner at Twenty-second and Palm, shearing off a fire hydrant.

Spook walked by Harry and dropped an old pair of eyeglasses on the counter in front of him, smiling phony.

"Maybe these'll help."

And so, it went until they slipped in their regular booths, sliding their coffee cups to the table's edge. Julie appeared with two full pots of the hard stuff, poring with both hands.

"Julie, my darlin', you're lookin' good this AM. Whatta ya got that's wet and hot?" Dago said, giving her a goofy smile.

"What, you didn't get any last night?" she shot back without a blink. three years in this joint and she heard it all.

The rest all sang in chorus, "Mornin', Julie."

As the cups filled, Dago took his cup and slid it back by the window, forcing her to bend way over thereby giving him a peek down her blouse. Yeah, she thought, like that's never been tried before. She glanced at his smile, daring her.

"You know, I can fill that cup, but if I do, you're goin' to be dunkin' those two doughnut holes between your legs in hot coffee."

"Oooh, good one, Julie," they all sing-songed together.

Dago surrendered, pushing his cup back to the edge.

"Julie, how's the sausage patties today?"

"Greasy, as usual."

"Great, gimmee a double order with a couple of butter pats in the middle."

She rolled her eyes knowing he wasn't kidding. She turned to Pop.

"How about you, George."

Pop looked up a little shy this morning. He liked the way she put Dago in his place.

"Just the usual, Julie, thanks."

"How's the kid?" Micky asked.

"Growin' like a weed. Can't fill him up. I gotta scrape plates and take 'em home.

"Is he playin' football this year?"

"Yeah, runnin' back, no less."

"Julie, meet the new guy, Joseph O'brien."

She smiled, catching his ghost-gray eyes.

"Hi."

No way he's Irish, she thought.

She memorized the rest of the orders and walked back to the kitchen with a smile, hearing Pop say, "Yes, sir, a fine-lookin' woman."

The rest of the guys quieted, looked at him, wondering, but not saying a word.

Julie was thirty-seven, the same as Micky. They went to high school together, and she married right after graduation to a guy that liked to use her as a punching bag. She finally dumped him and with some help from Micky, landed the job at the diner and the whole squad sorta adopted her as a sister.

Not bad looking with a Daisy Mae body, she always drew a second male stare, which used to piss her off. Now, she kinda appreciated it.

Fifteen minutes later, she stood in the back on a cigarette break watching them scarf up their heart-attacks-on-a-plate. Her eyes fixed on Micky. In high school she had a crush on him, but nothing came of it. As the years went by, they stayed in touch and were kinda like brother and sister. He helped her out of a bunch of messes and helped keep Billy, her son, in line. It was a shame he messed up. She thought his wife shoulda given him another chance.

"Hey, Julie, need more java."

She sighed, twisted her butt into the ashtray, and grabbed a fresh perked pot.

A half-hour later, the gang of eight marched down the hall to the squad room. Mabel held up phone messages with a bored look as they passed by.

"Hey, Mabel, how come no more sweets from your secret admirer?"

"He's probably dead," Dago said.

With that, she reached down and pulled up a dozen red roses sprinkled with baby's breath and smugly plopped them at the edge of the desk with a smirk.

"He's moved up to the next level."

"And what might that be?" Kraut asked.

"The pleasure of torture," she answered matter-of-factly.

They slipped into the squad room deciding not to push any further.

"All right, guys, gather round. Kraut, you start."

"Hey, sarge, I gotta good one," Dago said.

Micky looked up. "Okay, shoot."

"This copper was clocking a new souped-up T-Bird at a hundred. He gave him lights and a siren, and the guy stepped it up to a hundred and twenty. The copper started flashing his lights, and the guy hit one thirty. A mile later, the guy suddenly pulls over. The copper is pissed but he's due to get off, so he tells the guy, 'Buddy', I get off in ten minutes and about the last thing I want to do is paperwork throwing you in the can. So, if you got a good story, you gotta free ride.'

"The driver quiets and thinks a minute, then says, 'Well, Officer, my wife ran off with a cop last week, and I thought you were trying to give her back'."

"The cop says, 'Have a nice day'."

The squad groaned, disappointed it wasn't dirty.

Spook broke in, "Jezus, sarge, did you see the headline last night. that broad really hates us."

"We wouldn't have this problem if the sarge paid attention to the panty line," Grezer added.

Micky looked up surprised they knew about Cynthia's signals. The rest of the guys just smirked.

"Okay, knock it off. I got standards. I don't dip my wick in every inkwell."

They all glanced at each other with a knowing look.

"Oh shit, he's in love," Dago spoke for all.

Micky growled, "Kraut, whatta ya got?"

"Pop and I went to the library. The librarian started to kick us out until we ID'd ourselves. She apologized saying it looked like we didn't even know how to read. A real clown. After I schmoozed her, she confessed."

He turned, glaring at Spook returning an innocent look.

"She said a certain asshole out of this office put her up to it."

"Did you by any chance get around to doing any police work?" Micky asked.

"Yeah, sarge. All kinda stuff on cults. They all pretty much say the same thing. Some smart crazy convinces a bunch of dumb crazies to do somthin' stupid."

"This one is obviously related to Christianity based on the crucifixion. Also, the way everybody was laid out, it looks like there was some kinda worship leadin' up to the mass suicide. Might be some connection to the twelve apostles. We stopped on the way back and talked to Doc Bigelow, the guy that helped with our Lollipop creep. Anyway, it's his opinion they were all queer and used the place to have their orgies. They also had a lot of guilt and felt they had to make amends, punish themselves in some way."

"So, they zapped themselves with cyanide?" Grezer added.

"Looks like that's the way it's fallen," Micky said. "The FBI profiler says the same. How about you, Breed, whatta ya got?"

Breed stood, clearing his throat, a little nervous being the new guy.

"We identified six of the subjects. probably have three more by the end of the day. the high priest, or nut, is the only one with ID on him. He also is the owner of the house. They were all single, dainty and light, had good jobs. Four of 'em worked as hairdressers. We couldn't find any assets, no bank accounts, cars, property, furniture, or debt. It was almost like they plopped down out of nowhere."

"Spook, Cheeks?"

"Ditto with pop and Kraut, sarge."

"Dago?"

Dago shuffled his papers.

"County records list two other houses in his name. No known relatives yet."

"So whatta we got here," Micky said, "twelve queers, like the twelve apostles, having fun and games coasting the Hershey highway, feel guilty about their perverted behavior and sins against God, offer a sacrifice by crucifying one of their own and then make a toast with a delicious almond punch?"

"Works for me," Kraut said.

Micky quieted, looking out from the podium.

"That's probably it. Dago, check out the other two properties. the rest of you guys divide the names. I want proof our IDs match each stiff. Pop, Kraut, see if any other groups worship the same or related in some way."

He stopped, collecting his papers.

"Dago, anything on the calendar?"

"Not yet, sarge."

"Okay, other business. Cheek's bachelor party at Casey's this Friday."

"Ho-ho, I've been waitin' for this."

"I don't know, Sarge," Cheeks said. "Becky's pissed that you're throwin' one."

"What? You kiddin'," Spook said. "Why would she deny your last pleasure on earth?"

"Because she met you guys. Big mistake. She's pissed I even associate with you at work."

"Shit, guys, I think we've been insulted."

"I take it as the ultimate compliment."

"Shows she's got good judgment."

"We must be doin' somthin' right."

Kraut put his arm over Cheeks's shoulders.

"My boy, this is the first test of your marriage. The question you must answer: Who will be the pussy?"

After the squad room emptied, Pop hung back and wandered back to Micky's office.

"Hey, sarge, I gotta question."

Micky looked up at his serious face. "Shoot."

"I know you and Julie were high school buddies. I'm thinkin' about asking her for a date. Whatta ya think?"

Micky had to bite his tongue. His normal response would be, "*Pop, you kiddin', she's got more class than that,*" but he sensed this wasn't a smart-ass moment.

"Pop, just ask her. Julie's a great gal. She's lookin' for a great guy. Go for it."

"Thanks, sarge."

Micky watched him walk away standing a little taller. He wondered if he should warn Julie in case she wasn't interested so she could let him down easy. Just then, his phone rang.

"Sergeant Delaney."

"Hi dad, it's Cory."

"Well, what a surprise. How Ya doing? How's school?"

"I'm fine, schools great but that's why I'm calling. I need your signature on some papers for financial assistance."

"No problem, when?"

"As soon as I get them filled out, I'll give you a call."

"How's your mom and sister doin'?"

"Fine, Mom says hi . . . She's still seeing that guy, Jeff."

When he hung up the phone, his mind flashed back to the Lollipop series and how close he came to losing his daughter. He couldn't have been prouder the way she tripped up that asshole, a true Delaney. She was taking to St. Louis U like a duck to water, but his ex, Helen, was upset she left the nest rooming with four other students close to the campus.

He didn't like it much either, but whatta you gonna do. She has to grow up.

He sighed, his mind switching to his other daughter, Kelly, married with a baby boy already. Shit, he thought, he was a grandfather. She and her husband lived in Atlanta, and so far, he only had some snapshots. Maybe he and Kathy could drive down for a few days.

His phone rang again.

"Sergeant Delaney."

"Hi, good lookin', whatcha got cookin'?"

"I was just thinking of you . . . naked."

"How'd I look?"

"If you could see my lap right now, you'd see what's cookin'."

"Well, just keep it warm. How about spaghetti and garlic bread tonight"

"Sounds good. I'm on schedule."

"See you at home. You bring the sausage."

Micky leaned back, rocking back in his swivel, smiling. Sharp lady, she understood the pea brains of male macho cops. He and Kathy, a nurse, were an item for six months now. they met when she patched him up when he was nicked by a bullet. He let his mind picture the first time he saw her standing there, pixie cute with big blue eyes and dimples that could crack a walnut. He smiled remembering he finally figured out she was the one that made the move on him, and he didn't even know it.

Anyway, a classy lady with a body that wouldn't quit. She was even sexy in her white RN uniform and her little nurse's hat, but he liked her best in short shorts. He decided last week he was going to ask her to marry him but was scared to death, not about getting married but about her maybe saying no. It has to be unusual, something special.

Women liked special.

CHAPTER 10

RIGHT BEFORE THE plane touched down, Gabriel looked out his window at the nightlights of New Orleans and started thinking about the best way to get home. Grabbing his two bags, he followed the crowd up the gateway to the terminal watching the passengers hugging and greeting those waiting. Wishing for the same, he moved forward.

"Gabriel!"

He turned to the sound and a sight that stunned him. His sister, Angel, ran toward him, smiling with tears in her eyes, flying into his arms, squeezing him so hard it took his breath. They twirled around, her legs up, crying and laughing at the same time.

"*Ma cher*, finally, you are here."

He felt the heat of her body and her warm tears on his neck

as his own watered in relief and love. passerby's looked with a knowing smile at two lovers together again.

Pulling apart, holding hands, he looked at her as never before. She was beautiful, truly an angel, a grown woman with full thick hair falling midnight black past her shoulders. Natural curls framed sultry eyes black as polished ebony over a tiny nose and the fullest lips he'd ever seen. He stood back, holding her at arm's length, not believing this was his Angel.

She laughed, seeing his look and hugged him again. Her petite figure, slim and tempting, poured forth that rare essence that drove men wild.

Soon they were in a cab, both talking a mile a minute, and a half-hour later, she led him through the lobby of the hotel and to their room. He was amazed at her sophistication as she excitedly showed him around the small suite. Her yellow knit dress clung like skin, outlining every crevice, while cheekbones, slashed high under cat eyes, flashed black as sin. Her skin, the color of milked coffee, seemed soft as silk as she pranced around in her stiletto heels like she was born in them. He tried to keep up with her excitement suddenly realizing this was a different woman, and he became sad.

He missed his old Angel.

When Angel spotted her brother walking toward her in the airport, she felt faint, every nerve edgy and wiggly like a puppy greeting its master. Her stomach ached in want, tickling down to her center as she felt herself get wet just seeing him.

They were together again, just the two of them.

But now, in the hotel room, she quieted, sensing his confusion. She took his hand, turned down the lights, and melted in his arms. Her lips pushed hungry against his like all his dreams. His cock filled full, tasting her desire as his tongue probed for more. His hands roamed, feeling her pelvic bone push against his. Finally, like starving animals, they satisfied their hungry lust.

The next morning, Gabriel rolled over in an empty bed and smiled, listening to her soft song over the running shower. His sister, his lover, his bride, they were as one. The shower stopped and a minute later, she stepped into the room wrapped in a furry white towel. She smiled as their eyes caught. Her mischievous grin held him as she stopped at the foot of the bed, letting the towel slide to the floor. No words were spoken. She held his gaze, crawling slow forward straddling his middle. He felt the damp tickle of her kitten hair caress his chest as she scooted slowly forward over his face. Reaching down, she spread herself, and with a sigh, lowered over him, rocking gently back and forth. Animal desire wracked her body as she suddenly gripped the headboard, arching back, as the first spasm of pleasure shot through her. Her baby moans filled the room as her head fell forward, tossing in abandon.

She loved the feel of her brother's tongue inside her.

CHAPTER 11

AT 0800, THE Doom squad did their usual shtick working their way back to their booths.

Grezer started the roll.

"Hey, Dan, yer not supposed to wiggle little Danny at them like that. It scares 'em off."

Yesterday, Officer Dan Shlum and his partner were chasing a naked female nutcase down the street. Dan, yelling and blowing his whistle, tried to get her to stop. When he caught up to her, she tripped and he plopped on top of her.

"Dan, Dan, ya got it backward. She's supposed to blow YOUR whistle," Dago added.

"That musta been a real *wham-bam-thank-ya-ma'am* moment," Kraut said.

"A keystone cop moment," Cheeks finished.

"Screw you, I shoulda shot the broad."

"Hal," Spook said, picking up the slack. "Ya know you're not supposed to let anybody borrow your patrol car."

A drunk had wiggled out of Hal's cuffs and drove off in his cruiser while he was taking a report. Hal was seen standing in the middle of the street, screaming at the top of his lungs.

"At least I caught the guy. What about your savings and loan?" he shot back.

"Hey, the gentleman assured us he was just borrowing the money. Ya know, sometimes ya gotta have faith in your fellow man."

They made it to the booths, sliding across the slick plastic, leaving the crowd yipping and yapping.

"Do you guys have to do that every time you come in here?" Julie asked with her waitress smirk.

"Yes, Julie . . . we do. It's our responsibility," Grezer stated with a serious look.

Kraut looked at her, somewhat indignant.

"Julie, my dear, someone has to set the standard."

She moaned, pouring the coffee and took their order. As she walked away, Micky noticed that far-away look in Pop's eyes.

"I think I'm in love." Dago blurted.

"With Julie?"

"No, this gal I'm datin'."

Micky saw a relieved look on Pop's face.

"Again, that's three times this month."

"This time's different. She likes me the way I am."

"Nobody likes you the way you are."

Dago was the team's lover boy. The ladies dubbed him "Mr. One-Nighter". A good-lookin' wop, he had the smoky eyes and the whole bit. Women had to take a number.

"Dago, you know she'll try to change you. They all do."

"Yeah, why's that?"

"Beats me. Take me for example. I'm the typical macho slob, liar, cheat, leave-my-dirty-underwear-on-the-floor kinda guy. What's not to love?"

"Amen, brother."

"I don't understand women."

"That's because they're aliens," Micky said, adding his two cents.

"Whatta ya mean?"

"Well, you know that Adam and Eve story. The part where God took one of our ribs to make a woman?"

The group nodded.

"It's a bullshit story spread by aliens. Ya know how I know?"

The group quieted, nodding, expecting some words of wisdom.

"The last soft thing I had in bed, I counted her ribs and she had the same as me. Now if God took one of mine to make her, I should have one less, right?"

They all nodded their collective yes, made sense.

"So, it's a crock. Aliens planted the story. Females are from a different planet sent here to screw with us, and I don't mean just literally."

The booth stayed hushed, pondering Micky's wisdom.

His logic seemed sound.

Cheeks piped in, "Shit, yer scaring me. I'm gettin' married in a couple of weeks."

"Better count her ribs first."

Filing down the hall toward the squad room, tart coffee smells caught their breath, making them cough. They passed Mabel's desk noticing a fresh bouquet of red roses. They all thought the same, *Guess lover boy's still kickin'.*

None had the guts to pour a cup.

Grabbing a seat in the briefing room, Micky started by asking Pop for an update. Just as he stood, the phone rang and Dago picked up. Two minutes later, he hung up.

"Guess what?" he said.

"Seems our stiff wearing the high priest getup wasn't Jeff Holmes. Looks like old Jeff switched identities tryin' to make it look like he died with his followers."

"No kiddin'. Where's he at now?" Micky asked.

Dago shrugged. "Nobody knows."

Micky stilled, looking over the room, his mind buzzing.

"Okay, Dago, check his bank. Do another asset check. Kraut, Breed, snoop around his property at? What's the address, Dago?"

Dago shuffled through his notebook.

"One is at 8432 Upton and the other . . . 3845 Ashland."

"Kraut, Breed, you take the Upton house. Pop, Spook, take Ashland. Keep it on the QT. We don't want to tip him off we're on to him. Grezer, Cheeks, Dago, you guys stay on the ID's, get us somethin' solid from relatives or friends... questions?"

A couple of minutes later the squad room was empty.

Micky checked out a little early. It was the day he made his pilgrimage to visit his friend at Resurrection Cemetery. Every month, he visited Shamy's grave, making sure it was trim and neat, and spent some time thinking about the old days.

Standing in front of the grave, tears welled, remembering that day in the dark hallway searching for the Lollipop killer. Shamy, a step ahead, tripped the wire that pulled the pin on the grenade. He shoved Micky out of the way and took the full blast in his back.

Shamy died in his arms. Micky would give anything to change that day.

Finally, wiping his eyes, he stepped up to the gravestone, patting the top like he touched his friend's shoulder.

"See ya next time, buddy. Give 'em hell upstairs."

* * *

"Ah, hell, might as well, it's on the way home," Micky muttered and turned in the direction of his grandmother's beer bar. He was about due for his obligatory visit. Ten minutes later he swung to the curb in front of the tavern in a worn-out neighborhood. Those still here gave up on life a while ago, settling with their fellow losers, waiting to die.

Pushing through the screen door, the three stooges turned with beer-soused smiles genuinely happy to see him.

"Jackie, me lad, top of the evenin' to ya," they sang in chorus, raising their three-two beers like it was holy water.

Finny leaned back on the barstool, almost falling, squinting to look out the front door.

"It is evenin', ain't it?"

Micky grabbed a stool a few down from theirs thinking these yo-yo clowns not only never knew what time it was, they probably didn't know the year. Micky leaned forward, looking down the long bar, spotting the usual beer in front of an empty stool, and shook his head. As useless as these three were, they never forgot the daily offering to their friend Paddy who got drunk and run over by a streetcar right out in front. He was tempted to ask Finny to tell the story again but thought better of it. He knew it by heart anyway.

Sis, his grandma, poked her head from the back carrying a case of Falstaff.

"Micky, me lad, good to see ya... Yer regular?"

Sis was a feisty four foot eleven and a hundred pounds soaking wet, but she could toss a case of beer with the best of them. Plopping it down, she grabbed an iced Coke and slid it down the bar like a shuffleboard ace, stopping right in front of him. It was an art.

"Thanks, Sis, how's everythin'?"

"Well, guess what this crazy SOB here did?" she said, pointing to Finny with her chin, walking toward Micky.

"Ya got me."

"Now, Sis, darlin', don't start braggin'." Finny giggled.

She stopped in front of Micky, serious, but grinning.

"He comes in, pretty as ya please, grabs me from the back,

an' me with a case in me hands, kisses me on the neck an' asks me to marry him. Can ya believe it?"

She turned to Finny and said, "The crazy bastard, he knows he's too old for me, me wantin' little ones and all."

Micky choked on his Coke, nearly falling off the stool. The rest were laughing as hard. Sis was at least seventy-five with Finny in his late forties.

"Well," she said with a straight face and a wink, "he's gotta be man enough to give me at least a baker's dozen."

Micky laughed so hard his Coke was coming out his nose. Finally, Sis couldn't stand it anymore and started giggling too.

"Ya know, Jackie, ya gotta stop drinkin' that stuff. It's got cocaine in it ya know," she said serious. "What kinda Irishman are ya anyway, turnin' down the golden nectar of the gods."

"Nectar of the gods?" He was still laughing. "That's wine, not beer."

"Maybe for those pansy Frenchies, but beer's an Irishman's nectar. We would not be where we are today without the pause that refreshes."

"That's Dr Pepper."

"They stole it from the Irish. It's in the Bible."

Micky laughed again, but this time she was serious. She always quoted the Bible when she meant business.

A half-hour later, he walked out the squeaky screen door to a hearty, "See ya later, Jackie."

He sucked a breath of fresh air trying to get rid of the beer stink and listened to his grandmother declare her usual, "There's a good lad, he's a copper ya know, was almos' a priest."

Micky smiled. they lived in their own little world. He was glad he stopped by.

A half-hour later, he enjoyed spaghetti and garlic bread with his favorite woman in the world. He reminded her he didn't forget to bring the sausage.

Later, hugging under the cool sheets enjoying the comfort of each other's bodies. He turned, looked in her velvet eyes and flushed with love. He didn't think it was possible to find love again. He pulled her close, knowing how lucky he was.

CHAPTER 12

THEY LOUNGED, SHARING beignets with cheese and black coffee on the small balcony overlooking the French Quarter. The black wrought railing, swarming with tangled designs, outlined the French influence from long ago. The air, already thick as pudding, warned the citizens not to force the day as a young boy of fifty-seven varieties, hawked his ten-cent newspapers. His drawling holler echoing lazy off the narrow walls sounded sad with surrender.

Gabriel glanced down at dawn wet bricks with endless cracks and crevices paving the shiny streets slick as ice He wondered how the night sex navigated so tempting on stiletto heels. He shook himself, observing the morning streets were deserted except for those cleaning up after the night souls.

Their hotel, Bienville House, was old and quaint, sitting a block off Bourbon Street, close to the waterfront.

This was New Orleans, the Big Easy, where anything goes, for it boasted *laissez-faire*, as long as it didn't cross Huey Long and Big Daddy, for they were the unanointed king and prince of the city. They controlled the politics and booze, the city's lifeblood.

Gabriel leaned forward, reaching across the small cast iron table, taking her hand.

"Cheri, tell me everything from the beginning, leave nothing out."

Angel caught his eyes. Her body stiffened, dreading this moment, but she sighed, resigned.

"Well, when you left for the army, we managed okay. We missed you terrible but two men came every month and handed me an envelope with five hundred dollars. That plus the money you sent seemed like a fortune."

She stopped for a sip of coffee.

"The next year we moved here to New Orleans and rented a small *maison*. Everything was fine for a while until Marion became restless and unhappy. He kept complaining that he was *rien*. He was upset we were living off of your money and he wanted to earn his own way.

"On his birthday, we celebrated, just the two of us. He seemed happy when he held up his glass of *vin* and told me he had a job driving some *liquier* north for Big Daddy. *Sacrebleu*, we had a big *ènorme* argument. I told him it was how you got in trouble, but he would not listen. He wanted to earn his own."

She sighed, taking a sip of coffee.

"Soon after, he left one morning. He never said goodbye but left a note saying he would be back in a few days. He still was not home after five days so I went asking for him but everyone ignored me. Finally, a *prostituèe* took pity on me and whispered he was captured in St. Louis. I took a Greyhound bus and found him in the *bastille.*"

"*Pouvre ami,* he looked so *triste.* He told me *de* police arrest him with the *liquier.* When they were taking him in the police car, one police laughed saying he was a, a . . . How do you say *sot?*"

"Fool," he answered, feeling his blood start to anger.

"He told me Big Daddy told *de* police he was coming. That why he drove the small load. When de police went after him, the main trucks drove past on another road. They used him for a, a . . . sacrifice."

She stopped, tears in her eyes, and Gabriel remembered when he was arrested. He drove a short load also and the police seemed to know who he was. So, it was the same for him. Big Daddy, too, set him up as a decoy.

"Gabriel, he was *très* frightened. The magistrate sentenced him to the *bastille* for one year. I visited him the day they took him away. Gabriel, he was so scared. They should have not done that for such a *petit* offense. He made me promise not to tell you. He was so ashamed. He made me swear on our *méres* grave." Angel stopped, making the sign of the cross.

"He said he would be released before you returned. I went to the bastille to visit a month later and he was dead."

Big tears rolled down her cheeks.

"The only thing they told me was he was in combat with another prisoner. You know that is not true. He was small and his leg made him afraid to fight, *mon pauvre frère.*"

Gabriel, reached across the small table, taking her other hand. Looking up at him, she saw the tears in his eyes. What she did not know was they were not tears of grief but tears of anger and rage.

"I did as you asked. I *dècouvrir* he was driving the truck for Big Daddy. Here is the name of his attorney, the judge, and the *prosecuteur.* I failed to get a list of those on the jury or the name of the man that killed him."

Angel looked close into Gabriel's eyes.

"What are you going to do *mon amour?*"

He returned her gaze with a cold stare.

"I will set things right."

That afternoon, strolling around the French Quarter, she pointed out Big Daddy's warehouse nightclub. She had watched for several days, acting like a woman of the night, and learned he arrived every evening about nine, always with four bodyguards.

"I was so angry, I thought I would act like a *prostituèe* and kill him myself. But then, I did not know your plan and thought you might be angry."

Again, he took her hand. "I am happy you waited. I will set things right."

At eight thirty that night, the Ghost crouched behind the parapet on the roof of the building across from Big Daddy's nightclub. He scouted the area thoroughly that afternoon and was prepared, dressed all black in a tight-fitting bush suit with paper-thin leather gloves. Black camo grease covered his face as he carefully took his CIA military bow from the padded case. In a practiced move, he took the two halves and with a twist and snap, finished with a long bow strung with the best catgut.

He double-checked the tuning of his arrows, balancing the weight perfectly. They were the very latest military issue aluminum shaft and curled feather fletching. Polished mirror slick and camouflaged, they were fitted with smooth needle point tips ensuring a silent flight. He checked the numbered marking next to the fletching, making sure they were in the proper order.

At nine o'clock, the limousine pulled smooth in front of the warehouse. the curbside door opened, but no one stepped out until the four bodyguards took their assigned positions, glancing around for trouble. then, with a nod by one, Big Daddy stepped out to the sidewalk, arrogant and cocky.

Ghost smiled and in a fluid move, nocked the arrow, knowing exactly where he would place them.

He threw the half brick off the roof in the middle of the street, and as the bodyguards twisted to the sound, Big Daddy bent over trying to duck with his lard fat hulk.

The Ghost smiled, looking at the top of his head, and released his whisper of death.

The arrow pierced the top of his skull with a shlunk, sounding like a stick jabbed into a watermelon. the arrow's needle point sunk through his brain, his pallet, and continued down his throat, puncturing his guts. His body froze for a moment, not understanding it was dead but then plopped sideways like a tipped bike.

One bodyguard rushed to his side. Ghost strung another and let it fly striking him in the side of the head. The shaft poked through like a burning rod, stopping out the left ear. the second guard crouched low, searching, trying to figure out what was happening when the shaft struck him downward on the side of the nose continuing through his throat and out the back of his neck. The third and fourth jumped behind the Lincoln.

"Fuck, Ace, do ya see 'em?"

Ace hunkered down, scared to death, as number three scooted along the side of the car behind the hood. Squatting there, he took a deep breath, gathered his senses, deciding he'd take a quick peek, see if he could spot the fucker. On three, he popped up to eye level, and the death whisper struck him right between the eyes.

Ace screamed, jumped up, running down the street. Ghost's smile curled, nocking the last arrow, sending it on its way. The needle shaft sunk into the back of Ace's head, knocking him forward off his feet. His face ground into the rough cement tearing the meat off the tip of his nose, but he didn't feel a thing.

Ghost turned, calm, broke down his bow, slipped it in his case, and melted into the night.

At eleven o'clock, Gabriel and Angel boarded TWA flight nine twenty-three for St. Louis, Missouri.

CHAPTER 13

"SARGE, WE FOUND Jeffrey Holmes. Guess what?" Kraut said into the phone. "He's started another church. Got the lights up and everything. We saw him go inside. Do you want us to haul his ass in and sweat him?"

"No, which house you at?"

Micky's brain was turning.

"The one on Upton, 8432."

"You and Breed come back to the office."

Micky buzzed Mabel.

"Get a hold of Checks and have him return."

Twenty minutes later, the three grabbed chairs in Micky's office anxious to hear their leader's plan. After he spelled it out, two of them didn't like it one bit.

"Shit, sarge, I can't act queer," Cheeks complained.

Kraut, his hand over his mouth, snorted, holding back his giggles.

"Look, it's not that big a deal. You and Breed are young enough. Go undercover for a day, maybe two. Just knock on the door and tell the guy you want to join. You and your partner heard good things about his work. Just bullshit him. Get inside, snoop around. We need some hard evidence to nail this guy for mass murder. The fact he owns the house and his ID was in someone else's pocket isn't enough."

"But, sarge, if the word gets out around here, we'll be dead meat," Cheeks pleaded.

Breed just sat there, numb, thinking, *all this work to get assigned to the Doom squad, and the first thing I get to do is act like a fag. Shit!*

"Stop whining. This is your assignment. Kraut's your outside contact. Go home and dress right. I want you knockin' on the door in an hour."

"What's right?"

"You know, loafers, open shirts, pull over V-necks, slacks. tousle your hair. Use words like, wonderful, beautiful, amazing. Shit like that."

Leaving the office, Breed and Cheeks moaned like their moms died, and Kraut looked like he was going to bust a gut.

"Hey, guys," Micky said.

They turned, hoping for a reprieve.

"Be careful if ya' bend over."

That was it. Kraut laughed so hard he had tears.

CHAPTER 14

GABRIEL AND ANGEL checked into the Commodore Hotel on Jefferson Street. As she watched her brother write his name in the registration book, she thought how clever he was.

The manager swiveled the registration book around with a smile. Welcome, Mr. and Mrs. *Trompet*."

Gabriel returned his smile. "You pronounce our name Tropet. It is French."

"Of course, my apologies."

The manager couldn't keep his eyes off the young wife.

"We hope you enjoy your stay."

The first order of business was to familiarize themselves with the hotel and every way to escape including fire escapes and freight elevators. Then, he started a general conversation with the desk clerk about various tourist sights and things to do. He casually found out the number of employees on any one day and if they had security. When he walked away, he told the clerk cancel any maid service until they request it.

"As newlyweds." Gabriel winked. "I'm sure you understand."

After seeing the lucky bastard's wife, the clerk clearly understood.

After renting a car and getting a map of St. Louis, their first visit was to Attorney Christian Brunner, Marion's defense attorney. They went straight to his office, not bothering with an appointment, and after some insistence, sat in front of him wanting to know the details of their brother's arrest.

After listening patiently, Gabriel asked, "Who paid for his defense?"

"A friend. He asked not to be exposed," the attorney answered with a flat expression.

"Did you know he was only sixteen?"

"He insisted he was eighteen," he responded, forgetting to act surprised. He wasn't.

Twenty minutes later, they had their answers and Gabriel had the opportunity to case the building, the area, and the offices.

As they walked out the office door, Brunner chalked them up as southern hick trash. They didn't know who they were fooling with.

Their next visit was to city hall and the public works department.

"Excuse me. I wonder if you could help?" Gabriel put on his best smile as the bored civil service employee turned with a dull expression.

"I'm an engineering student and need to do a paper on the mapping of storm drain designs. Are maps available of the city's system?"

"Yes. Five dollars."

She reached down and pulled a prepacked blue-line blueprint in a cardboard tube.

Surprised, Gabriel dug out his five dollars saying, "I didn't think it would be this easy."

"We get all kinds of requests from contractors, construction people, city planners," she responded in a monotone voice, handing him a receipt.

The last bit of work for the day involved mailing a letter to the desk clerk at their hotel.

* * *

At 2:00 AM, Ghost entered a side window, twisted the locks off the filing cabinet, and removed his brother's file. He was calm, taking his time, moving with purpose. He sat at the attorney's desk and found what he wanted; the names and addresses of the twelve men and women that sentenced his brother to death. Then he dug out a copy of the arrest report and stumbled across a receipt for payment from a bank in New Orleans with a notation in the margin saying, "We do not want Mr. Dupre to return to New Orleans."

The amount was two thousand dollars. So that was what they thought his brother's life was worth.

His blood burned as he picked another file from the back and removed the jury list. He noticed they were handwritten and changed the defendant names at the top, switched the lists, and put the files back in their proper place. Before leaving, he broke the other locks, took a pillowcase out of his pocket and loaded it with the office radio, petty cash, a fancy desk set, and a thirty-eight four-inch Smith and Wesson revolver hidden in the attorney's desk drawer. He scattered papers around, tipped over a half-filled coffee cup, and took a bite out of a candy bar and threw it on the floor. He stood back with a quick glance satisfied it looked like a petty thief broke in.

Then he turned, leaving the same way, and melted into the night.

By 4:00 AM, they checked into a motel off route fifty-four just outside Jefferson City and settled in for a few hours of sleep.

By 9:00 AM, after a fast breakfast, they pulled into the parking lot at the prison.

It looked like a stone castle. Gabriel was reminded of the movie in the *Knights of the Round Table* looking up at gray stone turrets with thick merlons, ramparts, and corbels, supporting narrow wall walks.

When the front gate rolled open, they were first in the records department getting a copy of the official report of Marion's death. Before the report was handed over, the clerk blacked out witness names, names of the guards on duty, and the name of the convict he supposedly fought with. Gabriel started to protest but the stony face of the clerk glaring back told him it would do no good. they left, returned to the motel and grabbed a booth in the coffee shop for a cool drink and to plan their next step.

Angel, listening, observed her brother. He was not the same young boy she knew. He was calm, sure, and determined. She was surprised at his poise, the way he spoke with confidence. She felt very safe with her brother-husband.

"What are they trying to hide?" she asked.

Gabriel looked up from reading the report.

"This is useless. They do not list the events leading to the fight or where the fight occurred. It just has the date, time, cellblock number, and that he died of massive head injuries."

He glanced at the bottom half.

"They do list where he is buried. We will visit his grave later."

When they went to the register to pay, Gabriel smiled at the worn-out-looking waitress and handed her a two-dollar tip.

"Perhaps you can help us. My sister and I are supposed to pick up my brother from the prison tomorrow. Could you tell me which gate they come out?"

The two dollars brought some life back in a sad smile.

"I don't know the gate but they always bring them into town by bus and dump 'em off at the Greyhound about eleven in the morning . . . Tuesdays and Thursdays."

They both smiled, glancing at the other.

Today was Thursday.

At eleven o'clock, they watched the prison bus pull to a stop with a final hiss of its airbrakes in front of the bus station. Five men stepped off. the two Negroes and three whites moved tentatively toward the front door as Gabriel jumped from the car and cut them off.

"Excuse me, but were any of you men in cell block even?"

They turned and stared at him, suspicious.

He smiled wider.

"I'm just trying to find out some information about my brother."

He took a hundred-dollar bill out of his pocket.

"I will pay for any information."

A pasty thin white man answered, "I did my time on seven."

"Good, good, let me buy you lunch. After a few answers, the hundred's yours."

Gabriel made small talk until the waitress slid an open roast beef sandwich smothered in gravy-glue in front of the ex-con. Then, he introduced himself and his sister. Hearing the last name, the con's eyes narrowed, saying he would tell him what happened, but the sister would have to leave. Gabriel nodded to Angel and she reluctantly left to the restroom.

For the next ten minutes, Gabriel, quiet, listened to the details of his brother's shameful death. When he finished, Gabriel asked one question in a low and deadly voice.

"I want the name of the cell block supervisor that assigned him to that cell and the name of the man he fought with."

The con hesitated, his eyes raised from his plate to Gabriel. What he saw was sure death. He saw the same eyes in prison killers but none as cold and vicious as the man sitting across from him.

Gabriel pulled out another hundred-dollar bill and set it on the table.

"The cell block screw is Sgt. Al Blevins, a dirty bastard. Yer brother's cellmate was Sam Johnson. they call him 'Bubba'."

The con looked hard at Gabriel. He could read his mind.

"I wouldn't bother with Bubba. Your bro took care of him. The screws rub it in every day, callin' him Mr. Ballis or Mr. Dicklis. It's drivin' him nuts."

The con scooped up the extra hundred and slipped out of the booth.

"I gotta split. Blevins deserves whatever he gets," he said, turning to leave.

Gabriel's mind was working.

"One more thing, what shift does Blevin's work? Also, I need a description."

The con sat back on the edge of the seat, described Blevins and added, "He works days, gets off at five."

The con walked into the sunshine feeling good. With two large "C" notes in his pocket plus two bits from the prison, he could coast a bit. He walked away from the bus depot, heading downtown. He thought he'd get a cheap room and get laid.

It was hard but Gabriel told Angel about Marion's fate. Both were thrilled at his bravery and the way he fought.

Gabriel went to the pay-phone, swinging up the tethered phone book, but as expected, there was no Al Blevins listed.

He smiled, noting a Harry Blevins and dialed the number.

"Hello, Al? This is Charlie."

"I'm sorry, you have the wrong Blevins. You want my brother."

"I'm sorry, I'm an old friend. Do you have his number?"

"Sure, got a pencil . . . It's two-four-five, six-one-eight- five.... Got it?"

"Yes, thanks. Sorry to bother you."

Gabriel hung up and dialed the number.

"Hello, this is Parcel Post. We have a package for a mister Al Blevins but apparently it has the wrong address on Scottsdale Street. Could you verify the numbers for us please?"

The nice lady answered, "We live on Avalon, not Scottsdale."

"I apologize, ma'am. Someone must've messed up. If you will give me your address, we'll get this right out to you."

"It's five thirty-two."

"Thank you. Sorry for the delay but it might not get there until tomorrow."

At three o'clock, Gabriel and Angel stood at the foot of Marion's grave. Their poor brother never had a chance. The odds were stacked against him from the day he was born, but he always was a fighter and tried to make the best of it. With a sigh, Gabriel bent to his knee and cleaned the grass away from the simple grave marker.

Then, placing the flat of his hand on the cool stone block, he whispered, "My brother, I am proud of you. I swear I will set things right."

At five o'clock, Ghost sat in his car down the block on Avalon

Street about a hundred yards from Al Blevin's house. At five twenty, Ghost watched the nineteen fifty-four Chevrolet pull into the driveway and the prison guard slowly open the door and step out.

Gabriel calmly stepped out of the car, nocked his arrow, and let it fly. The needle-tipped shaft entered Blevin's left temple, drilling a round hole, and exited out his right ear. Gabriel watched him crumple to the ground without a sound, now with a three-eighth-inch hole through his head. The sadist prison guard would torture no one, anymore.

Gabriel picked Angel up at the diner and was back at their hotel in St Louis by 9:00 PM.

* * *

The next morning, the con rolled out of the sack close to eleven. He smiled remembering the drunken binge and the redhead split tail. He'd never did a redhead before. She was worth the twenty bucks.

A half-hour later, he cruised through the lobby and bought a paper. The headline of the day reported a supervisor at the prison, a Sergeant Blevins, was killed yesterday in front of his house with an arrow.

"An arrow? That's cool," he mumbled with a grin.

CHAPTER 15

F EELING   SORRY   FOR themselves, they rapped on
the door with dread. Seconds later, the minister opened with
a warm smile.

"Good afternoon, welcome."

"Uh, hello . . . Reverend. My name is Joseph and this is my
friend Bobby. We heard about your new church . . . and . . ."

Breed and Cheeks stood nervous, looking like a couple
of fresh preppies thinking the same thought, *I'd rather be in a
gunfight to the death.*

"Come in, come in. Welcome, friends."

Jeffrey Holmes's smile turned wider.

"Let me give you a little tour and tell you about our special
faith."

Jeffrey smiled inside, sizing up his two new parishioners. His day was complete. These two queers made twelve. I can move my special service up a week. I will observe for myself their sin against God and nature and dispense the ultimate penance.

God's will be done.

Two hours later, Cheeks and Breed sat across from Micky's messy desk, briefing him. But, first, they ran home to change back into their straight clothes and felt much better.

"Well, whatta ya got?"

"Sarge, the setup's exactly the same; the whole joints clean. The living room's bare except for twelve cushions, same print with small teacups and saucers. There's a big wooden cross, empty, hangin' on the wall. It was big enough to hold a body."

Cheeks piped in, "The place is spooky. The same purple curtains with all the shades pulled down. there was some kinda slant-eye music playin' soft and enough incense ta gag ya."

Breed continued, "Mister Swishy showed us the room upstairs with the wall-to-wall mattresses, saying it was their meditation space to experience complete rapture. I looked at Cheeks thinkin', Yeah, sure, I bet it's not spiritual rapture. The one wall had a built-in one-way mirror. He didn't show us any other rooms except the kitchen which was just ordinary."

"Somethin' we couldn't figure though," Cheeks said. "Holmes looks straight arrow. Looks like a truck driver. Big, husky, kinda burly, and a regular voice. Looked like my uncle.

"No doubt though, it's the same operation. I asked how many parishioners he had and he said it was a blessed day. With us, he had twelve, the same number as the disciples of Jesus."

* * *

Reverend Jeffrey Holmes was ecstatic. He now had his twelve sinners. He would observe and verify their perversion and then cleanse their souls with a special devotion before sending them to God so they would sin no more. He smiled, remembering the look they gave each other showing them the mattress room. He knew what nasty perverted thoughts they had. He knew every one of them.

As he puttered around making sure everything was in order, a niggling thought nipped at him. There was something different about those two. They looked butch enough, but he noticed they never stood close to each other. They never held hands or any show of affection while he gave them a tour.

He shrugged. They were probably a little nervous. One thing for sure, he didn't miss the look they gave each other visiting the mattress room. No matter, those perverted queer bastards would meet their maker like all the others.

The thought stirred him so he decided to retire to his bedroom to study. Thirty minutes later, he lay naked on his bed with the eight-millimeter projector whirring. After he chose his favorite male porno magazine from the stack, he sighed, plumped the pillow behind his head, and glanced up at the naked men on the screen.

* * *

"What's the next step, sarge?"

"When did he tell you to come back?"

"This Saturday, to pick up our vestments. He said they were gonna hold a special service Sunday evenin'."

"Sunday?...that gives us just two days. Get more history on this guy. I want everything, criminal, civil, bank accounts, family, occupation. I want it all by end of day.

"That gives us a day to plan and maybe get a search warrant. He just might be planning to off his fairy followers this Sunday."

"Should we go back to pick up the robes?"

"Maybe, first let's see what shakes out."

CHAPTER 16

"CHERI, I WANT you to go back to New Orleans and wait for me. It is too *dangereux*."

Angel rolled over. She knew he was suffering. He was the family protector since a young boy. It was tearing him apart he did not save Marion and he did not want anything to happen to her.

"But I can help. He was my brother too. I was also his protector and I also want vengeance. *Plaire á*, Gabriel, do not send me away," she said, tears rolling down her cheeks.

Propped on his elbow, he looked into her wet eyes and pulled her into his arms.

"*Mon amour*, we will do this together."

An hour later, spreading the map of the city and drain system side by side, they outlined a plan of action. Gabriel smiled, watching Angel's concentration, taking notes, making a list of the remaining targets in the order of their death.

That afternoon, they purchased a compass, a collapsible baby buggy, and a used green panel truck. The rest of the day was spent checking addresses and workplaces of everyone on the list.

Tomorrow, the reckoning would start.

Both woke early, their thoughts anxious about their mission. Angel lay there, spooned against Marion's back, afraid and excited at the same time. Her body flushed with fever as her heart thrummed. It was the same when her brother was gored and she sewed his arm. She needed relief from the edgy fear pulsing through her body.

Gabriel, sensing her need, rolled toward her. His hand petting her belly, coasting down to her wetness.

By seven thirty, they were following Harry Olmsted, jury foreman, driving to work. patiently, they watched him park his car and walk to the front door of his real estate office bearing his name proudly across the front.

At the same time, Gabriel parked at the curb about fifty yards away and as planned, told Angel to open the back doors of the van. As she jumped out, Ghost climbed over the seat to the back, sat down, and strung his bow.

When Angel opened the doors, Ghost had a clear shot out the back. He smiled as the four sides of the van centered his target like a picture frame.

Like Vietnam, like a light switch, his mind clicked. With

a silent breath, he pulled his arrow full length, holding just a moment before loosed. His three fingers then released and the death whisper flew. The slick needle shaft pierced the back of Harry's head, continued through his forehead, and disappeared inside his office. Harry crumpled gently forward like he was just going to lie down.

Angel closed the doors, hopped in front, and they drove off.

At noon, Angel entered Bettendorf's grocery store and asked to speak to the manager, Mr. Danberry. As he approached, she studied him close.

"Yes, ma'am, can I help you?"

He smiled, noticing how sexy she looked, petite, velvet eyes, hot body. Her tits could poke your eyes out.

She smiled.

"A friend of mine said to ask for you. You might have a job opening?"

He frowned with true regret.

"I'm sorry, not right now. But why don't you take an application and bring it back."

He bent to reach under the counter making sure he took a good look at her tanned legs and great ass.

He straightened with a smile.

"I get off at five and I could review it with you. I'll buy you a drink."

Angel smiled, hating him for what he did to her brother.

Five minutes later, she pushed out the front door, walked quickly down the street, and jumped in the front seat of the panel van with a curse, "*Le cochon* leaves work at five. He invited me to meet him."

"*Bein*, we will park over there. When he leaves work, you will wait at the corner and when he shows his face, call his name. I will take care of the rest.

"When he falls, walk around the corner and keep walking. I will pick you up, *comprendez*."

Angel nodded, wishing she knew how to shoot the bow and arrow.

At five, as planned, Angel moved into position.

Mr. Danberry walked out of the grocery store with four of his employees, looking around hopefully. planning for the best, he called his wife telling her he had to work late. Just then, he heard his name and turned, spotting Angel standing on the corner. He smiled. His last thought pictured her naked.

The needle-arrow hit him in the left eye and exited out the back of his head, disappearing into the empty lot.

The small hole bled very little.

The four female employees screamed.

That evening, brother and sister celebrated with a delicious meal and a fine cabernet.

*   *   *

The desk clerk opened the letter and three twenty-dollar bills fell out. The letter said,

Dear Sirs:

Please reserve room 365 for Mr. and Mrs. Marion Mortel starting on the date this letter is received. This particular room is important to us as we are celebrating our tenth wedding anniversary and we stayed in that room on our honeymoon. We may be a few days late in arriving but be sure to save it for us.

Sincerely,
M. Mortel

The desk clerk did some fast thinking. The room the Mortels want is right next door to the Tropets. They were ten vacancies on that floor, and he wanted one right next to them. What were the odds. Well, if necessary, he would move the Tropets when the other couple arrived. Until then, he would just keep the sixty dollars in his pocket and have the Mortels register on his other registration book, the one the owner didn't know about. He was tired of that jerk getting rich for not doing a damn thing.

CHAPTER 17

MICKY STOPPED AT Mabel's desk on his way to the coffee shop.

"Mabel, Cory's comin' down to get some papers signed. If I'm not back, send her over to Greasys."

At 2:00 PM, Greasys was quiet. The only customers were the Doom squad sitting in their usual booths.

Micky eyeballed Cheeks and Breed.

"So, what do you have on twinkle toes?"

"I'm bettin' he's not gay, sarge," Cheeks said. "Remember the preacher that started the crusade against queers about five years back?"

Micky frowned, trying to place it.

"Remember, he was preaching that all queers should be stoned and a bunch of guys rocked a queer bar?"

"Anyway, that's our guy's pappy. If he was queer, his old man woulda' killed him."

"What's the angle then?"

"Not real sure but it could be he just robs and murders 'em."

Micky thought a minute.

"This is what I want you guys to do. Go back Saturday to pick up your dresses,.. I mean robes."

The rest of the crew started chuckling, watching Cheeks and Breed turning red.

Micky smirked. He couldn't resist.

"One of you get him upstairs while the other one asks to use the head. Snoop around, see if you can find somethin' to cinch a search warrant. poison, ID from the dead guys, blood on clothes, jewelry, anything. I'm gonna call our shrink. Maybe he's got an angle."

Micky, sitting with his back to the front, heard the tinkle of the bell on the door. He watched Dago, Cheeks, Kraut, Grezer, and Breed freeze with a stare.

"Damn, don't look now. I'm in love."

"Too late, my dick's already hard."

"Oh, honey, come over here and sit on my face."

"Shit, she's comin' over. Me first. I hate sloppy seconds."

Micky turned to see what the furor was all about.

"Hi, Dad."

"Oh, 'Hi', Cory."

He glared across the table, slipping out of the booth, leading her back to the front.

The guys' faces bleached white as the sugar on the table. Groaning in unison, they slipped lower in the booth. The ones that didn't shoot their mouth off thanked God for his mercy.

"Oh, my god. We're dead."

"Whatta we do."

"Jezus, this is bad, real bad. What do we do?"

"Damn, does he have his gun with him?" "Jezus, this is bad."

A few minutes later, Micky walked slowly back to the booth with a flat expression. He was going to milk this till the cow's tits wilt.

"Sarge, we're really sorry. We didn't know she was your daughter."

"Chris, I feel like cutting my tongue out."

"Sarge, you know we were just bull-shittin'. We're really sorry."

Micky couldn't hold it anymore and started laughing. They looked dumbstruck, responding with a sheepish grin.

"You assholes, the look on your mugs was classic."

"You're not pissed?"

"What for? You didn't know she was my daughter. She couldn't hear you. I already know you perverts are harmless. And....I'd rather hear those comments of admiration than something like put a bag over her head or hand me my ugly stick."

The group gave a collective sigh of relief.

"Thanks, sarge," Kraut said. "She really is a beautiful young lady. You must be proud."

"I am."

Just then, Julie came over and told Micky Mabel called. Captain Barnes was trying to find him. they have a couple of fresh bodies. The team started dropping money on the table, sliding out of the booths, heading out the door.

Captain Barnes and Lieutenant SS were waiting in his office as Micky hot-footed it through the squad room. Barnes, Micky's boss, a good guy, was going to retire in about two months. That was probably why he was letting his handlebar mustache curl like a whip. He reminded Micky of the bad guy in black saying curses standing over the sexy broad tied to the railroad tracks.

On the other chair, sat good old Lieutenant SS, short for *Suck-up Sutton*, real name Stanley Sutton, the department joke and the resident Nazi. Prancing around in his crisp uniform like a storm trooper, he was a cop only because his daddy knew the mayor. Micky suddenly had a sick feeling. What if they promote the asshole and Micky has to work for him? If that happened, he swore right there he'd head for the San Diego beaches.

"Whatta we got?" Micky asked.

"We got two dead guys," Barnes huffed. "One in the morning, one late afternoon. No connection or relation except the wounds are the same. A small hole in and out through the skull. Homicide wants your team to respond to Bettendorf's, Taylor and Greer."

Micky grabbed his jacket, moving to the doorway.

"Guys, saddle up. We got a hot one. everyone at Bettendorf's grocery, Taylor and Greer."

Hustling out the door, Mabel, holding the phone.

"It's your daughter."

Micky grabbed the phone, thinking he forgot to sign something.

"Yeah, Corey?"

"Dad, I just wanted to tell you to never let me come down there again, for any reason."

"Why?"

He knew she couldn't hear those dip-shits.

"Just the look on their faces. I felt naked."

"Okay, I'm sorry. They didn't mean anything. They're harmless. They're really good guys."

"Maybe so, but never again, okay?"

"Yep, no problem. Sorry if you were embarrassed."

Handing the phone to Mabel, she had a look that could kill.

"I know, Mabel, we're pigs," he said, stomping off after his herd of swine.

The Doom squad arrived at the homicide scene at Bettendorf's at five thirty. The sun casted evening shadows as the homicide sergeant briefed Micky. Fifteen minutes later, he called the team over to take a look at the wound and make a cursory check of the area before the lab took over. Soon, they retreated to their cars, waiting for their assignments. As Micky walked over to join them, he glanced at the press, huddling, wanting a scoop.

Cynthia, front and center, no panty line, caught Micky's eye with come on smile.

As one, they started yelling questions.

"Here's what we got so far. One, a white male, Stanley Danberry,

forty-six, store manager, shot in the head when he left work. The exit wound is the same size as the entry. That's a new one for me. Two, no one heard a shot and there were four coworkers within five feet. Three, just before he got his ticket punched, a female on that corner over there called his name. She disappeared. Four, one witness clerk said she thought it was the same woman that stopped in earlier asking for him by name about a job. She's described as small, petite, dark, guys say sexy, women say attractive."

He smirked, thinking that's what he wanted to say if the pack of press was honest and had a little class, but nooooo…. They're all blood sucking assholes.

Facing them, holding the flat of his hands up, legs planted, he barked, "Quiet,… this is what we got. One white male is dead from a head wound. Our investigation is continuing. I will hold a press conference tomorrow. Thank you."

The press mob, yelling, expressed their unhappiness with a distant comment from the middle of the group.

"You're an asshole Delaney."

Micky walked away with a grin and a backhand wave, thinking, *he still had it.*

Micky made the assignments and an hour later was sitting in his office, pushed back in his swivel. He closed his eyes, a habit he always practiced, wanting the facts to cook quietly, figuring how they mix, and see what stays on the plate.

So far, he couldn't figure it. No gunshot noise, coulda been a silencer which means the killer was a pro, but exit wounds always leave a big hole. Coulda been a high-velocity steel jacketed bullet. that would account for the neat hole through and through.

How did the young woman fit? Was she just a coincidence? If so, how come she didn't stick around.

Just then, Mabel tapped on the doorframe, jerking his mind back.

"Sorry, sergeant, but I thought you would want these right away."

Stepping forward, she dropped the preliminary homicide reports on his desk from the real estate office that morning.

"How's your daughter?"

"She's fine. It was just a misunderstanding."

She humphed with a dirty look, and walked out the door.

Micky scanned the report noting the wound was the same, no gunshot heard. There were no witnesses, also no dark-haired woman. Micky closed the file knowing they were connected. It was a sense all good cops developed. He knew as soon as they connected the link, they'd have the killer.

An hour later, the team formed up in the briefing room and Micky filled them in on the church murders.

"Kraut, Breed, you two get me a full history on number one, Jeffrey Olmstead. Spook, Pop, you take number two, Stanley Danberry. Grezer, Cheeks, you go over the crime scene on Olmstead. Take a fresh look. Dago, contact the witnesses again on Danberry, work em dry."

Micky looked out from the podium.

"Any other questions or ideas?"

The seven sat quiet.

"Okay, go get 'em. Remember, Cheeks's bachelor party at Casey's tonight. Let's move it to nine so you'll have more time."

At six, Micky telephoned Kathy.

"Hi, good lookin', got bad news. I can't make dinner. We're workin' two cold ones that are really strange and Cheeks' bachelor party at nine."

"Welllll…,Looks like I'll have leftover spaghetti since you have the sausage with you."

Micky chuckled. God, he loved that woman.

"Don't despair. I'll get home early enough so it won't get cold."

"I'll probably be asleep. I have an early shift tomorrow."

It hit him between the eyes. He had the perfect way to propose.

"What time is your lunch?"

"At eleven."

"I'll come over and share a sandwich."

"Great, what's up?"

"A surprise."

He hung up, pushing back in his chair with a sneaky grin. He'd buy a dozen roses and surprise her at the nurses' station with all her friends and get down on one knee and ask her to marry him. Women liked that corny stuff.

All of a sudden, his stomach tumbled. He felt nervous and panicky. Opening his desk drawer, he pulled out the velvet box, flipping it open, twisting it a bit to catch the light on the diamond.

He suddenly wished it was bigger.

He swallowed hard. Tomorrow's the day, chickenshit, no excuses.

CHAPTER 18

A NGEL AND GABRIEL settled in for the evening, pleased with their campaign. They pulled out their hit list and crossed out Big Daddy, the prison guard, and two on the jury. That left four men on the jury, the judge, the prosecutor, the defense attorney, and the police informant.

"We will continue to hunt the remaining four on the jury first. That will keep the police guessing because they will have a difficult time finding a pattern or connection. Speed is more important than choosing the easiest method to strike. We must strive to do at least one a day because once we strike the judge or attorneys, they will connect our actions to Marion's death.

"We will save them for last."

He stopped and unrolled the blueprints of the storm drain system on the bed, laying the city map next to it.

"Hand me the list of names and addresses *s'il vous plait*."

Angel passed the papers leaning on her elbows across the mattress. As her brother studied, she gazed at him, admiring his determination and knowledge to defeat their enemies. *Père* and Palo taught him well. She would pray for him although she knew God abandoned them once they coupled. She sighed, resigned to her sin, knowing she could not resist him.

"It was a good day, *cheri*, but every day will be more difficult."

Covering his hand over hers, he caught her serious eyes.

"I am happy you are here with me. It gives me courage."

She smiled, feeling full, feeling needed.

That night, Gabriel lay restless, listening to his sister's innocent sleep as his thoughts moved to tomorrow's hunt. Staring at the ceiling, he pictured the storm drain system in relation to the city streets, remembering the first time he hunted the enemy underground.

New to Vietnam, he was the new boot on a routine search and destroy mission when the sergeant discovered an enemy tunnel. The sergeant, huddling his men close, knew if they continued forward, the gooks in the tunnel would surface and attack from the rear.

Crouching down with the rest, he said, "I need a volunteer."

Scanning each face, everyone stayed quiet. They knew better and would take their chances they wouldn't be chosen.

"What for, Sergeant?" Gabriel asked.

"A tunnel rat," he said, sizing Gabriel up. He was small

enough and dumb. Somebody's gotta go, it might as well be him.

"What is that?" Gabriel asked.

The sergeant explained and five minutes later Gabriel, stripped to his waist, lowered himself into the narrow tunnel, knife in teeth. Gabriel, flash-backed to the bayou, the total black and dank air surrounding him as he crawled slow forward. The sides of the earth scraped against his body in the dirt tube, ears tuned to the slightest sound. His breaths sounded like a wind tunnel and his knees scraped the earth like a dragging bulldozer.

Gabriel's only question before volunteering was.

"No women or children down there? Just evil men?"

Crawling, his senses sharp as the wild animals he hunted in the bayou. He felt strangely at home, calm, hunting prey in the wild, determining its master, the survival of the fittest.

Suddenly, stopping, alert, his nose flared, smelling the evil men. His muscles, blood hardened, and scrotum, sucked up close to his body.

Continuing forward, cat quiet, eyes straining against the black, ears perked sharp, he heard soft mumbling just ahead. Adrenaline cursed through his body like a drug, making every nerve raw and ready.

An unconscious smile turned. His every breath, every presence, and every fingernail scratching the dirt, flowed through his senses.

When the attack came, he charged forward, the thrill of danger consuming him like an orgasm.

The death of the two evil men went quickly. Their frightened and feeble attempts at defense were easily overcome.

He was disappointed.

His thoughts drifted back to his hotel room. He pulled his sister close, remembering happy memories of his brother.

CHAPTER 19

T HEY AMBLED THROUGH the front door, mouths watering for a cool one.

"Hey, Casey!" they chimed as one.

"Yo . . . the back's all set up."

Casey, a retired cop, a while back, took a bullet in the belly. After cutting out a bunch of guts, he had to take a medical. But he missed the guys so he bought this broken-down beer bar and put the word out.

Business was good.

The joint had a small room off to the side from the back door, closed off by a curtain for these *special* events. A couple of tables were set up with cards, poker chips, peanuts, chips, and dip. Just to be corny, he added a bunch of balloons.

Thirty minutes later, with two beers each, the party was in full swing.

"How about some penny-ante here?" Kraut, hollered over the buzz, jamming a cheap stogie in his mouth.

"I'm in if it's real poker, not this joker, one-eyed jacks, deuces wild crap," Pop said, grabbing a chair.

"Fuckin' Cardinals lost again," Kraut grunted, plopping down and started shuffling.

"I heard Stan was three for three, homered one?"

"The other eight ain't worth shit," Kraut added.

Kraut played triple-A ball before he got married, had a kid, and had to get a real job. At least that was his excuse. Now divorced, he since put on an extra fifty pounds. Cue-ball bald with zero neck, his eyes sat close separated by a skinny nose topped off by a bulbous tip. His bull chest and stubby legs sealed his image of a ticked-off gorilla.

Dago looked at Cheeks downing his third and pulled Micky and Grezer aside.

"Sally said she'd stop by around eleven and wiggle her tits in his face, but if we want extra, it'll cost."

"What, you don't have a coupon?" Micky asked.

"Does she give green stamps?" Grezer asked, thinking, hell, free wiggling tits ain't bad.

"We get to see 'em, don't we?"

Grezer didn't get many nights out. He was the only Spic on the department and the only one with a solid marriage with five boys, but that didn't mean he didn't like looking at a strange pair of wiggling tits when he could.

He looked like a bad guy dope dealer with shifty eyes and a nose that punched too many fists. But he was a hell of a scrapper in any fight.

Just then, Spook climbed on a chair, raising his arms.

"Cheeks, my son, step over here… Hey, you assholes, quiet down, I gotta say this before Cheeks gets drunk and can't remember this special moment."

Everybody hushed, waiting for words of wisdom.

"This is the time to toast the poor bastard and give him our sympathies for this night is his last, the very last. He has grown from baby to child, to boy, to teenager, to young man, to cop, and to asshole. Now he crosses over to the other side and leaves his balls behind. Our salute to an asshole lost. We mourn him for he could have been the biggest one of all."

"Hear, hear," the rest answered in chorus, lifting their mugs for a toast.

"Jeez, Spook, that was beautiful," Kraut said, half-drunk, getting sentimental.

Micky, thinking he saw a tear in his eye, clinked his Coke against Pop's mug.

Just then, a moth the size of a canary invaded the room and started flitting around the light hanging over the poker table. No one paid any attention until Grezer snatched it, stuffed it in his mouth and started chewing.

"Damn, Grezer, that's gross."

The rest made revolting faces as he opened his mouth to show the wings still fluttering.

"Jezus, yer gonna make me puke."

He smiled, continuing to chew with his mouth open so they could hear the crunching and cracking. He finished with a smile, washing the remains down with a swig of beer.

"Ya know, they taste better with a little ketchup."

"That's top sirloin in Puerto Rico," Pop said, throwing a nickel in the pot.

Out front, Casey swiped his bar rag over the bar top, smiling at their bullshit, wishing he could close up and join them. Just then, the front door pushed open and twelve members of the Mongol motorcycle club ambled in. All wore full leathers including leather hats with a cross-bone badge and black jackets sporting the half-moon Mongol name emblazoned across the back over a skeleton riding a Harley hog. Black T-shirts and double-soled engineer boots, with chrome spur harnesses, matched silver chains, dangling keys, and crap from different places.

Casey noticed most wore their colors. He didn't know what color stood for what, but he knew it meant a scarf rag tied around the bicep meant the bad-ass committed a rape, robbery, or murder. A few proudly displayed two or three. He also knew, as any cop did, most were ex-cons and mean bastards.

Casey watched them belly up to the bar remembering the telephone chain call from the other bar owners warning about this bunch, the gutter-trash of the hell's angels that usually skip out without paying.

He glanced under the bar, making sure his Louisville Slugger was handy.

Scanning the group, he picked out the leader, a cocky runt

who Casey sized up as all mouth but probably the brains of the outfit. He glanced toward the rear, thankful Micky and his guys were in the back room.

"What can I get you, fellas?" he asked, thinkin' they'll suck a beer or two and leave. Shouldn't be a problem.

"Well, barkeep, what say you fill some pitchers cold and foamy for me and my friends here," big mouth bellowed, slapping his hands on the bar top.

Casey, pouring from the tap, quickly had seven full pitchers decorating the top of the bar, but he didn't see any money appearing out of pockets.

Fuck these assholes, he thought, who they think they're shakin' down.

"Seven more, barkeep."

"No problem, my man, let's see the color of your money."

Just then, Pop pushed through the curtain lugging a fist full of empty pitchers to trade for full ones. Apparently, Casey forgot Micky's crew could drain them faster than he could pour.

"My man? Who you callin' my man? I'm not your fuckin' man."

Pop set the pitchers on the bar, turning toward the loudmouth.

"Okay, son," Casey said in a calm voice, holding up the palms of his hands.

"Have it your way, just pay for your beer."

"Whatta ya mean, we're good for it."

The punk, raising his voice, glanced at Pop, looking at him with a smirk.

"What're you smilin' at, old man, mind yer business."

At the same time, in the back, Micky's ears perked up, hearing the voices over the chatter of his guys.

He moved closer to the curtain.

"Smilin' at you, but I'll stop," Pop said in a calm voice, turning forward.

"That's more like it, chickenshit old fart."

Casey looked at the punk. "Oh shit, big mistake, numb nuts."

Suddenly, he started worrying about the new mirror he just put in behind the bar.

Pop turned, squaring off.

"Little man, I'm gonna give you one chance to back off and apologize."

The punk turned, faced pop with a sneer, sizing him up. He could take the old man easy. This was his chance to show the guys he could take care of business.

Pop and the punk faced each other about fifteen feet apart like western gunslingers in a showdown.

The punk sneered, grabbed a beer bottle by the neck, smashed it against the corner, and crouched low, stalking toward Pop, pointing the jagged edge.

"I'm gonna make you a redhead, old man."

Pop smirked, thinking the punk watched too many movies.

Just then, Micky and his guys filed out, forming up behind Pop. The punk hesitated with sudden doubt, knowing he couldn't back down. A quick count showed his guys totaled two to one plus they were a lot younger.

Crouching, he leaned forward toward Pop, knowing his crew would mop the floor with 'em.

Punk suddenly charged, swiping at Pop's face with the jagged bottle. Pop, a semi-pro boxer in the navy, with fists fat as ten-pound hams, sidestepped the lunge and planted his left on the punk's chin. everyone heard the jawbone crack like a bat hitting a home run. The punk's feet flew out from under him, landing him flat on his back, out cold.

The fight was on.

Casey grabbed his bat, guarding his mirror.

All of a sudden, a Mongol asshole pulled a switchblade.

Spook heard the familiar snap clack.

"Breed, watchit' . . . knife!"

Breed, turned with a sneer, facing the blade.

"That's not a knife," he said, reaching over his shoulder, pulling his Bowie.

"THIS…is a knife."

Wide-eyed asshole shrunk back, watching dim bar lights glint off Breed's steel-shined blade.

In the weeks and months to come, the tales would be tall about the next fifteen minutes that night in ol' Casey's bar, and all would be taller than the last. Suffice to say, the Mongols, forever after, gave that section of town a wide berth.

The four Mongols, left standing, with something cut or broken, were encouraged to pony-up money from the wallets of their fallen comrades to pay for the damage.

That done, Micky announced, "Party must be over."

With a good bye wave to Casey, the Doom team filed out, wishing him a good night.

"Now that's what I call a bachelor party," Cheeks said, sporting a black eye.

Walking out, Kraut asked Casey for an ice pick. Once outside, he walked down the row of Harleys, casually jabbing a hole in every gas tank hose. Reaching the end, he lit a cigarette, took a drag, and flipped the match in the gas-filled gutter.

In seconds, the row of bikes blazed away.

"Whoops," Kraut muttered, jogging to catch up with the guys, listening to Grezer complain.

"Gee sarge, we didn't get to see Sally wiggle her tits.

*   *   *

Saturday morning, they were stuffed in their usual booths, giving Julie a hard time.

She loved it, picked up her whole day.

"Lookin' good today, Julie," Dago said with his usual leering smile. "One of these days I'd like to see you wearing somethin' different than the waitress thing."

"Yeah, knowin' you, probably in my birthday suit." She shot back, noticing Cheeks' black eye, various scratches and nicks on the others including a splint on Dago's middle finger.

Micky's look caught Pop dropping his head with a mumble and thought he better change the subject.

"I checked with the head doctor on our reverend. It's his theory Holmes is a closet fag who's denying his queerness. He resolves his guilt by hating other queers and is determined to rid the earth of their perversion. In his twisted mind, this gets him some brownie points with the old man upstairs against his sinful thoughts. His father probably brainwashed him as a kid, and he thinks he's doing the Lord's work.

"I checked with the judge. He said we needed more info for a warrant."

Micky caught the eyes of Cheeks and Breed.

"When you pick up your robes, be careful. The guy's a nutcase. Try to do what I said the other day. One of you keep him occupied while the other snoops around. We need just one piece to show he probably did it. I want this guy behind bars before his service tomorrow night."

Micky looked at Cheeks' black eye.

"How you gonna explain that?"

"I figure I'll whine a little and say some guy punched me for no reason in the public restroom in the park."

Micky smiled.

"That should do it. You strapped low?"

They nodded as Julie returned to fill coffee cups.

Pop said, "Thank you, Julie."

The rest, again, looked at him with a questioning look. Julie walked away, also wondered.

"Whatta we got so far on the two with holes in their heads?"

"Sarge, we can't find any connection. The wives say they didn't know each other, went to different schools. There were ten years differences in their ages."

Spook read from his notebook.

"Had regular jobs, kids, different religions, one was football, the other baseball. Bottom line, we struck out so far."

"They obviously died of head wounds, but we don't know what caused it yet," Grezer added.

"A bullet doesn't make sense, but the lab hasn't ruled it out. We interviewed the witnesses again at the market and a couple said they heard a kinda whispering whoosh just before the guy went down. One said it was like a quiet low-pitched whistle. Except for the body, the scene was clean. The lab promised us somethin' by ten today.

"Nothin' more on the gal hollerin' at him. We did a neighborhood search and found a lady around the corner that saw a woman fittin' the description walkin' fast down the street and hop into a green panel delivery truck. No make, no license."

Micky was thinking. The broad was connected, he knew it. Years of police sense made it a fact, unproven yet, but a fact.

"Not much to go on." Micky grunted. "There must be a couple of thousand green panels in the city."

Micky looked at his group.

"Anything else?"

"Yeah, great party. It'll go down in history," Kraut said.

"Johnson told me this morning guys in blue went in after, scooped up the leather assholes and gave them free room and board."

"Double that," Grezer said.

"Dago, whatcha gonna do since your pussy finger is out of action? You need a new starter engine."

Dago stuck out his tongue. "I got a backup."

"Okay," Micky finished.

"Everybody in the briefing room at ten for the lab report."

Sliding out the booth, Kraut reached in his pocket for money.

"Shit, I'm short. Hey, Breed, you got any wampum?"

Breed turned, reached in his pocket, and pulled out a string of cheap beads, handing them to Kraut.

"Here, my treat."

Everybody cracked up as Kraut stood, speechless, with a dumbfounded look.

Walking away, Breed smiled. He'd been carryin' those beads for a week knowing somebody would bite. Julie giggled in the back. These guys are great.

Heading for the door, Pop hung back saying he needed to hit the head. He watched the team leave and walked over to Julie's station.

"Say, Julie."

She turned, smiled, thinking they'd left.

"Hi, George? Forget somethin?"

"Uh no, I was wonderin' if maybe I could take you to dinner and a movie or somethin'?"

He was really nervous, shoving his hands in his pockets because they were shaking.

Julie was caught off guard.

Over the years she grew to think of these macho clowns as brothers. Although his full head of hair was snow-white, she knew he was only forty-two and on his own for about ten years. He had lumberjack looks and eyes that twinkled with a secret.

He loved animals and was always rescuing strays. What the hell, she thought, a guy who loves animals can't be all bad.

Her smile widened.

"I'd love to, George, sounds like fun."

Pop felt his heart jump.

"How about Sunday?"

Minutes later, he floated out the front door, a new man with thoughts of love and fancy. He couldn't believe his luck. His belly churned like his first time; butterflies tickled his gut like never before.

CHAPTER 20

T HEY SPENT THE morning finalizing their plans and by ten o'clock, they were ready to go. Their targets today were two jury members, Donald Orlof, a telephone lineman and Arnold Shultz, a parcel post deliveryman.

Gabriel decided, and Angel quickly agreed, the men would not be killed at home in front of their families. This would have been the easier approach but cruel to the wives and children. It was the same as his decision not to wreak vengeance on the females serving on the jury because they were women, subject to the pressures of men, and maybe mothers to children. No, retribution against the evil men would satisfy his blood feud to set things right.

Passing through the hotel lobby, the desk manager noted

that they seemed like a nice couple. The wife was a real looker. He loved the way those Levi's fit around that perfect round ass.

"Good morning, Mr. and Mrs. Tropet."

Both turned, returning the greeting, the clerk just staring at the new bride.

He sighed, lucky bastard. They seemed like a perfect match, he thought. In fact, they kinda looked alike. If he didn't know better, he'd think they were brother and sister.

CHAPTER 21

A T THE SAME time, the Doom squad gathered their chairs around the podium with a cold soda killing time waiting for the lab report. Cheeks and Breed were anxious about going back to the reverend's house, mulled over the best plan. Pop was floating on air thinking about his date with Julie, and Micky, nervous about his proposal to Kathy at eleven. He hoped these clowns would cooperate.

The rest hoped the lab had some magic answers.

"Hey, Breed, what's your story?" Spook asked. "How did an Apache end up in St. Louis, Missouri, and a cop?"

Spook's history was simple. He grew up in the projects not far from the precinct. The only reason he didn't end up in prison with his buddies was because he was spit fast and never got caught. He was lucky someone with juice in high school noticed, so he went to college on a scholarship and made the Olympic team throwing the javelin and running the four hundred meters.

He remembered those hillbilly white-bread crackers saying, "That boy can toss a javelin a country mile and sprint like the clans' on his ass."

It was there he saw how the other half lived and a white buddy, half-drunk, suggested he take the test. He was one of twelve black officers on the whole department.

"Well, my dad worked for the Bureau of Indian Affairs and was sent to Arizona to work with our tribe," Breed said.

"He met my mom and they got married. But he started drinking and died when I was ten, so my mom moved back to the reservation. But I was lucky, I had five years in a good Catholic school and in high school got a scholarship for track to Wash U. Mom moved here with me and liked it. Since I had an Irish name, they hired me before they saw me."

He laughed.

"You shoulda seen their faces when I showed up."

"Track? No shit, we gotta talk," Spook said.

"Hey, sarge," Dago said, "did you hear on the radio that Irish sheepherders found a new use for sheep?"

Micky felt it coming. "That so, what might that be?"

"Wool."

The room cracked up, Mickey and Shamy groaned.

"Hey," Breed said, "should I be offended?"

"Just your bottom half."

Micky tapped the edge of the podium.

"Since we got some time, I have an announcement."

Looking out at them, he already regretted what he was gonna say. This was going to be worse than the proposal.

"I'm goin' to propose to Kathy today."

The whole room fell dead quiet.

"Propose what?" Grezer said with a cop smile.

Marriage, you dipshit." Kraut said.

Dago looked at Cheeks.

"This is all your fault, asshole."

"Sarge, sarge, sarge, say it ain't so," Spook wailed.

""Doom da doom, doom, DOOM," Kraut sang.

"Congratulations, sarge," Cheeks said, happy to share some of the ribbing.

"Thanks. I need three guys to do somethin' for me."

After he explained his plan, Breed, Dago, and Kraut volunteered.

"The only reason I'm doin' this," Kraut declared, "is to see your sorry mug when she tells you to get lost."

Pop sat there thinking it's probably as good a time as any.

"I got somethin' too," he announced.

The room hushed, all thinking, what the shit's goin' on.

"Julie and I are goin' on a date."

"What! MY Julie, at the restaurant?" Dago said, shocked.

"Jezus, what's the world comin' to," Spook said.

"I don't get it," Dago said. "I'm better lookin' than you. I dress better."

Dago was smiling, happy for his friend. Julie was a great gal.

"But Pop's dick is bigger," Kraut said.

"Bullshit, I demand a measurement."

Dago stood up and started to unzip.

"Right here, right now."

Just then, Mabel walked in with the lab report and stared at Dago's crotch with a smirk.

"I don't know what you yahoos are up to, but it looks like it's gettin' interestin'."

"Mabel, Dago says he's got a big dick."

"Well, whip it out, big boy, I always wanted to know if you were cut or au naturel."

Dago sat down, his face the color of a Jonathon.

There was nothing new from the lab and twenty minutes later they were out the door with Micky, Dago, Breed, and Kraut heading for the hospital and his big moment.

CHAPTER 22

A T TEN THIRTY, Angel saw Gabriel's nod and dialed. "Hello, this is Mrs. Orlof. Would you tell me where my husband is working today? It's a family emergency. I have to reach him right away . . . Okay, I'll hold."

She put her hand over the mouthpiece, whispering to Gabriel, "their checking."

"Mrs. Orlof, let's see . . . He's working poles number 1038 through 1045. Hold on . . . that's on the five hundred block of Somersett. We can have a supervisor get him for you."

"No thanks, I'm close by. I'll find him. Thank you, again."

Twenty minutes later, the green panel cruised to a stop on Somersett. They looked out the windshield at two men at the top of a telephone pole hanging out by their safety belts, foot spurs jabbed into the wood.

They planned for this situation.

Angel got out and walked over to the pole about twenty-five feet away.

"Excuse me, excuse me," she hollered.

Both men looked down at the attractive young woman.

"Which one of you is Mr. Donald Orlof?"

"I am," he answered.

His fellow worker wished she was asking for him.

"Which one? Raise your hand."

Donald Orlof raised his hand, wondering what was going on when the girl turned and walked away down the street. Both men looked at each other and shrugged as the Ghost stepped out of the van, letting his arrow fly.

Donald Orlof was aware, for a split second, of the intense pain right below his sternum as the arrow pierced under his rib cage through his lung, up his throat, through his pallet, and into his brain. His partner heard him grunt as his body slacked, falling back, hanging like a crescent moon by the safety rig at his waist.

Gabriel pulled from the curb, turned at the first corner, slowed for a moment and let Angel jump in the passenger seat.

Donald Orlof was transported to the hospital and pronounced DOA. From the coworker's description, it was thought he had a heart attack. When pulling the sheet over the body, the doctor noticed the small three-eight's hole under his sternum.

A half-hour later, they called the police.

CHAPTER 23

KATHY LOOKED UP at the wall clock. It was ten forty-five. the time dragged. She was looking forward to lunch with her man. This was the first time he ever suggested it. She of course, shared her excitement with her fellow nurses, and they teased her unmercifully. She remembered he said he had a surprise and felt herself wiggle in anticipation. She couldn't seem to sit still. She looked at the clock again. She groaned.

The minute hand hit ten forty-seven.

She smiled, thinking of him when they first met. He was wounded on the job and when she stepped through the curtain to put on a dressing, their eyes met and she felt a rush through her body. It was like a magic beam melding them as one.

Walking toward him, she felt the natural bond of one made special for her.

When she leaned close to examine his wound, the scent of his body heat from his recent fight roused her sex and the urge to want him.

She smiled, remembering he was so shy she had to do a little prompting until he finally took the hint. The rest was history. It was seven months next Friday. She was two months pregnant and thrilled at the feeling of his life within her. He didn't know. She refused to tell him, thinking he might think she was trying to trap him.

Brushing the thought aside, she remembered her birthday was this Wednesday. Maybe he was bringing her a gift. She was hopelessly in love with the big lug. He was a typical male and a cop at that, but what was one to do, she thought, her heart was his.

Wondering like a little girl what the surprise was, she glanced at the clock once more, ten fifty-two.

"Will you calm down," Suzie said. "He's just a man, just a handsome looking hunk making us all jealous . . . .. On second thought, you better stay nervous."

At five to eleven, Micky walked a step ahead of his honor guard down the long hallway. Their heels clicked in rhythm as his three cohorts, marching side by side, kept step with him. When they rounded the corner, Kraut whispered, "It's not too late, sarge. You can turn and run. We'll cover for ya."

When they came to a halt at the counter, Micky stood there with a goofy smile with his three soldiers behind, standing at attention. The six nurses gawked as Kathy stood and he handed her a dozen roses. Smiling, she took them and on que, the honor guard broke into a rousing chorus.

"*Shaboom, shaboom, ya, dada, da, dat, dat. Shaboom, shaboom, ya, dada, dat dat, dat. If life could be a dream, shaboom, shaboom. Ya, da . . .*"

The nurses started laughing, holding their hands over their mouths. Kathy stood there, stunned, flabbergasted.

He never did anything goofy or silly.

Looking at his smiling eyes, she wondered what he was doing, fumbling in his pocket.

Micky's heart, hammering like a woodpecker, took her hand, and lead her to the opening between the counters. His trio was still belting out *shaboom, shaboom,* shuffling hips in tandem like hulas, snapping their fingers, really getting into it, their volume rising, echoing down the hall.

Micky turned, motioning them to quiet down, and went down on one knee, holding her hand. Immediately, her tears started along with the rest of the nurses.

"Kathy, I love you. Will you marry me?"

The trio suddenly stopped and the whole floor went dead quiet. Kathy was so happy and choked up, she couldn't talk. She held her hand over her mouth trying to get her breath. The most she could manage was shaking her head "YES". He stood and she jumped in his arms, squeezing him to death.

Holding him close, she whispered in his ear, "I have a surprise too. I'm carrying a little Micky."

He set her down, shocked, thrilled, and speechless. He smiled, staying quiet, cherishing their secret.

Everybody was clapping. Suzie cut loose with a two-finger street whistle.

Dago took a closer look.

A half-hour later, they walked out of the hospital with Micky walking on air.

He did it. He was the master, a prince.

Climbing in the car, Breed said, "I think it was our singing that cinched it."

"Yeah, maybe we ought to start our own trio, you know, so we can pick up groupies."

"It must work," Dago said, "I got a nurse's phone number."

He waved the slip of paper in the air, cocky.

"This is definitely a good day," Micky said in a fog of happiness.

As soon as the motor turned over, the police radio caught their attention. Micky turned, heading for the other hospital.

Twenty minutes later, the emergency room doctor handed Micky the arrow that was buried inside Donald Orlof's body.

They now had the killer's signature.

In five minutes, Micky made the assignments and the team fanned out. Micky made a couple of calls and managed to get an archery instructor and hunter to meet at the department the same time the Doom team returned to the briefing room.

*   *   *

Micky introduced Mr. Heller Vogel who said he had hunted with bow and arrow for twenty years and was a frequent writer for Field & Stream on bowhunting. He made the Olympic team in nineteen forty-eight and taught at the local college until he retired.

The room fell quiet. The whole team giving him their undivided attention as he examined the arrow. He asked a few questions about the murder scenes, certain distances, and the damage it caused.

He quieted again, thinking.

The team waited, anxious.

"Well, sergeant. First thing is I've never seen or heard of an arrow like this. The camouflage paint is typical but not this pattern. Also, I'd have to measure, but I know it's a good four inches longer than the normal arrow. The material seems to be aluminum, with a polished slick mirror finish not available anywhere in the world I know of.

Feeling the weight, he said, "Aluminum is lighter, so I expect the tube is filled to make it more rigid."

He examined the head, close, the room dead quiet.

"This steel tip is tapered perfectly to meet the diameter of the shaft. The whole arrow seems to be designed like a big sewing needle. The design and polished surface reduce wind resistance dramatically, increasing the FPS."

Vogel quieted again, thinking.

"I don't have my tools with me, but I can assure you this arrow is perfectly balanced to a thousandth of an inch. Also, the feather fletching, with a slight curve, would cause the arrow to spin like a bullet in flight, increasing accuracy.

"The rigidity of the metal and the design of the head ensure the arrow would be very silent in flight."

Stopping for a breath, reviewing his thoughts, he spotted something and pulled the arrow close for a better look.

"Did you see this black mark on the shaft?"

Micky taking the arrow, looked at the letter "G" between the feathers.

Micky asked, "Does this mean anything to you? Like a type? Batch? Series?"

"Sorry, I have no idea but I know this arrow is foreign to this country. Aluminum is lighter than wood and makes a stiffer shaft. You see, when you shoot an arrow, it bends coming off the bow and wobbles slightly in flight, affecting the accuracy and sound through the air. This arrow is very light and strong. It will shoot further, faster, more accurately, with deeper penetration than any other.

"It's like a flying needle."

Micky starred at the man, thinking, why can't this just be simple?

"Mr. Vogel, obviously it's from somewhere. What's your best guess?"

Again, Vogel quieted, studying the arrow.

"Well, it could be military or a foreign government, like Russia."

"Military! Shit. I thought we graduated to guns and bombs. Why would they want a super-duper arrow?"

He shrugged. "You asked my opinion."

"Sorry . . . how about this Russian thing. We talkin spies, special ops?"

"Sergeant, your guess is as good as mine. All I know is this arrow is one of a kind."

Micky thought he'd check with a couple of other archery guys to make sure this guy knew what he was talking about. Russia, enemy powers, military, that's bullshit. One thing's for sure, though, he wanted those other two arrows.

CHAPTER 24

A T TWO THIRTY, Angel stood down the block outside "Sam's tailor" shop, making a call from the payphone.

"Hello, this is Cindy from Sam's tailor. We need a pickup. Yes, we are at 3165 Potomac. Thank you . . . How long will it be? Three o'clock? Thank you."

Sam's tailoring shop was closed.

Angel and Gabriel, quiet with their thoughts, waited in the green panel about fifty yards away. Finally, Gabriel, glancing at his watch, turned to his sister with a half-smile.

"It is time."

Her eyes, loyal to death, met his and nodded. She left to wait in front of the store. At four minutes after three, the Parcel Post truck pulled to the curb.

Gabriel watched the driver, jury member, Arnold Shultz, leave his truck and walk toward Angel.

As instructed, her eyes drifted to his name tag and she raised her right hand, pretending to straighten her hair.

Then, she apologized profusely for not having the package, but there was a sudden change. She smiled, letting him flirt before thanking him for being so nice and understanding.

When he climbed back in his truck, she quickly turned and walked away.

The Ghost, sitting inside on the metal bed of the panel truck, faced the rear, looking out the two open doors at the windshield of the parcel post truck. He checked the angle of the window, and as he suspected, it was large, flat, and perpendicular to the arrow in flight, eliminating any concern of a ricochet.

Ghost, nocked the arrow, pulled it to his chin, and when he started to release, the moving sun created a sudden glare off the van's windshield, blinding him, making him unsure of the shot. Holding the arrow, he felt the fletching tickle his cheek. The hundred-pound bow strained for release as he held it easy as a kite string.

Then, Arnold pulled from the curb and the glare disappeared. Ghost smiled, letting his fingers slip from the bowstring.

Arnold yawned; happy this was his last stop. The arrow punched through the windshield like a 45-slug, stabbing him through the mouth. The laminated safety glass slowed the arrow's velocity but still went through the back of his skull, pinning him to the partition behind the seat like a mounted butterfly.

With the feathered end sticking out his mouth, the truck continued forward, weaving out of control down the street toward the Ghost in the green panel.

Veering straight toward him, Ghost held his breath. There was nothing he could do, bracing for the impact. Suddenly, the UPS truck swerved away at the last second, missing him by inches. Gabriel sucked a breath, jumped behind the wheel, watching the Truck smash into a parked car across the street, shearing off a fireplug.

The fountain of water sprayed down on the green panel accelerating down the street.

As a crowd gathered, Ghost already turned the corner, looking for Angel.

CHAPTER 25

WITH A CUP of Mabel's poison, the Doom team faced Micky, anxious, ready to go.

"You first, Spook."

"Still don't know the connection between the three. Same wounds and the arrow today solve that mystery. Sarge, the usual greed and sex angle don't fit. These guys were Joe Schmo working stiffs. Olmstead was a model railroader no less; no way was he messing around with any darkhaired girl. Also, none of these guys had any real money."

Micky looked out from the podium.

"Makes sense. Any other questions or ideas?... A witness saw a female fitting the same description on number two. We got two witnesses placing her at the scene. Nobody..."

The phone rang and Micky picked up.

"Delaney here," he said, listening. Two minutes later he hung up.

"We got number four at 3100 Potomac. Driver took an arrow through the mouth. We'll meet there and decide how to work."

Micky raced to the scene, his mind mixing the facts. One thing for sure, at the rate this guy was killing people, it was getting real messy real quick.

Pulling up behind the police barricades, he still couldn't figure out a connection. Was it some crazy just shooting people at random? A thrill killer? Maybe there was more than one hit team.

He decided to call Tommy at Quantico when he got back. Climbing out of his car, he noticed the press pool and Cynthia smiling, wearing a shorter, tighter skirt.

He walked over to the parcel post van with the team and looked inside at the driver pinned to the partition, eyes and mouth wide open in shock. Micky thought it looked weird, feathers poking out his mouth like that. There was very little blood, probably because the arrow sealed off the veins.

As they studied the body, Dago asked, "Whatta ya think, Breed?"

Breed quieted, furrowed his brow, and pondered. The rest waited, expecting some redskin wisdom.

"I think he got shot with an arrow."

They all turned, looking at him.

"No shit, Dick Tracy," Dago quipped. "I mean you bein' a savage and all, what about this bow and arrow thing?"

"How should I know. My grandad was the last Indian that

killed you palefaces with arrows. We use thirty-thirty Winchesters now."

With a groan, they backed off, huddling with Micky making SOP assignments. With a last glance, making sure he didn't miss something, he turned to the press.

"Thank you for your patience," he said, thinking he better be diplomatic. He didn't need the grief.

"We've had four homicides in the last two days by the same method, an arrow. We're following up on all leads. Our investigation is continuing and we'll hold a press conference if there are further developments. Thank you."

Geez, he thought, that was really good. He had a talent. Of course, it wasn't as much fun as saying, "Fuck off," but, maybe next time.

Walking to the car, Cynthia cut him off. "Come on, sergeant, I'm ready to trade."

He bent sideways, obviously looking at her ass. Just what he thought, no panties.

"I just got engaged, sorry." He smiled.

"I didn't mean that, you asshole," she sputtered. "I can treat the department with kid gloves on this or gut-punch you. What'll it be?"

"Look, Cindy, you'll get it when we give it, not before."

She turned, huffing away, shaking it a little more than usual, putting her hand behind her back, giving him the finger.

Micky chuckled as he drove away.

An hour later, the team plus Captain Barnes and Lieutenant

SS formed up in the briefing room waiting for the first brave soul to take a sip of Mable's new brew.

"Pop, recap for us."

"Sarge, I found out a female saying she was Orlof's wife called his work sayin' she had to reach him about an emergency. I checked with the wife. She didn't make any call. A female also called the dispatcher at parcel post to find out what route Shultz was working and hinted she was a girlfriend. A half-hour later, he said a female asked for a pick up at Sam's tailors. Sam's tailors was closed all day. It was a simple setup."

"That confirms the mystery woman accomplice."

Pop shuffled through a few papers.

"The guys confirmed a green panel truck at both scenes one and two. Also, several people saw a green panel at number four because the parcel post van almost smacked it. The witness sharin' the telephone pole this morning with Danberry said a good-lookin' woman hollered from the sidewalk asking for Dan. Seconds later, he was dead."

"Okay, good, we're one step closer. Spook, Dago, find those arrows at scene one and two."

Collecting his papers, he added, "The press is getting nasty. Cynthia is getting pushy . . . Listen up."

Micky's eyes, serious, looked at everyone.

"Keep your mouth shut. Any press info will be released by me. Specifically, no mention of the suspect green panel or mystery woman . . . I don't want this guy to know what we know . . . Okay, that said, we have to find the connection.

"There's a reason these people have been targeted. I want that reason."

Captain Barnes and Lieutenant SS hung behind after the rest filed out.

"Delaney, this is making us look bad, real fast. I have to call the mayor as soon as I get back to my office. What can I tell him?"

"Damn, boss, tell him the investigation is goin' forward. No, we don't have a suspect yet. We're workin' on it."

Chris, he thought, that namby-pamby jerk-off isn't worth the powder to blow him to hell. He glanced at SS. The smug anal-retentive Nazi sat with a ha-ha-you're-in-trouble look with his spit and polish uniform. All he did all day was prance around, looking pretty. Maybe he should have asked for him to work undercover on the queer murders. He'd fit right in. There's somethin' about that prick he didn't trust.

Barnes broke his thoughts.

"Ya got anything on the side for me?"

"No, Captain, wish I did. What I got is what you heard. But have faith, somethin' will break."

Walking out, SS turned and gave Micky his usual smirk. Micky smiled back, fake, and when he turned, gave him the one-finger salute.

Reaching for the phone to dial tommy at Quantico, he remembered SS always bad-mouthing Jews and blacks. Micky bet the asshole had Nazi flags all over his house. He wouldn't be surprised if there was a Luger in his holster.

"Tommy, my man, how are ya?"

"Ah, shit, whatta ya want now?"

"Tommy, I'm hurt. I just wanted to let you know I got your stuff and to thank you. That's what friends do."

"First of all, I'm not your friend. You don't have any friends. The whole world hates you. Whatta ya want?"

"Well, I wish you were here to see the tears in my eyes, but since you ask, I need one who knows someone who could call someone who could ask someone and you're the one."

"Huh?"

Micky laid out the weird details of the arrow murders and asked if he could poke around to see if it had any connection to the military or anything else sneaky floating in the clouds.

"Okay, Mick, I'll check around but it sounds weird."

* * *

That evening the *Post-Dispatch* spared no expense on the ink for their front page.

Four Murdered by Invisible Ghost, Cops Clueless

CHAPTER 26

A T FOUR THIRTY that same afternoon, Cheeks and Breed knocked on the reverend's door.

Jeffrey Holmes, answering with a big smile, welcomed them inside, and escorted them to the devotion room. There, he proudly showed them the crimson gowns for the service the next day. They chatted about the weather and meeting the other parishioners.

Cheeks asked, "Reverend, I wonder if we might see the meditation room again."

Holmes smiled, noticing the glance they gave one another. He knew why these fucking queers wanted to see it again. They all did, imagining the fun they were going to have.

"Certainly, my pleasure," he said, heading up the stairs.

"Reverend Holmes, I need to use the head. I'll catch up," Breed said, turning down the hall.

Holmes was suddenly uncomfortable but continued upstairs with Cheeks. Something wasn't adding up. When he reached the top of the stairs, it hit him. He never heard a homo use the word *head*. It was always *restroom* or *little boy's room*. A tickle of fear started picking at him.

Shit, he thought, he'd just test them.

As they stepped into the mattress room, Holmes put his arm around Cheeks in a friendly manner. Cheeks jumped like he was bit by a rattler.

"Shi . . . Sorry, Reverend, You, startled me."

Cheeks smiled, knowing he screwed up.

"I guess I'm too serious in a house of worship."

"That's alright, just relax. You're in good hands here."

Holmes knew he was in big trouble. He didn't know who these guys were, but they definitely were not queers. Then it hit him. Shit, they must be cops.

"Here, Bobby, let me show you this," he said pointing to the side.

When Cheeks turned his head, he barely saw the sucker punch from the corner of his eye, but he felt the heavy fist, heard the snap of his jaw, and crumpled to his knees. His world was fading fast. He tried to shake it off but the same fist plunged down like a jackhammer.

Cheeks's world went black.

Holmes stood over him, huffing for breath. He bent, grabbed

Cheeks's wallet, flipped it open, and stared at the gold badge reflecting back like a laser.

"Shit, fucking cops," he muttered. He quick patted him down finding the two-inch Colt strapped to his ankle.

Panicked, he pulled it, holding it to Cheeks's temple, cocking the hammer. Hearing the two clicks, he stopped, thinking, *keep a cool head, be smart.* The gunshot would bring the other cop running. He better take care of him first. He kicked Cheeks in the gut for good measure, making sure he was unconscious, and headed down the steps.

Breed was excited. He thought he found the bottle of cyanide. A skull and cross-bone with all kinds of warnings and a bunch of foreign words on the label. The dumb shit left it right on the workbench.

He hustled up the basement steps to the kitchen.

"Hands over your head, Officer."

Breed froze, spotting Cheeks' gun in Holmes' fist, and raised his arms.

What happened to Cheeks? He didn't hear a gunshot.

"Real slow, pull the gun out of your ankle holster and kick it over here."

Breed's mind raced. He bent, unsnapped his holster and slid it over.

When he straightened, watching Holmes raise the gun to kill him, he heard his grandfather's voice.

"Remember, smile with the devil."

"Jeffrey, wait, don't shoot," he said, dead calm.

Breed, watching him hesitate, quickly added, "If you kill us here, you'll have to haul four hundred pounds of dead weight downstairs plus clean up a lot of blood."

Holmes smiled, lowering the gun to his waist, pointed at Breed's gut. The cop was right. He might as well do it the easy way. The other cop was still unconscious, and this one can carry him. Plus, no one will hear the shots in the basement.

"Good thinkin'."

He smirked.

"Move ahead, upstairs. We'll get your friend. You wiggle the wrong way, you're dead."

Breed moved steady up the stairs, thinking fast. He had to divert the asshole's attention for a second, just a second.

On the landing, Cheeks was down and out, moaning with a split lip. Breed didn't know why, minds were funny that way, but he thought of Cheeks not being able to kiss his new bride on their honeymoon.

"Help him up and drag his ass downstairs."

Breed bent, turning to his side, hiding his arm, putting his is left hand under Cheek's arm to help him up.

"Come on buddy, stand up."

At the same time, his right hand slipped up behind, under his sweater, in the arch of his back. In one smooth movement, he twisted, whipping around, snapping the ten-inch Bowie underhanded at Holmes and dodged to the left.

Holmes fired.

The gun blast echoed through the hallway as the knife sank in Holmes' heart, full to the hilt.

At the same time, Cheeks lifted up on his fours, shaking

his head, trying to clear it. As his eyes started to focus, he saw Breed's shadowed form standing over him and Holmes with his gun about eight feet away. Suddenly, there was a flash of movement. He heard a thump, looked up, and saw Breed's knife in Holmes's chest, falling back, firing shots into the ceiling, tumbling backwards down the stairs.

Breed helped him up and they stood, starring at Holmes in a heap at the bottom of the stairs, staring at the ceiling.

Then, with a look to the other, they started laughing like hell from the adrenaline rush.

"Shit, man, that was toooo close," Breed said.

"Amen. Ya know, Breed, I think this makes us blood brothers."

A half-hour later the whole team plus an army of other cops were crawling all over. Pop took Cheeks to the hospital to get patched up.

Kathy on duty, personally supervised, making the doctor nervous. After finishing, he stomped out and she wrapped his cracked ribs and dressed his stitched lip.

"Congratulations," he said, squinting in pain. "Sarge told us."

She smiled. "Thanks. Jack said you were getting married next week?"

"Yeah, she's gonna be really upset when she sees this."

As she looked at him, her heart reached out. Just a young man, full of it, charging ahead to get the bad guys, loving it, ready to risk his life to make the world safe for the rest of us. Thank God for men like him.

"Well, you know, sometimes women enjoy doing all the work on a honeymoon. Don't worry."

Looking at her, he blushed as bright as the Red Cross emblem on the wall. Five minutes later, he walked to the waiting room to collect pop, thinking the sarge was a lucky man.

Within a half-hour, Cheeks was whisked away by Internal Affairs to make sure the killing was within department policy and the officers' actions were warranted, which really meant, *do we have to do anything to cover our ass?*

CHAPTER 27

PLEASED WITH THEIR success, Gabriel decided to take Angel out that evening for a special dinner. Waiting for her, he lounged in the stuffed chair, reading about the four murders filling the front page. With any luck, he thought, they will complete the others and be out of the city before the authorities figure out what happened.

He smiled. The reporter, Cynthia Roberts, called the killer the *Ghost*. She'll never know she guessed his *sobriquet* correctly.

Just then, the bathroom door opened and Angel stepped into the room. Her body moved hot, silhouetted by the dim light sneaking out the cracked door behind her. His eyes roamed down, seeing every curve, imagining every crevice as the light shadowed the soft puff of satin between her legs.

His eyes lifted to hers, her sex smell flowed like sweet poison through the charged air. Her smile, curling with power, knew his thoughts. Walking slowly toward him in her stiletto heels, she hiked her skirt high, straddling one of his legs. He glimpsed a touch of white panties as she settled the softness between her legs on his thigh.

Slowly leaning forward, her smile turned wicked as her tongue slowly tickled inside his ear, whispering, "Later, it is yours, *ma cher.*"

They slept late enjoying the lazy Sunday morning. Angel opened her eyes first, blinking at the stringy light poking through the edges of the dark drapes. Stretching lazy, she remembered, with a purr, last night. She rolled, facing her brother with a contented smile, listening to his soft sleeping breaths. She admired his broad shoulders as the dim light outlined his back with every muscle burnt in a carved edge. Beneath the dusty skin, it seemed his body was molded like metal, poured from the finest male castings created by the demands of nature.

She resisted the temptation to trace the hard ridges connected by cabled ligaments. His body bore witness to a hard life of struggle since a child, fashioning him strong, able to survive better than any man.

Pulling the sheet down, she compared her form to his. Her body was smooth and firm with a female softness that teased. Her form was shaped and built to create desire, thereby ensuring her own survival. What she did not know though, was her female stink would drive any male to kill to possess her.

With a sigh, she spooned against him, hugging her arm around his chest, refusing to think about their sins.

After breakfast, Gabriel would scout the next two targets, taking some quiet time to plan the final kills, the last of the jurors, leaving the two attorneys, the police informant, and the judge. He did not decide yet, which of the last four he would kill first. These would be the most difficult as their death would tip off the police. They would quickly figure out the first six were jurors and trace the case to their brother. Then, they would have the motive, and Angel and he would be hunted.

After dinner, they discussed the final day and how they would disappear to start a new life. Their first thought was returning to the bayou, where they felt safe from the world. But then, they realized so much time had passed, and they were no longer children.

They had tasted a bigger world.

While her brother was away, Angel had saved most of the money from the government men. They let their fantasies roam, perhaps going to an island somewhere or Australia. Also, maybe Paris or French Canada. They were good choices. Gabriel watched his sister's eyes grow round with girlish excitement, thinking of their future.

He told her Paris it would be.

That night, holding each other, Angel felt a chill, a premonition of dread, feeling that God would soon strike.

She trembled, her tears starting, fearing they would never see Paris.

* * *

In another part of town, Pop took Julie to Rigazzi's for the best breaded veal cutlet she ever tasted. They took in a movie and finished with pie and coffee at Howard Johnson's.

When he walked her to the door, saying good night, she kissed him on the cheek.

Walking away, Pop felt like Sir Lancelot and Julie felt like a schoolgirl again.

* * *

Micky bought a good bottle of champagne to toast the good news. Getting engaged and finding out he was going to have a son all in one day deserved a special celebration. A quiet evening at home with the lady he loved was in order and champagne would create the perfect mood.

Opening the front door, he announced he was home, but the house was strangely quiet. As he tossed his jacket across the chair, he heard her voice.

"I'm in here."

"Where's here?"

"Your favorite place."

Heading for the bedroom, he found her naked on the bed in his favorite position surrounded by rose petals. He dropped the booze and started yanking at buttons, thinking, *Now, this is a woman that knows how to celebrate.*

CHAPTER 28

MONDAY MORNING, GABRIEL and Angel walked through the hotel lobby, greeted the desk clerk with a "Good morning" and continued down six blocks south and three west to the parked green panel truck.

Thirty minutes later, they parked, waiting for their fifth kill.

Both were not happy with the setup. Mr. Benjamin Gold, the proprietor of "Security Jewelry" located at Gravois and Utah, was on time like always for the last twenty years. Unfortunately, it was ten minutes to ten and the streets were already crowded with pedestrians and automobiles moving through the area.

"That is the man," Angel said.

She cased the store the day before, asking for Mr. Gold, saying he was personally recommended by a friend. He was very pleasant but became impatient when she told him she could not make up her mind on a necklace, promising to come back with her husband.

As he watched her leave the store, he thought it odd she was not wearing a wedding ring.

Angel jumped from her seat, went to the rear, and opened the back doors of the truck. Ghost moved to the back, sat on the metal floor, strung his bow, nocked the arrow, and waited for the perfect shot.

He watched Gold stop at the front door and raised the long bow slow, pulling the arrow full back. Just then, Gold bent over, apparently having trouble with the lock. Ghost held the shot, the arrow pulled to the needle point, every muscle frozen like stone. Gold straightened and Ghost's fingers started to relax, his arrow shaft aimed at the back of his head.

Suddenly, a female employee stepped in his line of fire, blocking the target. Ghost's fingers froze, barely holding the catgut. He cursed low with a relieved breath knowing the arrow would have killed the innocent female employee. His hands shook, realizing the near accident as Gold and the employee disappeared inside the store.

Angel, standing by the back door, saw the problem, slammed the doors, and climbed back in the truck.

"Let us go. This one is bad luck. I can feel it," she said.

"It must be done."

"But how? We have lost our chance."

"Take the buggy, create the *tumulte* as we planned."

She glanced at the set jaw on his face. His black eyes flashed cold and determined. She did not like his decision, but she again opened the back doors on the van, took the buggy out, unfolded it, and wheeled it to the corner. She watched the traffic lights, and when it turned green, she pushed the buggy free into the traffic. Cars in all directions began screeching and sliding trying to avoid the carriage. Horns honked and people yelled as it stopped on the other side without being hit.

The disturbance brought people running and others stuck their heads out of the nearby businesses.

Mr. Benjamin Gold was one such person.

Standing in the doorway, he looked down the street and Gabriel smiled, releasing his arrow. the needle shaft sunk into the side of his head, slicing through his brain and came out the other side, disappearing in the far wall.

Angel already returned, closed the doors, and climbed in the front. Gabriel had the motor running, and slowly pulled from the curb, ignoring the screams of the female clerk running out of the store.

CHAPTER 29

A FTER BREAKFAST, THE Doom squad left Greasys in the usual uproar heading for the squad room. They continued stirring the pot in front of the station, elevator, and through the hallways. They stopped at the coffeemaker, taking a whiff. Nobody coughed, so they poured a cup, giving Mable a snicker as if to say, "If you can brew it, we can drink it."

When Micky entered the squad room, he looked up checking the ceiling, noticing the skies were clear because no one worked yesterday. He had a quick thought about their poor ceiling fan. Maybe it was dying because of all the cigarette smoke it was forced to breathe all those years. That annoying click every third turn was merely its cry for help. The poor thing was hurting.

Walking to the front, he sometimes worried about the way his thoughts wandered to that kinda bullshit. He wondered if others did the same or if he was the only weird one. On one level it was scary.

"Okay, guys, grab a seat. Breed, what about the missing arrows?"

"We found the one on the first murder, Olmsted, the real estate guy. The arrow went through to the far wall into an office partition and was buried inside. It did have a mark. It was the letter 'G'."

"Grezer?"

"Sarge, we searched around the grocery store till we were blue, no luck. There're all kinds of undeveloped lots with heavy brush. It was impossible to tell from which direction the arrow came, but if we assume, the shooter shot from inside the van. The arrow's probably in the weeds somewhere. With the camo color, it's like the old needle in a haystack."

"Well," Micky said, "we got three arrows with the letters G, O, and R. Spook, whatta ya got on the backup archery expert?"

"I found a guy who's a big game hunter with bow and arrow. He even leads safaris in Africa plus he's a trick shooter. The bottom line. He backs up our Vogel guy. Never saw that type of arrow before anywhere and he's been to a lot of countries. He says it's definitely made for a special target. probably military."

"Okay, other business. Cheeks and Breed are cooling their heels in admin until IA finishes their review on the cult shooting."

"Yeah, hey Breed, that musta been some show," Pop asked. "How do ya work that knife?"

The rest of the squad seconded the question and Breed,

blushing a little redder, finally bent to their curiosity. Shrugging off his sport coat, he turned around, and centered between the straps of his shoulder holster, sat a sheath knife mounted with heavy snaps, balanced between his shoulder blades. At the bottom of the sheath, a one-inch-wide leather strap hung down and hooked to the back of his belt.

"Show us how fast yo . . ."

Breed had the knife out and ready.

"Whooo, that is fast . . . But Cheeks said you underhanded it?"

"It's reversible."

Breed slid out of the harness, unsnapped the sheath and turned it upside down, snapped it back, and slid his arms through the straps ready to go.

"This way, reaching back at the belt, I just pull down."

"Where didja learn to throw like that?" Pop asked.

"Jeez Pop, he's Indian for Chrissake. It's in their blood. Like Spook, he's a champion spear chucker. They're born that way."

"It's a javelin, asshole," Spook shot back.

"Spear, javelin, same difference."

"Okay," Micky interrupted, "enough fun and games."

Just then, the phone rang and five minutes later, the team was out the door responding to the fifth murder by arrow in three days.

CHAPTER 30

A T NOON, THE green panel
was in position.

Both, sitting quiet with their thoughts, stared out the windshield. Angel sensed Gabriel was uneasy from the morning kill. He was tense, on edge.

"Are you feeling well, *cher?*" she asked. "*Oui,* I am fine."

Knowing better, she moved from her seat and started rubbing his shoulders. His muscles felt like stainless and the strands from his neck to shoulder were tight as his bowstrings.

Dropping his head, he closed his eyes, thankful for the relief feeling her hand coast between his legs.

Her husky voice surged through him.

"Let me make you feel better, *frère*," she whispered, lowering her mouth to his freed cock.

She felt her own pleasure hearing his moans. She loved the taste of him.

CHAPTER 31

WORKING THE CRIME scene at the jewelry store went quick. Five witnesses gave good descriptions of the crazy woman pushing the baby carriage into traffic.

Also, a produce man saw a man sitting in a green panel truck with the back doors open. He, however, did not note the license number, and it was too dark in the truck for a description of the man. But he did see the black-haired girl climb in the passenger seat after the woman in the jewelry store started screaming.

Micky avoided the press and headed back to the station. He knew he had to put out an all units on the truck. He couldn't keep it back any longer. He just hoped it didn't scare the killer away.

He trudged past Mabel with a grumble, "Hold my calls."

Pushing through the squad room door, he headed to his

office. He needed some quiet time. He needed to let everything mix in the pot. He needed to make sense of the whole mess.

Plopping in his chair, he pushed back, closing his eyes. What do these people have in common? All males, different ages, some married, some not, different occupations, different interests, different religions, and different social standings. What was the common thread, the connection? How do they know each other? Maybe a school reunion, no. poker game, no. Volunteer group of some kind, common charity, maybe. He'll check it out. What else, what . . . ?

The telephone buzz broke his spell and he straightened with a curse.

"What part of hold my calls don't she understand," he growled, picking up.

"Sorry, sergeant, but I think you want this one. It's a lieutenant from the New Orleans PD."

Micky punched the blinking light. "Sergeant Delaney."

"Sarge, this is Lieuutenant Lapierre down in New Orleans. I hear on the national news ya'll have a series by arrow workin'?"

"Sure do, Lieutenant."

He wondered why all Frenchie names sounded girlie?

"Weel, thought ya'll might like to know we had one too. Five at one time, all with arrow."

Micky straightened, all ears. "Give me a rundown."

"Weel, one of Huey's cohorts by the street name of Big Daddy and four of his bodyguards got out of their Lincoln in the French Quarter about 9:00 PM and were felled right there. Funny thing, the bodyguards took it in the head, but we couldn't figure how Big Daddy stopped breathing until they cut him open. Dam'est thing I ever saw. The arrow entered straight on the top of his head, down his throat, stomach and stopped in his guts. Damn near came out his ass. I don't know how the guy did it, but it was a hellova a shot."

Micky knew it was his killer.

"Are the arrows camouflaged?"

"Sure are."

"Do they have any black letters on them near the fletching?"

"Fletching? What the hell's that?"

"The feathers." He started to think he was dealing with a dumb southern cracker until he realized he just learned the term too.

"Don't know. I'd hafta check."

"I'd really appreciate it. How long would it take?"

"They're just down the hall a bit. I'll give y'all a call back in about fifteen."

Micky sat there watching the clock. Let's see, he thought, we got five hoods dead in the Big easy and five in St. Louie Lou, all by the same mystery arrow. this is shaping up like a real cluster fuck.

Just then the phone rang.

"Hey, sarge, I found a letter on each arrow back by the fletching."

Micky could tell he was happy he learned a new word.

"They are E, S, E, S, and a M. Y'all know what it means?"

"Not yet, lieutenant, thanks, good info. By the way, way, do you happen to know in what order the arrows were shot?"

"Huh?"

"Never mind. Would y'all," *Damn, he's got me talkin' like a shit kicker,* "do me a favor and take one of those arrows to an archery expert in your town and get his opinion on the type?"

"Sure thing," he said, thinking, Shit, it's just an arrow.

"Sarge, if you nab this guy, give us a holler so we can wipe our slate."

"Will do."

Hanging up the phone, Micky suddenly felt pretty good. He glanced at his watch, eleven thirty. He thought he'd slip over to the hospital to visit his bride-to-be. He was getting good at this spontaneous romantic bullshit. Maybe he should write a book. His guys should be done with the scene by the time he returned.

Micky walked out finding Mabel's desk empty with her little sign saying "Lunch". Continuing on, he remembered he needed a large envelope and U-turned to her desk. When he opened the drawer, his mind jumbled, looking at a riding crop, a swagger stick, a ping-pong paddle, and a few silk scarves. All jet black.

What the hell? he thought.

Looking around, he closed the drawer, making sure no one saw him. He continued down the hall thinking maybe she really did kill her men. He smirked, happy there wasn't a bow and arrow in the drawer.

CHAPTER 32

AT TWELVE FORTY-FIVE, the Ghost patiently waited in the shade of the roof. He felt better after receiving Angel's special care. He was comfortable here, alone, invisible, like the summer woods, like the bayou. The weather, clear and crisp for September, held a scattering of puffy clouds. The view from the roof across the street was a clear straight shot into the third-floor window of the brokerage. The sixth juror, Lloyd Webley, a stockbroker, was due back from lunch.

Ghost checked the complete circle around him. There was a ten-floor building under construction to his right. He had a clear view through the skeleton framework. No one was working today. To his left was an open space. All the buildings in that direction were lower.

Behind him, it was the same.

He smiled, knowing he held the high ground. He glanced at his hand-drawn map again, checking his compass to be sure. Before settling in, he figured the distance to the kill. The street was fifty-two feet wide, standard, and the sidewalks eight feet each. The target would be no more than seventy-five feet away. The single-pane glass window would be perpendicular to the arrow. Again, a ricochet was not an issue.

It would be a simple shot. He looked up, checking the position of the sun, making sure he would not have to deal with glare off the window glass. The kill on the Parcel Post truck was almost a *dèastre*.

It was a clear view into the office. Webley's desk faced the window against the far wall. Webley would be looking toward the window when the death whisper ended his life. He again reviewed his escape route. Angel waited in the green panel two blocks away. After the kill, he would climb down the fire escape on the side of the building, walk toward the street, and continue down the sidewalk to the panel van.

By the time Webley was discovered, they would be enjoying a late lunch at the café around the corner from their hotel.

His mind drifted to his dear Angel. Her loyalty and trust gave him the strength of a lion but her safety nagged at him. He knew each kill presented an even greater danger of discovery. He wanted her to wait for him in New Orleans, but every time he mentioned it, she refused with all the passion in her small body. He smiled, remembering her tantrum when he tried to send her away the last time. She was like a child, stomping around, throwing things, her eyes flashing. Her feelings were hurt and her words were angry.

He soon gave in and spent the next day trying to make her happy again.

A shadow in the window brought his attention back to the mission. Webley, his target, entered the office, closed the door, and sat behind his desk. After looking around, he picked up some papers and settled back in his high-back chair.

Ghost was careful to stand back from the edge of the roof to prevent anyone spotting him from the street.

His mind clicked as trained as he raised the bow and nocked the arrow. His right arm curled back until the feather fletching tickled his cheek, and as his breath slowly released, his fingers slipped from the bowstring. Death Whisper was in flight.

Suddenly, a yell from the side, whipped him around, his heart doubling.

A construction crew, not fifty feet away, were yelling and pointing at him. At least six were going up on the caged construction elevator. Ghost cursed, quick broke down the bow, and slung it over his shoulder. It could not be worse.

The fire escape was on the same side as the elevator about ten feet away. He jumped down the fire escape steps.

Yelling workers, cursing, shaking crowbars and hammers, were hungry for his scalp.

The elevator jerked to a stop and started back down.

Ghost raced down the fire escape, listening to the yells of those pursuing him. They were young men, bigger, used to physical work. They were formidable enemy.

Taking the steps three at a time, he jumped, scrambling to the sliding ladder and yanked the lever. Climbing down as it lowered, he jumped the last eight feet, hitting the ground, sprinting to the rear of the building.

Running toward the front sidewalk would be suicide.

The elevator hit the ground, the gang yelled, piling out, hot on his heels. Reaching the rear corner of the building, he glanced back at the sprinting mob, closing, judging his time.

Sprinting around the back, he smirked. plenty of time.

* * *

Angel, waiting, nervous, heard the commotion and as instructed, left the van and simply walked away, frightened, saying a prayer for her brother. His directions were specific in this circumstance. He made her repeat them several times. Do not, under any conditions, return to the hotel. She was to go to the coffee shop down the street and wait. He would meet her there. If he did not contact her within three hours, she was to go to the locker at the train station, take the bag of money, new identification, and leave the states.

He suggested French Canada or even Paris.

She walked along, head down, remembering his serious eyes, rejecting her arguments and pleas. When she turned the corner, the breeze chilled the tears on her cheeks.

* * *

The six steelworkers were hot on his heels, not fifty feet behind. They felt strong with their numbers, like a wolf pack, wielding hammers and crowbars. Working the area for the last six months, they knew the neighborhood. He was trapped. The idiot ran right into a dead end. Subconscious thoughts relished the bragging rights about the hunt and capture.

Racing around the corner, they skidded to a halt.

The brick walls rose two stories boxing in the dead-end alley.

There were no windows reachable.

The Ghost vanished.

* * *

The whisper arrow hit Mr. Webley right between the eyes, punching out through the back of his skull, pinning him to the head rest of his expensive high back chair.

His secretary found him seemingly studying his very important prospectus held in his rigor-mortis hands.

* * *

The uniforms were on the scene within five minutes, sealed off the area, and notified the Doom squad. They arrived by one-thirty, separated the construction workers, and recorded their individual statements, which were exactly the same. The murder scene inside the third-floor office was like the others, nothing new.

Micky left his guys, wandering back to the dead-end alley, alone, standing there in the quiet.

Maybe the guy really was a ghost, *yeah right*. He walked slow along the edge of the walls, finally reaching the dead end. He turned, facing the alley opening where the construction workers stopped. His eyes scanned, confirming there were no fire escapes and all second-floor windows, mounting jail-type bars, were at least twenty feet from the ground.

"Shit," whispering to himself. "How'd the fucker do it?"

He shut his eyes, forcing them closed for a full minute. Then, he opened them for a fresh look. Nothing. Disgusted, he started walking back, wondering, and spotted the storm drain dead center in the lane. Bending over, he looked close and spotted the fresh pry scrapes.

"Son of a bitch."

Walking back to the street, Cynthia and her press mob were all over him and he proceeded to piss them off.

By 4:00 PM, the team formed up in the squad room, comparing notes.

Grezer started, "That storm drain was spooky man, even for me. I didn't think they were that big, but a small guy could make some real-time runnin' hunched over. The city crew said the pipes get even bigger downstream, reaching twelve feet round. They said you had to be careful of methane gas buildin' up in pockets. A couple of whiffs and it's goners. It's not a good place to chase a killer, especially a *hombre* like this Ghost nut."

Kraut stood up.

"We got a little luck. The foreman at the construction site left and the guys decided to hit the Philly sandwich joint and snag a couple of beers instead of their usual brown bag. Our Ghost killer was surprised."

"They described him as white male, twenties, five six or seven, slight build, dark complexion, black hair, dark clothing. The green van was found a couple of blocks away and impounded. The crime lab guys are goin' over it with a fine-tooth comb. The arrow from this hit matched the others."

Micky briefed everybody on the phone call from New Orleans and the letters marked on the five arrows.

"That gives us the letters, E, S, E, S, and M from there, and we have a G, R, O, F, and a D. But we're missing one. Let those rumble around in those mushy heads of yours. See what you come up with."

"Alphabet soup?"

Micky ignored him.

"Pop, hot foot it down to city works. Get a map of the storm drain system,"

Micky's mind was clicking.

"Spook, stay on top of the lab. Kraut, find some tear gas bombs, smoke bombs, and a dozen surplus gas masks. We might need 'em . . . ask Mabel. She's probables got a closet full of crap, or she knows were to get it. Get some heavy-duty flashlights and check about walkie-talkies. Grezer, find out what kinda tools we need to handle those heavy drain covers. We want to be able to get in fast. What other hazards are in those drains? Check power, bugs, rats. What about germs?"

He paused, looking at his guys.

Kraut had to ask.

"Hey, Grezer, what about gators. I heard stories."

"God, I hate small dark holes," Dago said seriously.

"That's not what your girlfriend says," Kraut quipped.

"Yeah, does your dick know?" Spook added.

"Is that why you're always tryin' to plug 'em up?"

"I'm serious, guys. I freeze up. I even hate elevators."

Micky recognized the problem.

"That's okay, if we go down the hole, we're gonna need a guy topside to coordinate, you're it."

Dago straightened with a sigh of relief.

"Cheeks and Breed were cleared by IA. They'll be back fulltime tomorrow . . ."

He looked around, thinking.

"Anything else?.... Okay, let's hit it."

Everybody split to do their thing.

CHAPTER 33

AT THREE O'CLOCK, Angel sat by the window nursing another cup of coffee, checking her watch again for the hundredth time. She was frantic, worried, and afraid. Her heart thudded, pounding her head, and her stomach roiled. She kept swallowing, not wanting to throw up. She wondered what happened? She heard a bunch of men yelling and people running toward the alley. She was afraid for her brother. She prayed, knowing God would not listen. She cursed her sin, promising to stop if he returned safe.

Just then, a tap on the window made her jump. She turned, seeing him grinning, safe and dirty. She laughed out loud with joy, rushing outside, hugging him, never wanting to let go.

Walking slowly back to the hotel, arm in arm, she noticed his limp.

The waitress moved to clean the table. She was watching the young girl for the last hours, knowing some jerk broke her heart. She was surprised to see him show up. They usually don't. At least hers never did.

She watched Angel run into his arms, feeling a twinge of jealousy as she sized him up. He was good-looking, dangerous, the kind of dangerous that makes a woman flop on her back. The plains and angles of his face framed deadly eyes that both frightened and drew women like flies to webs. Yeah, she knew the type.

She shrugged with a sigh.

At least she left a great tip.

*　　*　　*

After the Doom squad stirred the cop crowd, they slid into the rear booths as Julie showed up with the coffee.

"Julie, how come you're workin'?"

"I'm doin' a split."

She took their orders, surprised she didn't have to field smart-ass remarks. Maybe they're too tired or the murder series is bugging them.

"Let's see if I got this right," Kraut said. "Grezer's married, Cheeks is getting' hitched in a few days, the sarge is engaged, Pop and Julie are an item, Spook's got a steady, and Dago looks like he's in love. What the fuck's goin' on here? Is there somethin' in the water?"

"Just you and Breed left," Cheeks said.

"Damn straight, and we are stayin' footloose and fancy-free, right, Breed?"

"Whatta ya mean, we, white man?"

Kraut gave him a dirty look, but unwilling to give up, he turned to Cheeks.

"Shit, in no time you'll be pickin' out names for your rug rats."

Breed leaned forward, very serious.

"Do you guys know the legend on how Indians name their children?"

The whole bunch leaned forward, anxious to learn some real Indian lore.

Breed leaned in a tad more, voice low.

"In the beginning days, a young brave asked the medicine man how they choose names for their newborn. The medicine man sat him down and told him that when a papoose was born, the warrior father looked out his teepee and chose the first thing he saw."

Breed paused, starting to talk like an Indian.

"If warrior see great eagle in air," he stopped, looked up to the ceiling for effect. "He name papoose *Flying Eagle*. If he see deer, he name *Running Deer*. Why you ask, *Two Dogs fucking*."

The bunch moaned, laughing at the same time, knowing they'd been had. Julie giggled at her station.

"We hear you, Julie," they sang in chorus.

Julie came out with their orders, still chuckling, and slid their plates across the table with her usual expertise.

"Kraut, Kathy wanted me to tell you one of the nurses yesterday thought you were cute," Micky said.

Pop choked while Kraut picked up his glass of water, holding it up to the light.

* * *

Settling in his chair, Micky unrolled the paper to the full-page headline.

GHOST ARROWS KILL AGAIN

He noticed Cynthia had her own byline. She was moving up in the world. He skimmed down to the good parts blasting the police department for withholding information and putting the public in danger. But the next paragraph caught his rapt attention.

> *The Doom squad, headed by Sergeant Delaney, is nothing but a wild posse breaking as many laws as those they hunt. Their brazen attitude, along with their lynch-mob mentality, makes one wonder who are the true criminals. It is time for the mayor and the citizens of this city to rein in this gang that hides behind a badge.*

Damn, he thought, when that broad gut punches, she goes right for the gonads.

CHAPTER 34

THE NEXT MORNING, the squad sat there numb. They were looking at six murders in four days and had zero to go on. They weren't sure if it was a woman-and-man team or if more suspect were involved. They still didn't know the common thread tying them together or if it was a thrill killing.

The whole crew had their own fantasy on how to respond to that witch's article in the *Post-Dispatch*. The worst was probably burying her alive. Well, maybe it was burning at the stake.

Micky interrupted their thoughts.

"The lab lifted some good prints off the panel truck but no match to a suspect yet."

Grezer reported *nada* on the registration.

"The green van was bought in St. Louis at a car lot on Tamarack, *"Neal's Deals on Wheels"*. I drove by early AM hoping to get lucky, maybe find an emergency number or a cleanup guy sleeping in the back room. No luck. It's a schlock shop selling junkers, barely keeping the doors open. Attempts to find Neal at home failed. Nothing in the phone book, water department, or gas and electric.

"Ol' Neal ain't stupid," Grezer said.

"He's probably got a mob of pissed-off customers lookin, to tar and feather him for sellin' that junk. Anyway, I'm gonna be waiten' outside his office at ten."

Their toast was scooping up the last of the eggs when Cheeks and Breed came through the door, all smiles. IA was done. Julie filled their cups as they slid into the booths announcing they got a blank sheet, it was a clean kill.

By ten, Micky trudged over to the *Stalag* to visit the mayor. Like usual, he trotted up the rank of wide granite steps, noticing the stone lions gracing the entrance looked grim and figured it wasn't because of the blanket of pigeon shit.

When he entered the office, Margie, as usual, greeted him with a warning smile, whispering the mayor was in a foul mood. He kept moving, mouthing his thanks and with a deep breath, opened the door, ready for an ass chewing.

The usual crowd, waiting, sat stiff, ready to gang-bang him. The mayor, chief, and SS wanted a chunk of his ass. Barnes shuffled, looked grim.

After a half-hour of bullshit chatter, the bottom line was the mayor was not happy. The editor from the *Post* called him personally to complain about Micky's uncooperative attitude.

The mayor was not happy with the performance on the case. He was not happy because they were not keeping him updated in a timely manner, and he was not happy with Micky's attitude. Nothing new, Micky thought, same shit he's always unhappy about.

Micky watched the red-faced stumpy bastard pace in front of him chomping on a cheap-ass cigar. He glanced at SS drooling with admiration and fought hard to control his snicker.

But he sat there, forcing a pleasant expression, letting the little fucker get it out of his system. Also, Barnes gave him a stern look, a silent warning for him to keep his trap shut.

He knew Micky too well.

Actually, Micky felt very calm, resigned to the bullshit.

He did, however, have an irresistible urge to wipe that silly ass grin off SS.

Micky, glanced at Barnes again, read his thoughts, catching his stare, which said, *You do and I'll have your ass.*

A half-hour later, he tromped by Mabel's desk royally pissed thinking he'd ask Kathy if she wanted to move to San Diego. Pulling up at the coffee maker, now affectionately called the *nuclear plant*, he glanced at Mabel to see her *"I dare you"* look.

With a sneer, he filled his cup, thinking, What the hell, as long as it don't make my weenie weak. He pushed through the door holding it at arm's length remembering her desk drawer. As a cop's lingo would say, *"She had paraphernalia commonly used by sexual sadists in plain sight in her desk drawer."* He knew he had to talk to her but dreaded it. I mean, how does one approach a subject like that? He made a quick decision.

He'd do it later.

At eleven thirty, the team returned for lunch and briefing. Micky noticed none of them were balancing a cup of Mable's brew. Maybe they knew something he didn't.

"Grezer, you first."

"Sarge, we got the gas masks and bombs. I divided them up between the cars."

He glanced at Kraut.

"No alligators, least not big ones, but there are rats big as poodles. Then you got your roaches and those big black water bugs, which I personally hate. Some tubes have phone wires, but they're all sealed in their own pipes. Should be no problem. Typical germs you'd find in a rainforest. The biggest hazard was methane gas. They really stressed that."

Spook added, "Zero makes on the prints from the lab. We did find somethin' weird though. You know how ol' Chester is about his files. Nobody screws with his files. He's like a little mad scientist. Anyway, after classifying the whirls, swirls, and ridges, they went to the file where it should be if we had a card on the suspect. Nothin' there, but there was a yellow card with the words, *national security*. No name, date, no notations, nothin'."

"When Chester found it, I thought he was gonna have a heart attack. It was like he got raped. No explanation how it got in the file. Of course, there's no way to tell if it's our guy, some other guy, or if someone just screwing with Chester. I asked him to do a complete search to see if there were any more yellow cards. He said it'd take a day or two."

Spook took a breath.

"Personally, I think somethin' weird's goin' on."

So did Micky.

At two, he decided to zip over to the hospital to see his wife-to-be. She was good at crossword puzzles, and he wanted to get her read on the letters.

A half-hour later, sitting in the employee lounge in a back booth, they stirred their coffee, looking like lovesick teenagers. He really meant *sex-starved* teenagers. After the usual chitchat, he gave her the letters to see if she could figure something out.

She asked him in what order the letters were found. He didn't know the sequence of the first five, but he gave her the ones he had and told her about the missing arrow. There was no way to tell how long the word or phrase was or even if it was.

"You're not giving me a whole lot to work with here."

Micky noticed her cute little frown as she concentrated on the letters. God, she was sexy, he thought. She really turns me on. He quick looked around, making sure the room was empty. With the coast clear, he moved next to her, nuzzling her neck and slid his hand up her skirt, petting her leg. His fingers felt the smooth nylon as they moved slowly to the hooked garter belt.

"Jack, don't, not here." She giggled.

Nibbling on her ear, he continued petting the baby softness inside her thigh leading to her sex. Her breath quickened as his hand reached her panties, his fingers hungry for her as one slipped under the elastic, entering her wetness. He listened to her sighing breath as she whispered, "Jack, please, someone will come."

"I know," he whispered, nuzzling her neck deeper. She wiggled with a chill as his finger stroked and teased her swollen nub. She moaned, "Oh god, don't," closing her eyes, pumping against his hand.

In seconds, she gasped, shuddering against his fingers with a settling sigh. Then, turning to him with a guilty look, she giggled, relaxing against him.

"I can't believe what we just did."

He smiled cocky.

"Wanted to give you somethin' to remember me for the rest of the day."

She stood, straightened herself, and noticed him taking off his sport jacket.

Walking out, he carried it directly in front. She put her hand over her mouth, stifling another giggle, realizing his predicament.

"Serves you right."

She laughed, taking his arm.

"I'll make it all better tonight."

At four o'clock, he pushed back in his chair, waiting for the team. Mabel buzzed, informing him FBI Agent Tommy Jagger holding on line two.

Picking up the receiver, he told himself he would talk to her about the sex toys tomorrow. He also wondered why old Tommy was being so formal.

"Tommy, my friend, how they hangin'?"

"Right now, they're pinched up tight, buddy."

Micky stiffened. Something was wrong.

"Micky, I'm calling from a payphone. I'm taking a chance your phones not bugged because it goes through an operator. I'm not sure of mine."

"What's up, Tom?"

"I started asking a few people about that special arrow and within hours I was sitting in front of my boss. I was ordered not to ask any more questions about arrows and not to respond to any of your inquiries."

"You're shittin' me. Why?"

"Friend, I have no idea but my best advice is to cover your ass. Somebody's tryin' to hide somethin' and it goes high up the ladder."

Micky's mind raced. He knew Tommy was sticking his neck out by warning him.

"Tom, thanks big time. I understand the risk. Let's not talk until this thing shakes out."

"Okay, watch your back, friend."

Micky cradled the receiver slow, not knowing his next move. The yellow card in the fingerprint file now made sense. Now he knew, for certain, the prints on the missing card belonged to the killer.

Pushing back, he let his mind drift. They had five dead gangsters in New Orleans. They had six ordinary citizens dead in St. Louis. All killed with a special arrow marked with a different single letter. There was a missing finger print card with heavy interference from unknown powers covering, hiding information. It all spelled a mess that didn't make sense.

Shit, he thought, if we connect the dots on those six citizens, I know we'll have the answers.

At five, the gang dragged in. Micky decided to keep Tommy's call close to the vest for the time being. He already knew the clues left at the scene would be thin, if any, and was now certain there would be more victims.

The team looked down in the mouth. He needed a break in the case to get them back on track, but damn, he had zip, so he'd do the next best thing.

"Pizza tonight at Napolis, on me, no excuses."

"Shit, Sarge, parkin's a bitch."

"No problem. We'll pile in two cars."

"Dibbs on shotgun," Spook said.

CHAPTER 35

AFTER A FRESH shower, Gabriel felt like a new man. His ankle looked worse than it felt, but Angel treated it like a deadly injury. He smiled as she fretted over him demanding he stay off his feet. She insisted he stay in the easy chair and yelled fake angry when he didn't keep his foot propped up on the chair.

He remembered the injury to his arm as a boy and her tears of fear and worry tending him. She was so young and brave that night, sewing his arm. The thought of losing her caused a chill to climb his spine, tickling the hairs on his neck. Surprised at the strong reaction, he realized how much he depended on her.

Watching her move, preparing lunch, his eyes could not help coasting over her body, his thoughts drifting to the first time they shared their love.

He read somewhere some brothers and sisters experimented when they were young, but then, put it aside and went on with their lives.

As she puttered around, she bent over, picking something up and he felt his body stir. It was wrong, he knew, but also knew he would not stop. Their lives in the swamps, alone, dependent on each other, molded their behavior on this path. He loved and desired her as a wife, and when she turned, smiling at him, he knew she felt the same.

The next day, they sat at the table reviewing their actions and what was accomplished.

"*Mon amour*, please, let us stop. We have done enough. I had a dream our brother smiled and thanked us. He was avenged. The scales were balanced."

Gabriel looked at his sister. He wanted to do what she asked. He could tell she was afraid for them.

"*Cheri*, the worst of the men have not paid. If they are not called to answer, it will dishonor those less guilty who paid the ultimate price. If I do not complete my vow, they have died in vain."

He took her hand.

"You know if I could, I would honor your wish, but, if I do not honor my word, my life means nothing. You will grow to hate me and I could not live if I lost you."

Tears rolled down her cheeks. She felt trapped. There seemed no way out. Looking into her brother's eyes, she saw his only path.

The die was cast.

"*Cheri*," he said, "please listen to me. You must leave me for a while to finish this task. The rest will present unknown dangers I cannot prepare for. My mind needs to be free of fear for you. If I worry for your safety, I might make a mistake."

Angel lowered her head knowing he was correct, but then, she raised her eyes, determined not to leave him.

"I know you are trying to protect me, but I am staying. We will see this through together. I am more of a help than a hindrance. You know this is true. So, I will stand with you, come what may."

Her tears rolled again.

"You are my brother, my love."

They spent the day with a walk and lunch at a nice café, and as the day wore on, her good cheer slowly returned. They purchased another vehicle, a nineteen fifty-two Plymouth, dark brown in color, under a different name, from a different car lot. When the dealer asked for his driver's license to complete the paperwork, Gabriel dropped cash on his desk and it was forgotten.

The next stop was an army surplus store. It was time to prepare a backup escape route. A half-hour later, the trunk on the Plymouth was stuffed.

On the way back to the hotel, he drove to an ice cream parlor, finally bringing a smile. He promised to stop the hunt until his ankle was better.

Licking their cones, he laughed at her childlike smile and the *choclat* on the tip of her nose.

He loved to see her happy.

He would make good use of the time. He would be more thorough in his planning and choosing the place of the kill. It would give him time to scout his targets and map his escape more carefully for he knew now the hunter was being hunted.

CHAPTER 36

AT FOUR THIRTY, the Doom squad of eight proceeded down Jefferson in two unmarked cars looking forward to pizza. Micky, driving, followed pop, as they crawled along in the rush hour traffic. It seemed every red light was conspiring against them.

"Big surprise," Micky muttered, stopping at the next intersection.

"Shit, Sarge, put the flasher on the roof and run it." Suddenly, a city bus behind them started leaning on his horn. Micky glanced in the rearview mirror.

"What's with that asshole? Nobody can go anywhere."

The bus driver kept blaring, causing them all to turn around with an appropriate remark. Then their heads jolted back. The driver tapped their rear bumper. Micky threw the car in park and jumped out, wondering what this guy's problem was.

Knowing his temper, the rest bailed out to make sure things didn't get out of hand.

The bus driver, folding his door open, yelled, "I got a lady havin' a baby."

Micky groaned, climbing the steps. The driver was right. There was a negro lady ready to pop, and no time for a code three run to the hospital.

While trying to figure the best course of action, Kraut elbowed through, taking charge.

"You guys get everybody off the bus," he ordered.

He helped the lady lay in the aisle, telling her he was a police officer and everything would be okay.

"Cheeks, you might as well get used to the drill. Get up behind her head, prop her up, give her some support."

Mickey backed off, radioed for an ambulance while the others emptied the bus and tried to get traffic moving. A crowd gathered, talking all at once, while cars honked their impatience.

"How'd the bus driver know we were cops?" Breed asked.

"Let's see," Spook said, putting his fist to his chin. "Four big lugs in cheap suits stuffed in a stripped down Ford decorated with dents and an antenna on the trunk lid. Gee, I don't know. Musta been a lucky guess."

Breed flushed, going to direct traffic, muttered "These guys have no mercy."

Inside the bus, Kraut had things well in hand. For a big guy, he moved sure and gentle, giving soothing encouragement to the mother. Micky returned to tell him the ambulance was on the way, code three, hoping he didn't have to lend a hand.

Hell, he thought, I'm the supervisor. I supervise.

He decided to take a quick peek. In all the years in the department, he never helped with a birthing, which he was always thankful for.

Looking over Kraut's shoulders, he heard the mother grunt and push and the top of the baby's head appeared. He stood there, transfixed, amazed at the event. He felt his body rush realizing the importance of new life coming into the world. This was really something, he thought. This was as simple and as complicated as it gets.

Micky watched the baby's head push out, stopping momentarily at the tiny shoulders. Kraut's rough hands, steady as a surgeon, made sure the head was supported and the umbilical cord was not wrapped around the tiny throat.

The mother, sweating, tried to make the best of things. Micky was sure she was not happy with all this attention and men gawking, but life had its own timetable. Everything else, a hundred people standing around, traffic halted, cops everywhere, and every other pressing need would just have to wait because this baby demanded center stage.

Finally, the mother's next push freed the soft body and the little boy slipped into Kraut's waiting arms. He quickly slipped his fingers around the baby's ankles, hoisted him upside down, and smacked his butt. No one said a word, the silence dragged like days waiting for the magic cry. Nothing. Micky started to panic. Kraut smacked him again. Nothing. Micky, glancing at

Cheeks, saw real fear. Micky started to turn when he heard the most beautiful god-awful scream. Whipping back around, he saw the caramel gunky baby raising hell and Cheeks, grinning ear to ear.

Micky was conscious of Breed right behind him, hearing the ambulance in the distance.

Grezer poked his head in the door.

"The cavalry's comin'."

Breed jumped, turning.

"Jeez, Grezer, don't ever say that to an Indian."

Micky snickered and the rest chuckled. The new mommy looked at Breed and smiled. She even got the joke.

Micky stuck his head out the door of the bus.

"It's a boy," he yelled to the cheers and clapping of the crowd.

He turned back, feeling the depth of the event. He couldn't help thinking of the old joke about the little five-year-old boy witnessing the birth of his little brother. The doc had a hell of a time, but finally the baby came out and when the doc smacked him on the ass, the little boy said, "Smack him again, he had no business crawling up there in the first place."

Micky thought he had a weird sense of humor as he watched Kraut lay the baby on the mother's chest, congratulating her. He stalled cutting the umbilical cord hoping the ambulance guys would handle it.

"Traffic's messed up, Sarge. The ambulance's havin' a hard time gettin' through."

The afterbirth was being expelled. Kraut knew the cord needed to be cut.

"Sarge, gimme your shoelaces. …Breed, gimme your knife… fire the edge first."

Micky stooped, fumbling with his laces as Breed pulled his knife and ran the flame of his Zippo along the cutting edge. In minutes, Micky watched, fascinated, as Kraut tied the cord in two places and cut between them.

Finally, the first aid guys jumped aboard and everyone scrambled to get out of the way. In seconds, the new mother and baby were strapped on a gurney and out the door. As they rolled her away, she took Kraut's hand, thanked him, and asked his name. Five minutes later, the mother was gone with her newborn son and the crowd cheered the cops.

Grezer raised his arms, smiling, relishing the spotlight saying, "Thank you, thank you. It was nothin', really."

"Grezer, what the hell you doin? All you did was stand around," Pop said.

"Hey, man, don't melt my moment in the sun," he shot back, taking another bow.

Micky wished he'd had a camera to capture the smile on Kraut's face. He thought this was just what the doctor ordered to get the team's juice back. Something like this reminded them all why they were cops.

A half-hour later, they sat in front of cold beers and peperoni pizza talking about the baby, life, and other meaningful bullshit.

"Hey, Kraut, the mother said she's gonna name the kid after you."

"They're gonna name the poor kid, *Kraut?*" Spook said.

"Hey," Micky put in, "I furnished the shoe laces."

Kraut was floating on air. He loved kids any size, any flavor. Micky remembered when Kraut walked a beat, he witnessed an accident ending with a Buick on its side pinning a little girl by the legs. The girl was screaming in pain, and he ran over, stooped with his back against the car and lifted it up to all four wheels. The crowd couldn't believe their eyes. It was an impossible feat.

Later, when interviewed by a reporter, he said he didn't remember doing it. the only thing he could remember was the little girl being afraid and screaming.

The guys on the job dubbed him "Mighty Joe Young". He was not only strong as a gorilla, he was kinda built like one with a heavy chest and thick muscles causing him to walk ape-like. Although not a handsome man, with a bald head, eyes too close, and a nose that met too many fists, he was a gentle giant born with a tenderness for women and children like his namesake.

The team ragged him unmercifully, but loved the hulk. He was a solid friend and a police brother and as they held their mugs high in a toast, he was a hero this day.

CHAPTER 37

ANGEL WAS AS happy as she was in the bayou with just the two of them alone in the hotel suite. With the small kitchen, she was able to cook for them like when they were young. They played cards and tic-tac-toe, giggling like children until she caught him cheating. She knew he did it on purpose so she could catch him and get angry, which led to wrestling and making love.

There was no rush of time, no crowds, no killing, and no one to judge them. She wished with all her heart it would not change but watching her brother working with the maps and reading the newspapers, she knew it was not to be.

CHAPTER 38

T HEY TRIED TO make it back to their booths without a lot of fanfare, but it was not in the cards.

"Hey, Kraut, you finally get to see what a pussy looks like."

"Yeah, and it don't run sideways like you thought."

"Why didn't ya tell the kid to hurry, yer pizza getten cold."

"Hey, I did and all I heard was this distant echo saying, 'tough shit'."

"Central said you guys can't direct traffic worth crap."

"Hey, we only had six fender-benders and one fatal."

"Hey, Sarge, what'd you do?"

"I boiled water."

They rolled in their booths with a chorus of "Hi, Julie."

As she started pouring, the guys noticed the special smile pass between Julie and Pop and lamented their loss.

Their male code prevented any sexual jokes and remarks as long as the two were an item. they would miss bantering with her for she was a good sport. She understood their bullshit male pea-brains and was their equal. Yes, although happy for Pop, it was a sad time.

She filled their cups understanding the unwritten rules, wishing it could be different. But Pop was worth it.

"Cheeks, my boy, next week's the big day."

"You're throwin' in the towel."

"You're puttin' on the blinders."

"You're leashing the weeney."

"You're takin the fall."

"OK already," he said. "I get the message. I'm haven' enough trouble. Sharon's starting to weird out because you guys are coming."

"What? why's that?"

"Well, for one, she knows your reputation. For two, she's met you. Number three, she saw me after my bachelor party. She's sure you're goin' to mess up the reception."

"Well, son," Spook said, putting his arm over his shoulder, "you tell that pretty little lady of yours that in her honor, we will be on our best behavior. Please assure her that instead of our usual five fights, we will have no more than two."

Cheeks gave a sarcastic, "Thanks."

"Hey, what are friends for."

The first thing Kraut did after settling in at his desk was to telephone the hospital to check on the mother and new baby. After he hung up, he smiled, sorting his mail.

* * *

Micky filled his cup and sighed, knowing he couldn't put it off any longer. He trudged to his office, settled in, and buzzed her desk.

"Mabel, will you come to my office, please."

"Please?" Shit, she thought, she never heard the man say please before. Must really be heavy.

She walked through his office door, careful, with a flat expression. Micky asked her to sit down while he shuffled a couple of papers. She started to get a little nervous as he looked up at her.

"Mabel, the other day, I needed an envelope and went to your desk when you were at lun—"

"Ohh, shit, you didn't?"

"Fraid so."

"Sergeant, you're not going to spoil it, are you?"

"Well, I—"

"I mean, how often do you get a chance to beat on a Nazi."

"Nazi!...SS?"

"Oh shit, you didn't know, did Ya? Damn, I just copped out."

He smiled, "Well, I am a great interrogator."

"Yeah, sure. Now what?"

"Dammed if I know . . . Say, you wanna borrow my handcuffs?"

"I got some."

"How about spurs?"

Her eyes widened. "Oooh, spurs sound interesting."

"I'll see what I can do."

"Is that all?"

"Yep, keep up the good work."

She stood up, heading for the door.

"Mabel, do you by chance have a couple of black and white glossies?"

She turned with a smart-ass smile, raising an eyebrow.

"Of me or him?"

"Get outta here."

Well, he thought, that wasn't as bad as I figured it was gonna be.

At ten, Captain Barnes and Lieutenant SS paid Micky a special visit. The FBI district supervisor contacted the chief in person within the last hour requesting they take over the lead in the investigation of the Ghost series.

"Delaney, do you know somethin' I don't?"

Micky thought of Tommy's phone call. Those fuckers don't screw around. They want to stonewall this mess for some reason.

"Captain, the only new info I have I just received from a lieutenant in New Orleans."

Micky spent the next ten minutes explaining the probable connection to the mob murders by arrows. He conveniently left out the yellow card found in the fingerprint files and the phone call from Tommy.

"Cap, they had five murders in one day. The main target was a local hood with connections to Mayor Huey Long by the name 'Big Daddy'. The description of those arrows matches ours and were marked with a single black letter like ours, but we don't know why yet. That's it. I'm keeping my mouth tight with the press on New Orleans, the marks on the arrows, and the description of the woman. If the killer knows we know, it might run him to ground."

Barnes sat there, thinking, while SS held his usual blank expression, sitting ramrod straight. Micky would bet if he pulled up his pants cuff, he'd find Jack Boots. He allowed himself a fast flash of Mabel beating his ass with the riding crop and ordering him to lick her black stilettos.

"What do you ya think they're up to?" Barnes asked.

"Beats me, cap, but keep 'em out of my hair, okay?"

The two stood to leave.

"I can bullshit 'em a week or so, but I gotta have somethin' at the end."

Micky watched them leave, deep in thought, and forgot to give SS the customary salute. Whatever was going down, it was big to involve the attention the Feds were giving this. His mind skipped around, terrorists, spies, subversives, political intrigue, rogue nations, invasion.

He finally gave up. He didn't have a clue.

Maybe the arrow was some sort of secret weapon or better yet, it was magic. All you had to do was wave your hand over it and say "Abracadabra," and it would go off by itself and kill someone. One thing for sure, starting for the door, the whole mess pissed him off, putting him in a foul mood.

Just then, his phone rang and he picked it up with a growl.

"Delaney here."

"Hi, bro, brother Mike. Havin' a bad day?"

Micky plopped back down. He hadn't heard from his brother

in a while, hadn't seen him in a year since the diocese sent him to Arizona to spread the good word.

"They finally install telephone poles out there?"

"Yeah, wanted to let you know I'm coming for a visit next week."

"Great, I'll hide my *Playboy* magazines."

"Why?"

"So, you won't get any impure thoughts."

"Too late."

"Man, I don't want to hear that. You're a priest now dummy."

"I see you're finally cleaning up your foul language. You usually refer to me as "asshole". I kinda miss it."

"Well, I want you to avoid temptation."

"You know, I'm a priest and a guy, but unlike you, I have good judgment, common sense, and willpower."

"Okay, asshole. You have a place to stay?"

"Thought you'd never ask."

"That's settled. What time and date. I'll pick you up."

After hanging up, Micky sat back, remembering when they were kids. He bought comic books with his hard-earned money and his younger brother would read them but never buy any of his own. It ticked him off so he locked them up. But his wise-ass brother, saint that he is, buys the same cheap lock, keyed the same, and kept reading his comics on the sly. Micky couldn't remember him ever buying one comic. He wondered if he confessed because he was sure it was pretty close to a mortal sin.

Thinking back on their growing up, he wondered how he

ended up a cop and his brother a priest, besides the obvious, being Irish and Catholic.

He remembered those Irish days with mixed feelings, recalling Dad's side of the family raising hell. The beer-drinking, the arguments, the fights, but also the good times, laughing, the picnics, and simpler times. Every special occasion was an excuse for a party, be it a wedding, baptism, or funeral.

The Delaney family crowd would gather in someone's basement with washtubs of iced beer. It always surprised him no matter how poor they were, there was always money for beer and cigarettes.

At every shindig, his grandma Sis met everyone at the door, reminding the men, whether cop or crook, to leave the guns on the bed in the bedroom with their coats. He was only five or six when he was wandering around and discovered the guns, handcuffs, brass knuckles, and saps thrown on top of the bed.

But for those few hours, there were no sides, no rights or wrongs, and differences put on hold for a good time. If a drunken temper did flare, a handful of Irish priests stepped in to negotiate the peace.

Micky's thoughts drifted back to the present as he flipped his sport jacket over his shoulder and turned out the lights. He looked forward to his brother's visit and the good times they used to have.

* * *

The police informant closed his office door, telling his secretary he did not want to be disturbed. He had to calm down. He forced himself to sit back and think. He wondered which kid they framed was doing the killing. He knew it would create suspicion if he tried to find out which jury the dead guys served on. Tomorrow, he would feel around the edges. Shit, he thought, it could be any one of a dozen guys. He thought he would shit when Delaney briefed them on the killings in New Orleans. Big Daddy paid big for the last five years helping him move his booze.

There's a good chance the killer don't know about me, he thought. Maybe he's just pissed at the jury. Besides Big Daddy and his thugs, the jury's the only ones being hit.

No. He couldn't take the chance. The thought of an arrow sticking through his head made a chill crawl up his back. Shit, I have to protect myself. If I knew who he was, I would arrange an accident. He reached for the phone and dialed, thinking the best thing to do is scare the guy off.

"Cynthia, hi, how ya doin'?"

"Well, stranger. I haven't heard from you in a while. You got something for me."

As she listened, her eyes narrowed and her whole body wiggled. This would put her at the top of the game. She scribbled furiously, not wanting to miss a word. The best part is she can screw Delaney into the ground.

"Great stuff. Call me if you have anything else . . . Yeah, okay, I'll meet you for a drink…at the same place."

Hell, she thought she could get out of it this time. Oh well, all he ever did was play with her tits.

She giggled, *What a deal.*

CHAPTER 39

GABRIEL MADE HIS decision. He would kill the crooked defense attorney, Cristian Brunner, next. He was the logical choice because it was the best chance his death would not trigger the motive and give him enough time to complete his vow. After his death, there would be just three remaining, the prosecutor, informant, and the judge. The judge would be the most difficult.

He checked his watch. It was midnight. Tomorrow he would strike. He rolled up the line drawings of the storm drain system and folded the city map. When he reached to switch off the light, he glanced at the bed and his sister sleeping peacefully. He did not tell her he would continue his mission in the morning. He wanted to give her one more day not to worry.

She faced him, sleeping on her side with the sheet slipped

down to her waist. Her arm, folded over her chest, did not hide the pink nipple of a breast peeking with an innocent tease. Her skin, copper in the light and soft as the finest silk, flowed over her female curves in a perfect design. Her eyes, closed with dark feathered lashes, hid the passion in her soul. Gabriel smiled, gently pulling the sheet to her shoulder, bending to kiss her cheek.

He must make sure her life was not in danger.

CHAPTER 40

WHEN MICKY UNROLLED the paper, he choked, spilling his coffee all over the desk. He jumped up, cursing a mile a minute at the spill and Cynthia Roberts.

Muttering, he soaked up the mess and grabbed the paper again, staring at the headline, unbelieving.

GHOST MURDERS LINKED TO NEW ORLEANS

This reporter has learned that the six murders in our city are connected to five murders of underworld figures in the Big Easy. The arrows have been identified as the same and each has a single black letter mark by the fletching . . .

Fuck, Micky thought, we got a leak. I'm gonna kick the shit out of the asshole when I find him. He kept reading. His hands shook; he was so pissed.

> *One suspect has been described as a white female, attractive, dar . . .*

Shit, who coulda done it? His mind raced. She even knew the word *fletching.* He knew it wasn't his guys. Maybe someone from New Orleans called. Naw, didn't make sense. Couldn't been a beat cop? The only other two that knew were Barnes and SS, but he told them he was keeping it hush-hush. He threw the paper down and stomped out. He needed to get a little air, calm down and figure his next step. Maybe the killer won't read the paper. *Yeah, and shit don't stink . . . or is it cows don't fly?*

Scooting out the front door, he took the steps two at a time, barely trading a couple of insults with his comrades.

CHAPTER 41

AS THE TWIN-ENGINE Cessna touched down careful as a sparrow, Stan Levy closed the file folder on Sgt. Jack Delaney, thinking the agency hired the best pilots. Snugging his tie, he gathered his suit coat, and snapped his briefcase closed while the plane taxied to the rear tarmac and a private hanger.

Ten minutes later, he merged into traffic in a nondescript newer Chevrolet, driving carefully. He always made sure he never broke the local laws, not even speeding. He didn't exist and he wanted to keep it that way. There were no fingerprints, social security numbers, internal revenue records, or anything else that would allow someone to identify or locate him.

It was a while since he last visited to St. Louis. He noticed the weather was always pleasant in the fall, remembering those great chili-macs at Steak 'n Shake.

He hoped he would have the time to grab one before leaving. He thought of White Castles but knew his stomach could not handle the belly bombers. A shame, he thought, but he was getting older and his body didn't work as well as it did years ago.

He settled in at the Roosevelt under an assumed name and went to the hotel restaurant for a bagel with cream cheese and coffee. There he reviewed the sergeant's file once more, taking pride in knowing his adversaries' thoughts and motivations better than they did.

A passerby that would bother to take notice would see a slight man, well-groomed with wire-rimmed glasses making him look older than his thirty-four years. Their eyes would first be drawn to his nose not because it was large, but because it was prominent and strong, if one could use such a word as strong to describe a nose. His gray-blue eyes were intelligent and reflected a man who wrestled with the meaning of life, weighed its philosophies, and chose his course with total conviction.

What an observer could not see, though, was his history. Levy was born of parents who were very religious ascetic Jews. During the war, they were interned by the Nazis and killed in Auschwitz, which convinced him beyond any doubt that there was no God.

He was saved from the gas chamber at the last moment by the Americans who brought him to their country with new hope. It was in its interest he now devoted his life as a Central Intelligence Agent in charge of a special division dedicated to destroying America's enemies.

At 10:00 AM, he started up the steps to the precinct when he spotted the man matching the picture in his file.

"Sergeant Delaney, a moment please."

Micky turned to face a man he didn't recognize.

"I have some information on the man you seek for the murders by bow and arrow."

Levy watched Micky's immediate interest.

"Perhaps we could sit at the park bench over there. It will just take a moment, and we will know someone will not hear our conversation."

As they walked across the street, Micky sized up his newfound friend. He was wearing a Brooks Brothers dark-brown suit, matching tie, shoes, and white shirt. He looked bookish with those glasses, but he could tell there was not a timid bone in his body. He had a little accent, but the guy was smart, cagey, sneaky, stealthy, and manipulative. There were other words meaning the same but Micky couldn't think of them right then.

As Micky sat, he watched the man do the same in an easy manner, cross his legs, and turn to him.

"I want to tell you a story. It is a short one but interesting. I would appreciate your letting me tell it completely before asking your questions. I promise I will answer all those I can, but you must know there will be some I will not, even though I know the answer."

He paused. "Do you know the story of *Mulan*?".

"Never heard of it."

"Most haven't. It is the story of a male baby raised by a pack of wolves in the jungles of India. Abandoned, it suckled a bitch and survived under the worst conditions. He grew to manhood and then leader of the pack. I always thought the story a myth, but now I know otherwise."

Stan Levy lit a cigarette before continuing.

"The man you hunt is equal to that wolf boy and much more. He grew up in the bayou swamps as a child and survived. He survived the bugs, snakes, alligators, cougars, and grew strong. There was some help from an Indian that guided him in the old ways, but it was his cunning, intelligence, and strength that saw him through. He not only thrived, but he also raised and protected his younger brother and sister.

"He came to our attention after being arrested in this city. He elected to join the military in lieu of going to prison and there we discovered his talent with the bow and arrow. He was transferred to our services where he graduated with honors and served his internship in the jungles of Vietnam."

He paused, saying with admiration, "He is so much more than Mulan. He is the perfect assassin."

"You mean you created a trained killer."

Levy gave the smallest smile.

"You must know of the problems we are experiencing in Vietnam. Its importance to our national security and democracy in the world cannot be overstated. Unfortunately, at present, we are not in a position to commit our forces, other than military advisors, mainly because of an ignorant public. We needed a plan to stall the intentions of the Vietcong. This man helped us create chaos in the North Vietnamese officer ranks and village elders sympathetic to their cause. It was designed to delay and discourage their aggression toward the south until our country was ready. This man was the best we had for that job."

"Why bow and arrow? Snipers make more sense."

"Yes, I thought the same and it was what we used in the beginning. It was very effective at first, but soon the enemy became used to the hazard, understanding it for what it was, a mere physical aggravation. But the arrow created fear and panic. There was something ancient and mystical that affected the people. At some primitive level, there was a fear the gods were intervening, and they started to question the righteousness of their cause.

"Our man had one hundred and fourteen kills and became a legend in the country. He was also the most effective tunnel rat in the division. He seemed born to rooting out the enemy from their burrows. They named him *le Revenant*, which is French for the 'the Ghost'."

Levy, blowing his cigarette smoke to the side, smiled.

"I found it an unusual coincidence and very perceptive of your local newspaper reporter that also dubbed him the same."

Micky grunted. He just wanted to kick her in the balls if she had any. He now understood the killer's escape in the storm drain. He read about the tunnel rats in *Life* magazine. Now those guys had huge steel *cajones*.

"So why did you come all the way, from wherever, to tell me this beautiful fairy tale?"

"We want him back and need your help."

"You're kiddin'? You want me to catch a cold-blooded killer

responsible for at least eleven murders in the last week and hand him to you? Why would I do that?"

"We need his talent. The situation in Vietnam is worsening every day, and the United States is still not ready. We need him to upset their momentum and buy more time. Otherwise, I fear, the lid will blow off, the south will be invaded, and thousands of our young men will die."

Micky was thinking.

"What's his name?"

"Come now, Sergeant, you know better."

"Why is he killing these citizens?"

When Captain Sanders informed him that Gabriel insisted on leaving to take care of some family business, Levy's people went to work. They learned of the brother's death and the link between New Orleans and his subsequent arrest in St. Louis.

Levy knew exactly why Ghost killed the men in New Orleans. He knew why he was killing the male members of the jury and the prison guard. He also knew the judge and prosecutor were next.

"I don't know, but I know how he thinks. He believes they deserve it. His moral code is not like yours or mine. His is more simplistic, born from the conditions he survived in the wild. Without getting too complicated, it follows pretty much the law of the jungle. The protection of the pack, or family, is paramount. Not only would any threat be met by the alpha male's deadliest force, he would seek revenge for any in his care."

"But why these people?"

Levy shrugged, tapping out his cigarette.

"Who can tell. For some reason he views these people as evil. Perhaps they have wronged him or his charges in some way."

Micky shook his head.

"I can't give a killer away."

"Why not?"

"Because he's killed eleven people!"

"But they are already dead. His death or imprisonment will not bring them back. We will take him back to Vietnam. We now have the noose to control him with the threat of arrest and death here. And, when he serves his country and no longer of use, he will be terminated."

Micky looked hard at this little man talking of killing people like stepping on a bug.

"Man, that's cold."

"Come now, Sergeant. You and I, along with others, make decisions all the time on who lives or dies."

Micky turned to him to protest.

Levy held up his hand wanting to continue.

"I've studied your life with great interest, Sergeant Delaney. I'm familiar with your childhood, your military service, and your best friend, Danny Murphy, that you affectionately called Shamy. You are a police officer on the front lines and I know you to be an honest man but a man no less. You have administered your own brand of street justice as your fellows have. I might mention the unusual suicide of the Lollipop killer not so long ago as an example."

Micky was shaken, this guy probably knew when he took a piss.

"You believe the killer you hunt today deserves death. But his death does not have to be tomorrow, a month, or a year from now. It can be after serving his country, helping us destroy its enemies, and, in the process, save the lives of countless American soldiers."

Micky was getting worried. This guy started to make sense.

"It will be easier if you agree to work with me. That way we will not be competing. You must remember you are up against a formidable foe. He has the cunning of an animal and the intelligence of man. He can go weeks without eating and exist indefinitely on sewer water, eating rats and bugs. He can smell you a hundred yards away, and his depth perception rivals that of an eagle. He can stalk the wiliest animal and has the patience of the alligators he grew up with. His immune system has handled the worst this world can deliver from fever to maggots. Add to this, with gun or arrow, he never misses. This is a man like no other. He will not die easy."

Levy's eyes zeroed on Micky.

"I know this man. I know what motivates him. I know what has to be done to capture him, but I need your help."

"I got a couple of loose ends to clear up.... How come the headshots?" Micky asked.

"In my humble opinion, I believe it is related to a casual comment he made one day. He said his mother told him that evil springs from the minds of men. I think he wants to strike at the heart of the evil."

Humble opinion, my ass, Micky thought. You, arrogant SOB. You don't have a humble bone in your body. You enjoy playing God.

"Why come directly to me and ignore the chain of command?"

"This operation is on a need to know. Also, the character of some of those above you leave a lot to be desired."

Micky couldn't argue with that.

"You know I'm a cop and my name. Seems only fair I know yours and who you work for."

Levy smiled. "I could give you my name but it would mean nothing. I do not exist. I lead a special cadre of men of like minds who also do not exist."

Micky stared at the little man's steel eyes unsure of his position. This was heavy shit. He believed the guy but trusted him as far as he could throw a Greyhound, the one with wheels. This fanatic is playing God and enjoying it. He reminded himself when in doubt, punt.

"I gotta have some time to think about it."

"I understand."

Levy smiled.

"But I will require your answer by tomorrow at this time."

He glanced at his Rolex.

"Fourteen hundred hours."

He stood to leave and Micky followed suit. He offered his handshake and Micky took it. It felt firm and solid with purpose.

As they separated, Micky asked, "Why do you do this?"

Levy turned; his smile curled.

"Love of country, sir…. Love of country."

At two thirty, Stan Levy went to a payphone and placed six ads randomly spaced under personals in the classified section of the *Post-Dispatch*. The wording was simple and straightforward. He asked the ad taker to read it back to make sure there were no errors. He listened as the young man cleared his throat.

"Ghost, please come home. Your friends will protect you and yours. Telephone collect, (347) 648-7746 . . . Yes, sir, you made it in time for the evening edition. You want it to run for a week, right?"

At four thirty, when the evening paper hit the newsstand; he checked the personals and placed a call to Cynthia Roberts.

"Hello, Miss Roberts, this is Charlie Tanner calling. I have a bit of information on this Ghost killer. I'm a big fan of yours. I think you're the best reporter in this town, bar none. Anyway, I know you're a busy lady but I wanted to tell you, if you didn't know, someone's runnin' a bunch of ads in the personals for this Ghost fella. Yeah, thas right. In your own paper. Well, yer welcome, Miss Roberts. Keep up the good work. Bye now."

Stan Levy hung up the payphone, smiling. It was almost too easy. Cynthia would find the ads and mention it in her story on the front page. She'll get an atta-boy or in this case an atta-girl because it will sell more papers and keep her editor happy. Gabriel, he was positive, read her coverage because it was the most complete. Her article would lead him to the personals and hopefully, he would call.

He was prepared to guarantee the death of the prosecutor and judge if Gabriel returned. He also would ensure the financial security for his sister for life in a country of her choice.

Unfortunately, he did not know Gabriel's state of mind and the kind of stress he was under. Hopefully, it was sufficient and he would seek refuge.

Levy prepared three questions to be asked by anyone calling to ensure the real Ghost responded. If the voice answered the three questions correctly, he would be given further instructions for a clandestine pickup. The answering service had no knowledge of who hired them.

Later, sipping his evening cocktail, he wondered which way the sergeant would jump. If he came on board, his job would be easier. If not, he would still succeed even at the expense of Delaney's life.

He raised his arm, catching the bartender's attention.

"Toss an extra olive in the next one."

* * *

When Angel saw the headline, she panicked. She read the full article, trembling with fear. they described her perfectly and connected them with the killings in New Orleans. Soon, all would be lost. We must run. We must leave now.

She listened to the shower running. She was afraid to show it to Gabriel. She didn't know what he would do. He surely would agree they must leave at once. Her mind raced. At least the killing would stop. They will go somewhere safe. Paris!

They will start over. They will finally have some peace.

The shower stopped. Her hands shook.

Gabriel stepped into the room with a towel around his middle. Angel handed him the newspaper, standing quiet, while he read the article. She already decided she would take just one suitcase and leave the rest. She hoped the weather was nice in Paris.

"We will have to modify our plans."

"We are not leaving?"

"*Certainement pas!* We must complete our mission."

Angel started to argue but saw the anger in his eyes. She turned with tears, knowing she could not reason with him. With a sob, she rushed to the restroom, knowing the end was near.

Gabriel began pacing the room. He would move on the next target tomorrow. With luck, he could finish both attorneys on the same day. That would leave the judge and informant. They connected the New Orleans hits but didn't know why yet. He would make sure Angel stays out of sight. He would not depend on her to help with the next kills.

Gabriel spread the maps out again. Tomorrow he would strike.

CHAPTER 42

AT 8:00 AM, Marion's defense attorney, Christian Brunner, was running late for a deposition at eight thirty. He cursed, pissed he allowed himself to be talked into meeting this early. He preferred the normal hours of the court, ten to four.

Resigned, he scooped up the morning paper, tossed it on the front seat, and pulled out of his driveway. As usual, he couldn't help glancing at his new, very expensive, two-story Victorian home with a sense of pride and satisfaction.

Merging onto the highway, he switched on the news as he mentally prepared some meaningless questions designed to impress his client. He knew the client was going to lose and in fact, he already met over a cocktail with the opposition. They agreed on a number and he would sell it to his guy after the deposition. He quickly ran some numbers through his head figuring he should net about six grand. Not a bad number for a few hours of work.

He absently listened to the news as his Mercedes hummed down the road. He drove past the construction site of the new downtown renewal project and glanced out the windshield to see how much higher the arch was today. He'd seen the master plan and model at the last Chamber of Commerce luncheon, and was impressed. It was going to be something with that stainless steel arch reaching over six hundred feet in the air.

Over the months, he watched with passing interest all the construction and demolition going on daily. When he lowered his eyes to the highway, he glanced at the good old *Admiral* tied at the levee with hawse lines thick as fists.

St. Louis, Missouri, gateway to the west, soon would be worthy again.

The radio commentator announced a special report and he turned up the volume. He listened as the perfect radio voice listed the names of the recent victims on the bow and arrow series. Brunner stiffened; a sudden chill crawled up his spine. He jerked the car over to the shoulder, sliding to a stop.

He listened as the announcer repeated that the Ghost killer committed two more murders. Listing the first four and adding the fifth as a Benjamin Gold, owner of a jewelry store, shot in the head entering the store. The sixth was a Loyd Webley, a stockbroker, shot in the head sitting at his desk.

Brunner wiped the sweat from his brow as the other four victims fell into place. When he heard one or two names, it struck a chord, they were familiar, but he didn't know why. But listening to them as a group, he knew it was a part of a jury panel on one of his cases. But which one?

Grabbing the paper, he scanned the front-page coverage by Cynthia Roberts.

"Shit!"

He threw the paper on the seat and pulled into traffic just missing a honking pickup truck. ten minutes later he was at his desk calling to cancel the deposition. He was sorry, but he was too sick, a twenty-four-hour flu or something he ate.

He sat back in his burgundy leather chair, forcing himself to calm down. His secretary wasn't due for another hour. Which case? Which case? He didn't have many jury trials. He knew it was fairly recent.

Suddenly their faces came into view matching the names. It was the fucking Dupre case. His hands shook fumbling with the keys to the file cabinet. Finally, the drawer opened and he finger-walked to the file. Pulling it, he flopped down, and pulled the jury list. They were different names. He stared at the sheet, confused. He could swear it was the Dupre case. Dammit, which one was it?

Plopping the jury list on the desk, he sat back, thinking. His mind blank, starring at the list trying to remember as light through the window lit the paper from a different angle.

Humm, he thought, leaning forward, that's weird. He picked up the list, staring at the heading. As he studied it, he felt his body stiffen realizing it was doctored. Suddenly, the visit from Dupre's brother and sister flashed in his mind and then, a spike of fear, recalling the break-in at the office.

Grabbing the magnifying glass, he turned to the light trying to figure out the name that was written over. Whoever it was, he thought, did a shitty job.

His mind raced.

"It was that fuckin' brother, I know it."

Finally, he guessed at a couple of possible letters of the last name and frantically searched the files. It seemed like hours but in a few minutes, he had the folder and the jury list that was switched. With that part of the puzzle solved, he pushed back, closing his eyes.

Think, think, what does it mean? Am I in danger here?

He forced himself to calm down. He didn't think he was in danger. After all, he defended the kid. His brother couldn't blame him for anything. But, as planned, he lost at trial. The kid went to prison. He remembered the day the two came to his office. The sister was a looker. He remembered the two questions. Who paid for the defense and if he knew he was only sixteen? Of all the questions, why those two.

There was no way he could know Big Daddy foot the bill.

Wait a minute.

He jumped from the chair to the dead case files. His hands shaking.

"Fuck me."

There it was; he handled the older brother Gabriel three years ago. Shit, how could I forget. Because it was a slam dunk, dummy, just like all the others, Big Daddy solved his booze-running problems this way for a decade.

He sat down with Gabriel's file trying to figure out what

the asshole was going to do next. He obviously was going to kill the whole jury and probably the prosecutor and judge. The two questions kept bouncing back. He grabbed Marion's file reading everything close to see if he could be connected in some way. He was sure the brother suspected something fishy was going on.

He heard the front door open and his secretary going to her desk. He quick went out, said good morning, and told her the deposition was canceled, and since it was Friday, he decided to take the day off. There were no other appointments so he told her to take a long weekend. She deserved it.

She looked at him, wondering, but wasn't going to turn down a free day. Suddenly, her day became a little brighter. She would scoot over and pick up the waffle iron on sale at Walgreens.

Rushing back to his desk, he pulled the numbers for New Orleans from his Rolodex. He needed to verify the deaths of Big Daddy and his crew. He dialed the first two numbers, disconnected.

"Fuck."

A film of sweat covered his forehead.

A rough voice answered the third number and after a lot of fast-talking. Dropping a few names, he learned the bad news. Big Daddy and the bodyguards were, in fact, killed a few weeks ago by bow and arrow. He hung up feeling sick. He needed to call the police, but shit, if he did that, they'd poke around, maybe discover he was on Big Daddy's payroll.

He had to take a piss. He was in big fucking trouble.

Goddammit, calm down. You're okay. You're one up.

He doesn't know you know. Make a plan. You're smarter than that cracker hick. Jezus.

Grabbing Marion's file, he started reviewing it very carefully like he did when first studying law. He assumed the brother read the arrest report. Was there anything there? Five minutes later he relaxed back. Nothing that would anger the brother toward him, but he noticed the police informant's name clearly listed. He was in danger. He better call him right away plus he'd know how to deal with the asshole. After all, he was in the business.

Dialing the number, the edge of his eye caught the notation in the margin on the money receipt noting they did not want Mr. Dupre returning to New Orleans. Shit, shit, if he saw that, I'm fucked. He'll know I was working with Big Daddy.

The informant wasn't in. He left a message to call with the secretary, saying it was important.

Again, he forced himself to calm. He couldn't think straight. His armpits soaked his shirt. He had to pee bad. The brother Gabriel probably didn't see it. It was dark. He probably only had a flashlight. He would be nervous, in a hurry, and more interested in the jury list. He probably read the arrest report, switched the jury lists, and split.

Brunner, dropping the file on the desk, ran to the john.

When he came back, he dialed information and soon had Missouri State Penitentiary on the line. Ten minutes later he was back in the john hanging over the toilet with the dry heaves.

* * *

Gabriel, taking his position at nine o'clock, was surprised to see Brunner's car. When he researched this kill, he cased the area as usual and called his office a few days ago asking to speak to him. The secretary said Brunner did not get in until ten.

"Wow! He's got banking hours," he said, joking. "Are those his regular hours?"

He had Angel call the next day. She was told the same.

As Ghost was deciding on his next move, he watched the secretary arrive, go inside, and leave five minutes later.

Something was different, out of the ordinary. He started to abort but decided to wait and watch. He hated to miss this target. Time was running out. He did not know if he would have another opportunity. Taking a breath, he knew he was safe in the brush and trees. Someone would have to be within a foot to see him.

He forced himself to rethink the hunt. It was early, no one on the street. He felt certain Brunner was still inside, alone. He could be in and out of the office in one minute. Weighing the options, he decided it was worth the risk.

Ghost left the security of the brush, walking normal, toward the attorney's office, holding his bow alongside his leg.

Brunner called the informant again, no luck. Bullshit, he thought. Fuck him, I tried. Brunner decided to skip town for a while and go to Bermuda or Miami. He'd lie in the sun until the crazy SOB was in jail or dead. Shit, what a mess for a lousy two thousand bucks.

As he stuffed papers in his briefcase, he heard the front door open. Damn, he thought, why did she come back.

"Terry?"

No response. He turned, looking at his office door, wondering. He watched the door knob slowly turn and the door coasting open.

He froze.

Ghost stood there, legs spread, eyes locked on Brunner, bow bent and arrow strung.

Eyes wide, Brunner fell back against the office wall, his heart revved so fast it caused a sharp pain. His fear, so intense, he felt his shorts fill.

"No, no, please don't. I didn't mean it. Ple—"

He watched the bow slowly raise with the steel tipped arrow. His eyes locked, holding Ghost's cold and frozen eyes.

He did not see the arrow pierce his face, impaling him between the eyes.

His last millisecond thought was the strange sound his sinuses made as the bones cracked. The force of the arrow at such a short distance punctured through his skull, through the sheetrock, and three inches into the two-by-four stud.

There he hung, the fletching sticking out between his eyes, frozen in shock.

Ghost walked to the desk, picked up the three files, and stopped, starring at Brunner hanging like gutted game. He stood, quiet, waiting for his final death rattle.

Seconds later, Brunner slumped in death. Ghost turned and walked out, shutting the office door behind him.

Stepping outside, glancing around, he turned back, locked the front door, and faded into the brush.

He was wrong, it only took thirty-eight seconds.

When Gabriel returned to the hotel, he stopped at the gift shop for a rose to cheer Angel up. He unlocked the door, stepped inside, and froze. For a second, he thought he was in the wrong room when the blonde sitting on the bed, turned, smiling at him.

It was his Angel.

He was speechless.

She came to him with a big smile.

"Now I can stay and help. Do you like it?"

She twirled toward him, her full skirt billowing with her blonde hair swaying like waves against the morning sun. Spinning, her skirt, swirling up, showed white bikini panties.

Gabriel felt the static of her sex fill the air.

Stopping before him, she looked up with teasing eyes, daring him, wanting him.

Gabriel flushed, drinking in her love potion, took her there on the floor.

CHAPTER 43

WHEN TERRY, BRUNNER'S secretary, returned to work that Monday, she unlocked the door and reeled from the smell. She hesitated, but entered slowly, thinking some animal had somehow gotten inside and died. The smell grew stronger approaching her boss's office. She started to back off until he arrived. But then, she reached for the doorknob knowing he would raise hell with her for not taking care of the problem.

When she pushed the door open, she didn't even scream. She just stared a moment in shock at her boss, hanging, drying like an old scarecrow with a feathered stick stuck between his eyes. Her eyes followed the trickle of blood that flowed and dried around the curve of his nose, painting his lips black.

Then, Terry screamed.

*   *   *

Micky and the team arrived the attorney's office by nine forty-five. Micky looked at Brunner stuck on the wall and made assignments. On his way out the door, he stopped the lab guy and told him to check the rear of the arrow right away for the letter. Fifteen minutes later he headed to the mayor's office with the letter "E".

As Micky walked into the mayor's outer office, he greeted Margie in his usual flirty manner.

"Margie, my love, what's a nice lass like you doin' in a place like this?"

She smiled. She liked his teasing.

The mayor was red-faced. Micky sat there hoping he'd have a heart attack. If he did, he was sure SS would be the first one to give mouth to mouth. He glanced at Barnes who just sat there with a flat expression. The mayor kept ranting but Micky wasn't paying attention. He was thinking about the last victim and hopefully finding something in the attorney's office that would break the case. He looked over at SS. For once he didn't have that smug look.

"And another thing, sergeant. Your assignment and that so-called Doom squad of yours, your days are numbered, you hear . . ."

Micky's ears perked up at the threat and he planted a worried and scared expression on his face. That should do it, he thought, his mind wondering what it would feel like to plant his fist on that fat, red, booze bulbous nose of his. He started to smile at the fantasy when he caught Barnes warning glare. Damn, he thought, he knows me too well.

Figuring he'd better play the game or he'd never get out of there, he planted a remorseful look on his face and made some positive bullshit comments. The mayor finally hitched up his pants and dismissed them, except for SS.

Walking back to the precinct, Micky thought it was weird, but Barnes said the Nazi had a daddy with deep pockets and the mayor didn't care whose ass he smooches to get reelected.

That conjured up a horrible sight. He wondered if Mabel was the jealous type.

Hopping up the steps, Micky decided, as usual, it was shaping up to be another shitty Monday.

* * *

Micky was settled back thinking about the case when the buzzer snapped him back.

"Sorry, Sergeant, but I think you want this one. It's a lieutenant from the state prison in Jefferson City."

Micky punched the blinking light.

"Sergeant Delaney."

"Yeah, sarge, this is Lieutenant Burke out of Jefferson City. I read an article about some murders you guys are having with some arrows. You know, we had a prison guard killed on Thursday, September twentieth."

Micky shot up, all ears.

"He got an arrow through the head after work goin' into his house. No suspects."

"Do you have the arrow?"

"JC homo has it. They handled the investigation."

"What's his name and duty?"

"Al Blevins, he was a cellblock supervisor on seven."

"I'll have one of my guys there in two hours. Really appreciate the info. This might be just what we need. How does my guy find you?"

Micky jotted the address, thanking the lieutenant again.

Fifteen minutes later, Micky had Dago on the horn.

"Dago, shag your ass to Jefferson City and contact their PD homicide about an arrow murder of a prison guard. First thing I want you to do is call me with the letter. Then, do your usual and contact a Lt. A. Burke at the prison for a follow-up . . . Got it?"

"Ten-four, sarge. I'll pedal it to the metal."

Micky hung up the phone suddenly feeling pretty good. He glanced at his watch, thinking he'd slip over to visit his wife-to-be. He was perfecting this spontaneous romantic stuff. A book was definitely called for. It would undoubtedly be a best seller.

Driving along, he thought of their expected baby son. He was going to be a family man again, a second chance to hopefully get it right.

* * *

At eleven thirty, the squad returned from Attorney Brunner's office with not a whole lot.

Micky pointed to Kraut. "Whatta ya got from the scene?"

"Sarge, you already know we got the letter "E" off the arrow.

The big difference between this and the others is it was a close-up hit. The killer came into the office to do the deed. We had the secretary look around and she said there was nothing different in the office she could see. Brunner was a criminal shyster. She said he wasn't too smart. Handled a lot of slam-dunk cases."

Bam! Micky had it.

"Shit! Our victims are jurors," Micky nearly shouted.

"It's gotta be."

The whole team sat straighter, minds connecting the dots.

"Grezer, Cheeks, Breed, call the wives of our victims and ask if they served on a jury. Kraut, Dago, Pop, go back and search Brunner's files."

His mind was chugging.

"Also, check the courthouse. Look for any cases connected with New Orleans and Big Daddy."

* * *

At two o'clock, Mabel transferred the call from his special secret government friend.

"Sergeant, as we discussed, it is fourteen hundred hours and I need your decision."

"You know, you got your job and I got mine. Mine is to arrest murderers and bring them to justice. Your guy killed again. No deal."

"I regret your position on this matter. I feel I must inform you of something I failed to mention when we met. Our "R" and "D" people furnished the Ghost the finest laminated one-hundred-pound longbow made in the world. The arrows are aluminum, lighter than wood, and four inches longer with the tensile strength to ensure their silence. They have been perfectly balanced and tipped with steel tempered needle-heads. The arrows travel at more than four hundred feet per second and were designed for human game. As our Sherwood hero of old, he can literally split another arrow at a hundred yards. With that bit of information, I suggest you reconsider."

"Your guy may be king of the bayou and Vietnam, but he's in my jungle now and there's no room for the two of us."

"Well then, sergeant, you will not hear from me again but I will attend your funeral."

"Fuck off, asshole."

Micky slammed the phone down.

A half-hour later, Mabel brought the newspaper in telling Micky about the classified ads. He read Cynthia's copy plus the personals, dialed the number, and learned about the three questions. When he hung up, he knew his special friend was determined to win this contest at any cost.

He needed to brief the squad.

He dialed Lieutenant Burke at the State Penn to pave the way for Dago knowing they'd give him a ration of shit.

"Lieutenant, we need a current roster of all inmates on cellblock seven. We also need a list of inmates that were on that cellblock for the last two years. One more thing, I want any incident reports of death or injury during that time."

"Hey, sarge, you're askin' a pile here. I can get the current roster on the cellblock, but anything else has to go through channels. I can tell ya right now those incident reports will not be given up without a fight. You understand what I'm sayin'?"

"Sure do, Lieutenant, but see what you can do. It was one of your guys that bought it, remember. I've got an officer by the name of Tony Angelo in your city now, and he'll be contacting you. Thanks for your help."

He hung up, thinking, See, he could be nice and polite.

He settled back in his swivel.

They were close, he could taste it. He just started a slow rock when Mabel buzzed to remind him to pick up his brother at the airport.

Grabbing his suit coat, he scooted out the door satisfied things were rolling. He felt pretty good.

CHAPTER 44

"HI, BEAUTIFUL, WATCHA doin'."

"Who is this? Tom? Dick? or Harry?"

"Very funny. I wanted to let you know Father Mike's here and I got him settled in the guest room."

"Great, I finally get to meet a sane member of the family."

"I got a few more letters for you. The letter N as in Nora, which comes before the G, George, and the letter E as in easy, which is after D, David. Have you come up with anything yet on what you already have?"

"No, but this will definitely help. We should have some possibles soon."

"How about I come over for another cup of coffee?"

"Oh no, I know your coffee."

"Then how about counting the broomsticks in the broom closet?"

She giggled.

"Elevator, basement, how about the countertop where you are right now?"

"You are soooo bad. I like it."

"Father Mike's got some things to do tonight so I thought we'd take you out for a good steak at Riley's tomorrow."

"A date with two good-looking Irishmen and a steak too. How could I refuse?"

"You know, I fell in love with you on that first date when I watched you attack that hunk of beef like a cowboy."

"And here I thought it was my boobs."

"Boy, you are in rare form today."

When he hung up, he had to admit he was the luckiest guy on earth.

* * *

Dago called at 6:00 PM.

Jesus, Micky thought, he musta did ninety all the way.

Dago told him the letter on the arrow was an N. He was on his way to the prison but was already told the guard was a cell block boss and a real hard-ass. Any con would have loved to take him down.

"They probably won't want to give it up, but ask if there were any recent incidents on cell block seven. Also, Burke should give you a list of prisoners serving on that block . . . and drive slow comin' back."

CHAPTER 45

WHEN GABRIEL AND Angel walked through the lobby; the manager did a double-take. The sexy wife was a blonde.

"Good morning, Mr. and Mrs. Tropet."

They answered their hello, continuing out the door, and as usual, he stared at her ass.

He greeted them on purpose because she always turned and smiled, and he got a better look. He thought she looked better with her full black hair. He remembered as she walked, it swayed, the light shining it in sexy waves to match the movement of her hips. With big eyes, turned up like a cat, she filled the air with sex. Some women were born with more of that essence than others, and she had an extra portion poured into a body that wouldn't quit.

An hour later, he opened another letter from Mr. Mortel with another sixty dollars to continue reserving the room. The enclosed note apologized for not arriving earlier, but they would arrive soon. This is shaping up to be a good day, he thought, another sixty bucks in the old pocket. He just might spring for one of those new transistor radios he had his eye on.

*　　*　　*

At 8:00 AM, Miss Abigail Dobbin spotted the young Tropets leaving their room. For a second, she thought he was with another woman and wouldn't have been surprised knowing the way men were. But when they smiled, passing by with a good morning, she noticed it was the same woman, but now blonde.

What a lovely couple, she thought.

Abigail, a maid at the hotel for ten years, was in her early fifties and disappointed with her life. She never married. In fact, she did very little except work and go home to her apartment and five cats.

Because of her dull life, she was curious about those in the hotel, wondering about their lives. She would imagine all the wonderful places they traveled, whether newlyweds or not, where they were from, or where they were going.

It was great fun cleaning the rooms, playing detective and figuring it all out. She was particularly interested in the sexual antics. She would see if there were sexy nightgowns, rubbers, or vaginal gels. She sometimes discovered black rubber stuff, rope, paddles, and things she just couldn't figure out what or how they would use them.

She did though, one day, find a dildo in a nightstand and took it home knowing they would be too embarrassed to report it. She washed it really good and used it, fantasizing about the couples in the rooms.

But the young couple in room three sixty-five were a mystery. Refusing maid service, the young woman always brought the dirty linens to her in the hall and trade for clean. They were a mystery all right. She thought it strange that as newlyweds, they never hugged or held hands outside like most young couples. She did admit they were a handsome pair and was dying to get a peek in their room.

As she continued down the hall, cleaning the other rooms, she slowly hatched a plan. Hotel policy stated rooms were to be inspected when occupied at least once a week to ensure there was no damage.

Well, it had been two weeks without an inspection. They might be tearing the place up, she reasoned. She had a duty to check and could not be blamed for invading their privacy.

Her mind made up, she went to their door with the passkey, a little nervous. She told herself she'd just take a quick look around. Maybe something needs to be repaired or maybe beds made.

She tapped on the door, "Room Service."

No answer.

Looking from side to side, she twisted the key and slipped inside. Turning around, she saw everything clean and in order. Beds made, bathroom straight, and kitchenette clean. Not as clean as she would have left it, she thought, trying to justify her actions. She stepped to the bed and looked in the nightstand finding nothing but the usual Gideon Bible, hotel stationery, and envelopes.

Disappointed, she started to leave but decided to take a fast look in the closet. The clothes were neat and orderly, shoes lined up and suitcases stacked in the corner.

Her eye did catch an unusual case in the back. It was soft padded, long and narrow, and looked like a fishing rod case her father had when she was little. She decided on a fast peek because sometimes guests hid money and valuables in unusual places thinking no one would think to look. Abigail had taken a few things over the years. A few bills out of wallets, some jewelry, and even some cosmetics, but never enough to cast any real suspicion.

So, unzipping the bag, she was surprised to see the funny colored arrows and bow. Suddenly, she was frightened. She did not at that instant, why, but she was, so she hurried out of the room and went about her chores.

A half-hour later, it dawned on her what she discovered, and shook with fear. She didn't know what to do. If she told the manager, she might get in trouble for going into the room. Maybe she should just forget it. It wasn't her problem. Let someone else catch them.

But as the morning wore on, the thought of someone else getting killed weighed heavy. Finally, she went down to the front desk.

A half-hour later, the call was transferred to Captain Barnes.

Ten minutes later, he called Micky, ordering him and his squad to sit tight; he was on his way.

Barnes and SS briefed Micky in his office while the squad cooled their heels in the squad room. They knew something big was going down.

After Barnes briefed him, Micky called the desk clerk and determined the suspects left at 8:00 AM and hadn't returned. Micky very carefully explained if the couple returned before the police were in position, he was to act normal and call him immediately. He was to send the maid home and a detective would contact her there. That done, he headed for the briefing room with Barnes and SS on his heels.

Briefing the team, he felt their spirit rise to the hunt. These officers, hand-picked, battle-tested, would charge forward without question. They were old school, street hunters, men who thrived on stopping the predators of the city. This was why they were cops.

"Gentlemen, we are goin' to box him in before takin' him down. If we try to take him on the street, the lobby, or the halls, it could get real messy. Once we know he's in the room, his movement is limited. We got tear gas if we need it."

"Pop, get over to the hotel and size it up for us. Find a place close to form up before the takedown. I want everything. All escape routes, which rooms are occupied on that floor, pass key, door, how thick, hollow or solid core in case we have to kick it down."

Pop headed out and Micky told the team to draw shotguns.

"I want everybody at Fourteenth and Chambers on the

southwest corner. We'll meet there to be close and wait till Pop picks a spot for us."

"Sergeant, I'd like a word," Barnes said.

Micky stepped aside; Barnes leaned on the podium.

"Men, I want to move real careful on this one. Take your time, no mistakes. This guy's probably the toughest killer we've ever dealt with. Make sure you know what your job is and do it."

Barnes straightened and stepped back.

"Okay, guys, hit it, Fourteenth and Chambers," Micky ordered.

The room emptied.

Barnes asked Micky how long it would take to get in position. Micky said it could take upwards of an hour. Hopefully, the suspects wouldn't return until they were in place.

"Okay, we'll brief the chief and mayor."

Five minutes later, Micky, driving to the staging area, received a radio call. The female suspect just returned to the room. Micky cursed, hoping the asshole wasn't out killing someone.

Everyone formed up at Fourteenth and Chambers. Pop showed up twenty minutes later and briefed the squad.

"They're registered under the name of G. Tropet. No first name, just the letter G. There're two fire escapes at both ends of the hallway. Access out a large window. There's one stairwell, a housekeeping elevator, and two elevators for guests."

He stopped, checking his notes.

"There're only three other rooms rented on the floor, the rooms on either side of the suspects are vacant. It's on the third floor, the suspect's room is in the middle of the hall. It's a long run, maybe seventy-five feet, either way to fire escapes. The elevator's about twenty feet from their door. They're in a kitchenette, which means two rooms and two windows."

"The only one they could climb out is in the bedroom, and it's a hell of a jump to a concrete alley. I've got a passkey. The door's solid pine backed up by the usual deadbolt and viewing chain."

He stopped and looked up.

"That's it. This spot's good as any for the command post."

"Okay, thanks Pop. Here's an update. The female suspect has returned to the room. The clerk will call as soon as the guy shows up. I've got eight uniforms standing by for backup. The entry team will be Kraut, Spook, and two blues. Breed, you take the left fire escape with one blue. Grezer, take the right side with one blue. The elevators will be shut down. Dago, cover the stairs with Pop. Cheeks, back up the uniforms covering the alley."

He stopped, catching every eye.

"Here's the plan. When he returns and everyone is in position, we'll go to their door, announce our presence, and try the passkey. If that fails, we'll break it down. We've got two blues with the entry team. Everyone will wear a vest but keep in mind all victims were head shots. We don't know if he's armed, but I'm told he's as accurate with a firearm as a bow . . . Any questions so far?"

Everyone stood quiet, anxious to get moving.

"The best time to hit the door is when he just gets inside, we catch him off guard. We're goin' to move in close as we can. The clerk said there's a small room off the lobby we can use."

Micky instructed everybody to split up and walk casually to the hotel by ones and twos. When he climbed in his car, he received a radio call.

The male suspect just returned.

He jumped out of the car, hollering, "Guys, suspect's back. I want everyone in position in exactly five minutes. Pay attention, be careful."

In four minutes, Micky and the team hustled up the three floors and thirty seconds later, were huffing in the hall outside the room.

*   *   *

On the roof, across the alley from Gabriel's room, the police informant waited. He figured he had plenty of time.

It's gonna take the Doom squad about an hour to get everything in place. *He had plenty of time.* He wished there was some other way, but he couldn't let the asshole start talking to the cops. If they tie him in, it's five to ten in the big house.

Sighting down the Hensholdt scope of his sniper rifle, he had a clear view inside the room.

"Shit," he muttered, scanning through the kitchenette and the bedroom. He wasn't there, just the girl. At this angle, he could only see the bottom of the door to the hall.

"Shit. This is gonna be close. I gotta wait until he walks a few steps into the room for the best shot. The Doom squad's gonna be right behind him. I got maybe two shots before I hafta split."

Forcing deep breaths to calm himself, he watched the girl putter around through the eight-power scope. It'd been a while since he did this kind of shooting. He practiced following her in the crosshairs, deciding to take the guy first. When she ran to his side, he'd get her.

He'd be gone before the Doom squad made it through the door.

* * *

Ghost finished checking the area for his next kill sooner than he thought. He was tense and edgy. Like a wild thing, he was wary, sensing forces closing in, wondering if he could complete the three remaining kills. It would be difficult. He wished he could stop and go away with Angel to a place with few people. He shook himself, dismissing the thought, knowing he would not fail his brother. He would complete his vow.

He would set things right.

Opening their hotel room door, he decided he would take Angel to lunch and maybe take a tour of the city. Both needed to relax. He must keep his mind clear. He worried for her. He wished again he could convince her to leave.

Closing the door, he automatically wedged the piece of two by four in place against the doorknob. Hearing Angel call his name, he turned toward the small kitchen.

* * *

The informant tensed, watching the bottom of the door open and the Ghost's feet entering the room. He could see from his calves down, watching him put the brace against the door.... Good, that'll fuck up the entry team.

His target, the Ghost, came into view.

"Closer, closer, that's it."

Feeling the pressure of the steel against his trigger finger, he squeezed off his first shot.

* * *

At the same moment, Angel rushed from the kitchen to greet him. As his eyes admired her beauty, the shot rang out. The bullet pierced the window glass striking dead center in the middle of her back.

Gabriel watched her welcome smile twist to pain as she fell forward, vomiting blood.

Gabriel screamed, diving forward to catch her.

The glass splattered again; the bullet missed by inches.

Gabriel belly crawled to her, grabbed her wrist and pulled her to the shadowed wall, away from the window.

Two more shots ripped the floor missing by inches.

* * *

The informant, cursing, continued squeezing off shots, hoping for the best. The fucking broad stepped right into his line of fire. He saw her go down, but he was pretty sure he missed the guy.

He could hear the cops pounding on the door through the broken window. He had to get the fuck outta here.

* * *

Micky and the entry team, hearing the shots, yelled, "Police officers, open the door."

Weapons ready, they tried the pass key but were stopped by the wood brace.

"Take it out," Micky ordered.

The battering ram, swinging like a pendulum, smashed against the lock, cracking the door. The crash split the door.

The second one would do the job.

* * *

Gabriel, sitting on his legs, cradled Angel in his arms as she choked, trembling, blood gushing from her mouth like a fountain. Smelling her death, her last breath sighed away forever.

The Ghost howled his loss as a gray wolf.

* * *

The blood scream and wolf-howl of grief filled the hall. Micky and the rest, looked at each other, never hearing such a wail.

With Micky's nod, the blues reared back with the ram for the second blow. The crash echoed down the hall but the door held, split and cracked, leaving a round hole waist high.

Quick, Micky stooped, eye to the hole and a sight he would never forget.

The Ghost, crouched in the corner on the far wall, cradled the bloody body of his sister, drooped in death. Hunched on his knees, snarling his hate like a trapped animal, demanding blood revenge, the death of his enemy.

Micky would remember forever the fury and rage coated on the Ghost's face as his black eyes bore through him like bolts of fury.

Then, in a flash, Ghost leaped to the side into the kitchen and disappeared.

* * *

The shooting through the window stopped. Gabriel, crazed and wild, rose to kill as many as he could before he fell.

He would die next to his sister.

The second battering ram crash jolted his mind, clearing his thoughts. His human mind clicked. Instant satisfaction for revenge was tempered by the sudden logic of fighting with a cool head to ensure that complete revenge would be his.

He decided he would leave so he could kill all of them instead of the few at his door.

* * *

Micky yelled, "He's in the kitchen."

The third smash of the battering ram tore away the door and half the frame. Kraut, Spook, and the uniforms charged inside, jumping behind furniture, sliding to the floor. Micky followed their lead with his Colt, covering the kitchen.

He glanced at the woman, slouched against the wall, head hung, staring dead, laying in a pool of lung blood. He knew she was moved by the blood drag. The window, blown away, left bullet holes peppering the floor.

What the fuck happened?

Kraut hollered, "It's over, asshole. Come on out."

No sound or movement. Spook belly crawled to the kitchen doorway, took a fast peek at floor level.

"The fuckers gone!"

The Ghost vanished.

* * *

After the second crash, Ghost grabbed his bow bag, jumped to the kitchen, and opened the double doors connected to the empty room next door and slipped through. He planned this escape route by reserving the adjoining room and made sure the connecting doors were unlocked. Once through, he closed and locked both doors and stooped to pull the nylon fishing line strung along the floor under the doors and tied to the kitchen table leg. By pulling the nylon line exactly three feet, the table was pulled in front of the door in the kitchenette. Then, letting loose of one end of the line, he pulled it to him.

Silent as a cat, he put his ear against the hallway door before cracking it open an inch, watching the last officer rush into his room.

He heard one ask, "Did ya get him, sarge?"

"We got the girl."

The Ghost fought against the urge to attack and tear them apart. He would charge with bare nails and teeth. He would make them pay with their death.

Again, his training made him think and reason. They would not die today, but soon.

He swore on his sister's death. *The sergeant would be first.*

In the next breath, moving like a shadow, he crept to the linen chute and disappeared.

* * *

Micky and the four cops stood in the tiny kitchen, not believing their eyes. There was no hole. No windows except the small one high and still locked. The only way out was the adjoining doors blocked by the kitchen table. Spook twisted the knob, locked. They couldn't figure it. Micky's mind couldn't connect what he saw. The killer went in the kitchen; we were only seconds behind. The adjoining doors were locked, blocked by the table.

The Ghost couldn't go that way without moving the table.

Shit, he thought, maybe he is a ghost.

Micky was pissed, walking further into the room, looking close. No crawl space in the ceiling. One thing sure, no storm drain. The sugar bowl, napkins, and salt and pepper shakers on the table.

As Micky started to turn, he noticed the salt shaker tipped over by the table's edge with a few grains sprinkling out. Bending down, he patted the floor under the shaker with his fingertips, feeling more grains. By touch, he followed the short trail three feet away.

"Son of a bitch!" he said. "Spook, cover these doors....Kraut, on me"

Micky ran to the hall to the adjoining room with two blues and the battering ram. He tried the passkey and the door slid open.

Seconds later, the room was cleared.

Kraut bent over, saying, "Hey sarge, look what I found."

He held up the fishing line lying by the adjoining door.

At the same time, the teams covering the fire escapes arrived, confirming the Ghost didn't escape their way.

Everyone stopped, scratching their heads.

As Micky walked back to the room, his eye spotted the linen chute.

"Fuck!"

He sent Breed and Grezer to investigate the shooting from the roof on the other building and Pop and Dago with four blues to search the basement, knowing the fucker was long gone. He then organized the crime scene follow-up, coroner, and lab guys before heading back to the station to try and make sense of this monumental fuckup.

Walking out of the hotel, Barnes was waiting for him, tie loose, cockeyed, and out of breath.

"Shit," he said. "I'm getting' too old for this bullshit, runnin' around with you guys."

"What brings you here, Cap?"

"I thought as heavy as this one was, I'd cover your ass with the press or whatever, but when the shootin' started, I ran up the stairs to the room.... the girl bought it, huh?"

"Yeah," Micky said, a little puzzled, "I didn't see you?"

"I stayed in the hall. Didn't wanta' mess up the scene any more than it already was."

"Where's your shadow?"

"I sent him over to city hall to keep the mayor happy and out of our hair."

Micky climbed in his car with a hundred questions buzzing through his head. Who the fuck was on the roof? Could it have been his special government friend? Who the fuck are these guys anyway?

Micky bit the bullet and put out all units for the Ghost, advising he was armed and dangerous.

CHAPTER 46

THE GHOST RAN blindly through the underground veins of the city. His grief and self-loathing crazed his mind like a rabid animal, plunging in any direction, splashing through the trail of drain water. Tears washed his face, thinking his mother named him wrong. It should have been Lucifer, the archangel that defied God and banished from paradise to the bowels of hell.

His legs pushed him forward, ever deeper in the drains, laughing hysterically at the irony of his fate. His brother and sister were dead. He failed them both. They followed blindly with trust and loyalty, asking nothing but to be with him, to be cared for and loved by him. He was their leader. He was the strong one charged with protecting them.

Now they were dead.

Ghost, stumbled ever forward through the round concrete guts of the city, knowing it was the road to hell.

After a while, his body weakened. He did not know how far he ran or where he was. He stopped, falling against the round cement wall, heaving for breath. His heart pounded like a jackhammer and he prayed it would break. He wanted to die. He wanted peace from this agony, his loathing, his loss.

It hurt too much.

Hours passed. Finally, he calmed, knowing he would not die yet. Thoughts and reasoning began to form as the difficulty of his situation sunk in. With no map to guide him, he pulled out the compass and straightened, knowing he must find his lair. The place he prepared for this moment.

CHAPTER 47

THREE HOURS LATER, the squad room was stuffed with his team, the blues, SS, and Barnes.

"Grezer, what's the story on the roof?"

"We found where the shooter set up, scuff marks an such. Gravel surface, so no footprints. A witness saw the guy going up to the roof from an interior hallway. He thought it was a maintenance guy. Normal height, weight, said he didn't see his face. The shooter took the shell casings with him."

Micky thought something stunk real bad, *was it a cop?*

It didn't make sense the government guy did it. He wanted the Ghost alive to take back to Vietnam.

"Kraut?"

"The suspect escaped through the adjoining doors to a vacant room. He pulled the kitchen table in front of the door with a clear fishing line. When we were picking our noses in his kitchen, he went out the door into the hallway and disappeared down the laundry chute."

"The desk manager said he received a letter shortly after they moved in asking to reserve the room."

"Cheeks?"

"The woman took one in the back, high-powered rifle with a lead bullet. It blew up inside her body. Five other shots fired, hitting the floor. Prints all over. Labs workin' em'. We found maps of the city and storm drains."

"Dago."

"Basement checked negative. Laundry thrown around and a broken lock. It's the way he split."

Micky checked his watch. It was two o'clock.

"Well, the asshole's hidin' in a sewer somewhere. This guy doesn't panic so he won't do anything stupid. He's goin' to stay invisible for a while. Pop, anything yet on the files from the attorney's office?"

"Didn't get a chance to really start when this went down. I told the secretary to start searching."

"Cheeks, what about the court case the victims were on?"

"Me and Dago got city court clerks checking. Problem is their records don't track which trial they sat on. They can tell us when the jurors were told to report and what jury pool they were in. they gotta search that time period in all the different courtrooms. There's thirty-four of 'em. They won't have anything till tomorrow. We talked to the four wives; they confirmed their husbands served on a jury during that time but couldn't remember which case."

"Okay, let's call it a day. Everything's bein' done that can be done."

Walking back to collect his jacket, he remembered the dinner date with Kathy and his brother.

He could use a good steak.

CHAPTER 48

FINALLY, GHOST WAS there. Standing with a resting breath, he looked, surveying the square concrete room with a ceiling fifteen feet high. Three storm drains converged at this point, their streams mixing in whirlpools only to continue flowing out a larger drain leading to the river. Aged concrete walls were covered with a cushion of moss matching straggly strands hanging from the ceiling. A ledge ten feet above the water held his supplies and gave easy access to the streets of the city. In the shadows, one was reminded of a natural cave.

The air, heavy and wet as the bayou, were lit with dim strands of light squeezing through heavy grates above, painting the witch's cavern a safe but eerie place.

Ghost bent down, cupped his hands, and drank deep. Then he stood, surveying his den, thinking it looked like a cavern he visited that once was a silver mine. It was cool, smelling fresh from the flowing water. The rushing water soothed like jungle rain in contrast to the stillness of the swamp.

Climbing the iron ladder to his perch, he slumped weary to the cement and dozed. While he slept, he tossed and shifted for comfort as his dreams, starting soft, remembered his brother and sister and the good times in the peace of the bayou. Marion and Angel's faces appeared smiling, grateful, and trusting, before him. But suddenly, human devils with twisted thoughts and evil promises pulled his kin away with sneers of hate, knowing he had no power to defeat them.

He first withered, accepting their fate until Angel cried out for his help, and Gabriel hardened, standing tall to her call.

He jerked awake not knowing where he was. Shaking his head clear, the death of his brother and sister flooded back. Rolling to his haunches, he tossed his head back with wails of despair, filling the air like a wolf to the moon. Moonbeams streaming through the grates above, glowed him ghost white, rocking on his haunches, arms spread, beseeching God's justice. Perched on the ledge, he swayed and shuddered, crying with howls of loneliness echoing through the cavern, begging to be heard, begging for his family's return.

Finally exhausted, he curled in a ball, hugging himself on the damp ledge, and slept.

In the morning, he woke slow with rods of light piercing through the grates like spotlights on the stage at the Bijou. He rose stiff from the night but refreshed with a new resolve.

Resigned to his fate of death, he welcomed it, feeling his body feverish, soaked with the obsession of revenge.

He would punish those that killed his family with ecstasy and delight. His brother and sister would smile at him knowing he set things right. All that he was and all that he learned, would be channeled for this single purpose.

He would kill the police sergeant first. He would not fail.

He began pacing the edge of the ledge back and forth like a caged animal, his thoughts savoring the attack. From below, he looked like a lone wolf, loping, cunning, impatient for the kill. His eyes glowed with the single instinct to kill or be killed.

The purity of this calling soothed his soul.

His decision made, a calm settled and he went to work preparing his narrow shelf with the items from the army surplus store. In short order, he had a sleeping bag, cot, alcohol stove, K rations, and clothes laid out along with the portable table. A backup set of maps for above and below the city were rolled out for study. His rifle and pistol, cleaned and oiled, were covered in waterproofed canvas. His knife and bow were cleaned, oiled, and placed in easy reach.

Setting them aside, he knew his task would be simple if he just killed the evil men with a bullet. But he felt compelled to complete his crusade with the weapon of old. He needed to feel the hunter's spirit.

He must feel the sacrifice of their death. There was no other way for him.

CHAPTER 49

AT TEN THAT evening, Kathy was slicing an apple pie while Micky and Father Mike sat at the kitchen table nursing a cup of coffee.

Her sides still ached from all the laughing over dinner.

Between Micky, his brother, and Riley, they managed to get the whole restaurant worked up with one smart remark after another.

Riley started as soon as they walked in the front door by congratulating Micky on their engagement. He then took Kathy's arm, ignoring the men, leading her to their table.

Walking along, he leaned over and whispered, "Our Lord has smiled on that lunk of an Irishman, but you, lass, have made a terrible mistake. But it's not too late as I'm still available."

She started giggling and didn't stop all night. Irishman, she decided, are full of blarney big time.

After placing the pie in front of them and filling their cups, she handed them a sheet of paper with the results her gang of nurses worked up on the riddle of the markings on the arrows.

"Okay, we started out with several assumptions. Number one, we have twelve letters. There are very few words with twelve letters or more so we assumed it is more than one word. Two, the sequence of the words is important because if the killer is spelling something, he would do it in sequence otherwise his message had no meaning."

She stopped, sipping her coffee. The two men listened close.

"Three, the phrase or sentence would also be related to what the killer was doing, which was killing. This is what we started with . . . Look at the top line."

E S E S M N G [] R O F D E [] [] [] [] [] []?
(mixed seq.) (fixed sequence.)

"That done, we worked as many possibilities as we could think of by rearranging the first five letters trying to determine the sequence and dividing the letters into possible words. At the bottom is what we came up with."

M E S S E N G [] R O F D E [] [] [] [] [] -- ?

Micky and Mike starred hard at the block letters.

"We think he's saying *messenger of death*."

Their frowns suddenly changed. She smiled, imagining she

could see little light bulbs blink over their heads as they yell, "EUREKA."

"Damn," Micky said, "you got it."

"Was there any doubt?" she added, a little smug.

"It's Gabriel," Father Mike added.

"Gabriel? What do you mean?"

"The archangel Gabriel was one of the four archangels. The others were Michael, Lucifer, and Raphael. Gabriel was the trumpeter, the messenger. He was the angel heralding the Annunciation. The Bible says he will trumpet the end of the world and final judgment."

"Some call him the 'messenger of death'."

"Do you think it's the killer's name?"

"Could be."

"You know, the killer was registered under the name G. Tropet. the G could be Gabriel," Micky said.

"Tropet, what is that, Italian, Spanish, French?" Father Mike asked.

"Desk clerk said they were French."

"How does he spell it?"

Micky pulled out his notebook.

"It's TROMPETT. I guess the *M* is silent."

"I'll be darn. I don't know French but the Latin root would say it means 'trumpet'."

"You're kidding? Gabriel Trompet?" Kathy said.

"I'll be damned," Micky added.

"I know," Father Mike said, smiling. "That's why you should go to confession."

"Very funny."

"Gosh, I feel just like Sherlock Holmes," Kathy said, excited.

All three sat, just thinking. It was another piece of the puzzle, but what did it mean?

Another half-hour bantering the facts back and forth yielded nothing further, so they went to bed.

When Micky snuggled up to Kathy, he let his hand pet her stomach.

"How's our baby boy?"

"He's kicking already. He's going to be ornery as his father."

"Your tummy feels flat."

"That's because I'm lying down."

"I reeeally like your tummy," he said, scooting closer, letting his hand roam lower.

Kathy whispered, "Jack, no, your brother's sleepin' on the other side of the wall. He'll hear us."

"He knows about sex," he whispered back. "He used to be the biggest cock-hound around."

"You're kidding?" She couldn't believe that; he looked so innocent. He was a priest.

"That's right. He taught me everything I know."

"You're kidding? But, he's younger than you, right?"

"Yep, he figured he'd get as much as he could before he took his vows."

"You're kidding?" She was shocked.

"No, he invented the old Adam and Eve scam."

"What's that?"

"Well, we'd go out and talk to some girls, and he'd be

drinkin' his Coke, not smoking, with his innocent face and mention he was in the seminary. Man, you wouldn't believe the change. Those girls transformed into Eve, determined to tempt and seduce him. I swear, if there were any apples around, they'd be cored. He never struck out."

"You're kidding?" She couldn't believe what she was hearing but a part of her knew how women could be.

"And he said the best part was they did all the work. He acted dumb and innocent and they couldn't wait to teach him."

"You're kidding?"

"Scout's honor."

Kathy's mind spun as Micky hugged her, standing ready, hoping she would change her mind.

No luck.

At breakfast, Kathy was at the stove making scrambled eggs. Micky was drinking coffee, unrolling the paper when Father Mike walked in.

"Mornin' all."

Kathy turned, giving him a studied look.

"What?" he said.

"Oh, nothing. How much younger are you than Jack?"

"Four years. Why?"

"I told her you taught me everything I know," Micky said.

"Well, that's true. You're a real dummy."

Kathy whipped around, spatula in hand.

"You admit it?"

"I told her you even taught me about Adam and Eve."

"True enough, plus much more," Father Mike said, thinking they were talking about Bible study.

"What? You didn't?"

Micky couldn't hold it anymore. He choked on his coffee, laughing so hard.

Kathy turned to him.

"You were lying, weren't you?"

She felt like throwing something at him.

"I couldn't help myself, hon, it's the Irish in me. 'Tis a curse."

"Why do I get the feeling I've been set up," Father Mike added.

"Scout's honor!" she said. "I should've known they would never let you be a boy scout."

She turned back to the stove with thoughts of revenge.

"I'll Irish you," she said, reaching for the chili powder when he wasn't looking.

CHAPTER 50

TWO ITEMS IN the paper wiped the smile off Micky's face that morning. The first was the front-page coverage from his nemesis, Cynthia Roberts.

THE GHOST VANISHES

Again, the Ghost has outwitted the St. Louis police Department. the so-called elite Doom squad received information that the killer was staying at the Commodore Hotel. After they determined that he was in the room with a woman, they surrounded the hotel and broke in only to find he disappeared. However, they did manage to kill the young woman.....

*It seems the killer escaped through an adjoining room
and merely walked away....*

*This special squad, led by Sgt. Jack Delaney, apparently
did not consider this obvious escape route....*

*The mayor and police chief have refused to comment
saying the incident is being investigated.*

It is this reporter's opinion that . . ."

Micky threw the paper down, not really interested in her
fucking opinion. He turned to the personals and there it was.
A new notice for the ghost, repeated six times.

*Ghost, let me help you set things right. S. L. Call
(347) 648-7746*

* * *

By the time he walked in Greasys, Micky was not in a good
mood. As he ran the gauntlet, apparently the cops lining the
aisle sensed his lack of humor and kept their mouths shut. Julie
had a full cup waiting when he slid into the booth.

"Mornin'," he said grumpy. "Whatta we got on the files and
the jury?

"Nothing yet, Sarge. We should have it wrapped up by ten."

"Kathy and the girls solved the mystery of the letters on the
arrows," Micky said. "He's spelling out the phrase '*messenger of
death*', which my brother says is the Archangel Gabriel. It's a
good bet the killer's name is Gabriel."

The group mulled it as Kraut leaned over with a lowered voice.

"Sarge, we got a strange twist. I went back to debrief the desk clerk when Dago came up and asked me something about the shooter on the roof. The clerk overheard us and said he thought it was a police officer. He got our immediate attention and said a plainclothes officer came into the hotel just before our raid, flashed a badge, and told him he was verifying some information. He wanted to know the room number and how to identify the room from the outside. Specifically, he wanted to know how many windows it was from the south corner of the building."

"That was Pop."

"That's what I thought but the guy had dark hair and came in before Pop."

Everybody sat quiet with their thoughts, *a dirty cop.*

This was one of the few times an officer's blood would start pulsing. This was the one-time emotions weren't capped. This was the one-time there was no tolerance. A rogue cop in the ranks deserved no mercy.

Micky starred at Kraut, dreading the next question.

"Did he get a name?"

Kraut hesitated, hating his next words.

"Yeah, he said it was Captain Barnes."

Micky felt sick. He and Barnes went way back. They walked adjoining beats. They covered each other's ass daily. Barnes never hesitated to come to his rescue.

But it fit. Barnes was at the scene in the thick of it. As a captain, his job was giving direction and let the troops fight the battle. He warned us to go slow, take our time. He was out of breath. He didn't have SS with him. He said he ran up the steps when the shooting started.

He said he went to the room. Micky didn't see him in the area. None of the other cops mentioned it. They would have because it was unusual. But why? What's the connection? Shit, this is fucking bad.

"Can he ID him?"

"He said probably not. He was scared and so shook with everything goin' on. It was all a blur."

"Shit, how can you forget a handlebar mustache. Go back this morning and press him. We need an ID . . . Until I say so, that name doesn't leave this booth. Are we clear on that?"

Micky made sure his eyes met theirs, seeing their nod.

He took a swallow of coffee not looking forward to his visit to the mayor's office. He didn't want to look Barnes in the eye. He didn't want to play dumb. He wanted to pull him aside, look him straight, eye to eye, brother to brother, cop to cop.

Cheeks' question broke his thoughts.

"Sarge, is this gonna mess up my wedding Saturday?"

Micky looked at him, changing gears. "Why? No . . It's two days from now. I'm sure a few hours to get hitched won't change anything."

"You lookin' for an excuse?" Pop asked. .

"No, I was just wonderin'."

Julie came over and refilled their cups. When she left, Kraut leaned forward and asked Dago, "I know I'll probably regret this but since everybody's got a woman in their life, I need to know what I'm doin' wrong."

"Well, your approach is all wrong," Dago said.

The whole booth leaned forward wanting to learn how this cock-hound was so lucky.

"When you meet a young lady in a bar," he continued, leaning forward to meet them, "You can't just walk up and say, 'Hey, ya wanna fuck?' You have to go slow, be sensitive, show you care, have a little class. When you approach a doll, you smile and say, 'Hi there, my name is Kraut, ya wanna fuck?' See the difference, more class."

Everybody moaned, slipping out of the booth, with Kraut calling him a dumb shit.

* * *

Margie, the mayor's secretary, gave him that *I'm-sorry* look as he smiled, winked at her, and walked into the bowels of hell.

Micky was quieter than usual sitting in the hot seat facing the mayor. He avoided Barnes's eyes and concentrated on a fantasy of screwing SS around in some way. He was way too happy with the ass-chewing Micky was getting.

Then the bomb fell.

"I have received a personal phone call from the director of the FBI in Washington to take over the case. They claim jurisdiction because the murders occurred in more than one state. They informed me that they will be on board Monday, the twenty-third, at 9:00 AM."

Micky sat there, stunned. He glanced at Barnes for support, but he stood, staring at the floor. He thought SS was going to giggle.

Micky wondered how he'd look without front teeth.

"I will not tolerate your attitude any longer, sergeant. Your squad's dropped the ball and given the city a black eye. Your so-called Doom squad has failed miserably with this case. When the FBI reports, I will disband the squad and the chief will reassign all officers."

Micky looked up mean. He wanted to throw his badge at that pompous SOB and tell them all to fuck off. He looked at SS's smirk deciding he would look great without front teeth. But he held back. If he did anything stupid, his guys would suffer. He told himself to play it cool. Tomorrow's another day.

"Is that all, sir?" Micky said firmly.

The mayor was taken aback.

"Yes . . . yes, it is."

Micky stood up without another word and marched out.

Back at the office he slammed the door, telling Mabel to hold his calls.

"And I mean it this time!"

She grumbled, holding back a smart comment.

Micky knew he had a real mess. There was a total of thirteen murders involving gangsters from New Orleans, citizens from St. Louis, and a prison guard all done by a professional killer trained by the United States. But if that wasn't enough, a secret government agency was using the Feds to mess him around, keeping him from solving the case. Last but not least, there was a crooked cop leaking information to the press and killing people. Worse, the cop is probably his boss.

Micky opened his eyes and straightened in his chair.

He had a week and a half before the Feds knocked on the door. Everybody's playing hardball. The murderer, the mayor, Barnes, the Feds, and his secret government friend.

Then, Micky smiled. He grew up working the streets, he fought across Italy and France, he walked the toughest beats in the city, and he ran the best squad on the department.

"They wanna play hardball. I'll show 'em hardball," he muttered.

At ten, the squad gathered with a cup of Mabel's famous brew. Micky decided to keep the mayor's threats under his hat for now.

"You clown's better have somethin'."

Grezer stood up.

"The secretary found eight files in Brunner's cabinet connected to Big Daddy in New Orleans. I got 'em here."

He held them up.

"But better than that, she remembered a visit by a brother and sister asking about a case Brunner handled. They stayed about thirty minutes, and that same night they got burgeled. That was a week before he bought the farm. The name of the brother was Marion Dupre. She can't find the file. It's missing. They do put jury lists in their files. She didn't remember the names of the brother and sister, but they fit the description of our suspects."

Pop stood.

"The court clerks tracked the victims to a jury that heard the case on a Marion Dupre two months ago. He was found guilty of transporting booze from New Orleans. They gave him a year at the pen. I got his file here."

"Dago, get to a phone and call Burke at the state pen and ask if a Marion Dupre is on cellblock seven."

Dago moved to the phone as Breed took the floor.

"The fingerprints in the room matched the van. The female matched the room and the van. We still have not IDed the male."

"So, we have a professional killer probably named Gabriel seeking revenge and he's somewhere in our sewer system. Am I missing anything except we still got shit and the item we discussed in Greasys?"

"I think that says it all, Sarge."

"Okay, I will get two teams from patrol for twenty-four-hour protection for the judge and prosecutor. Those are the last two targets that were connected."

One thing didn't quite fit, he thought. It was one letter short to finish the phrase *messenger of death*.

Dago hung up the phone.

"Sarge, Burke said not only was Marion on cellblock seven. He was killed by his cellmate on the second day."

"That cinches it. Gabriel's our guy. Now if you guys can figure out how to smoke him out, we'll be heroes."

With the squad room empty, Micky retired to his office, dropped the files on his desk, and reached for the phone.

Thirty minutes later, Micky was sitting in Dan's coffee shop across town in a rear booth with high backs watching Cynthia Roberts step through the front door. He waved, catching her attention, and seconds later, she sat across from him with a look of suspicion.

"Thanks for coming. I know this is weird."

"No shit. Why am I here?"

"I'll cut to the chase. You think I'm an asshole and I think you're a bitch. That settled, I have a scoop for you that will make you queen of print and help me solve a murder. Interested?"

"I'm listening."

"I'm jumping off a building here. I don't like some of your crap but at least you play by your rules. the only thing I ask is, I stay an unnamed source. Agreed?"

She thought for a moment.

"Agreed. Don't try to kiss my ass. Whatta ya got?"

Micky spent the next thirty minutes connecting all the dots on the series plus his secret friend, the personal ads, and the Feds. As he talked, she scribbled so fast Micky thought he saw smoke. He could hear the wheels grinding away in her pretty little head.

Finishing his tale, she asked a couple of questions.

"Okay, all I need is another source to support your story."

"What! There's no other source." Shit, he thought.

"This is heavy. My editor will demand back up."

He started to argue but had a better idea.

"Okay, I'll have Tony give you a call."

"Tony! Tony Angelo?"

He saw the little light in her eyes.

"Yeah."

Micky figured Tony could sell it and maybe score on the side.

"Shit, that's stretching it." She quieted, mulling it over. "Okay, if I run with it, I want an exclusive at the end."

"You know I can't do that . . . but I'll give you a twenty-four-hour jump."

"Deal."

When he returned to the office, Spook called.

"Sarge, Burke called back. He checked Marion's file and found the next of kin listed as Gabriel and Angelica Dupre. He also checked the visitor's log and found the sister's name about a month after he was killed."

"Great, that nails it down."

He made a mental note to write an atta-boy letter to Burke's boss when this was all over.

The next phone call was from Kraut.

"Sarge, went back to talk to the desk clerk for a better ID on our mystery shooter, but he flew the coop. The owner was there. He came down because of all the commotion and started checking around. When he wasn't looking, the clerk walked out the front door with the cash from the till. The owner knows he was cookin' the books."

"Shit, we need him. Have a uniform take a theft report and put out all units for a material witness. Find his ass."

CHAPTER 51

G HOST SLIPPED INTO the storm drain like it was his front door. His mind was intent, focused, excited. He finished his reconnaissance and found several target spots that would work. He lit the lantern, settling back with the newspaper and a deli sandwich. Seconds later, he bolted upright, staring at the headlines covering the full front page. Adjusting for the light, he read every word thoroughly and carefully. Reading further, he felt his blood start to churn in anger. He always suspected there was a hidden agenda. When he read the ads in the personals, something told him it was a trap.

Well, it was time to set things right once and for all.

Starting his sandwich again, he paid particular attention to the parts about Sergeant Jack Delaney, the cop supervising the raid at the hotel. He remembered the voice. The day his sister was murdered.

The day the sergeant hollered, "We got the girl."

This was his third day on the ledge, no TV or radio, the evenings dragged so he passed the time reading the newspaper cover to cover. That was how he stumbled on the announcement giving him the idea for the ideal way to kill the sergeant. It would be perfect, dramatic.

"Sergeant Delaney will die in front of his friends."

CHAPTER 52

MICKY ACTUALLY GIGGLED when he read the headlines in three-inch wide black letters.

GOVERNMENT ASSASSIN KILLS CITIZENS

He read the whole article twice. She had it all, even the tiny fib about how a secret government agency and the FBI were working closely with the local police to capture the killer. He read the best part twice.

> *Sergeant Delaney was contacted for a statement and*
> *refused comment but said he welcomes any assistance*
> *in bringing the killer to justice . . .*

And of course, there was the news of Senator Thompson from Missouri declaring,

"I will demand answers to some very tough questions."

Leaving the squad room, Micky switched the lights off and started whistling, strolling down the hall.

"Now, that's hardball, assholes."

*　*　*

Stan Levy prided himself on his self-control. After all, he was a doctor of psychology and witnessed firsthand the folly of humans letting their emotions run unchecked. But this was too much, he thought, throwing his martini against the wall of his hotel room.

"That fucking sergeant doesn't know who he's dealing with," he said aloud in the empty room.

Just then the telephone rang as he knew it would. He picked it up knowing the man at the other end would not be happy and he would be given strict orders to remedy the situation, immediately.

After hanging up, he plopped down in the chair with a curse and dark thoughts. Stan Levy was a man in a rage wanting payback.

Stan Levy lost control.

*　*　*

That evening, the new personal ad in the newspaper read:

Ghost. Do not believe the lies. S. L. will help. Call (347) 648-7746.

* * *

Ghost called the number, answered the three questions correctly, and was instructed to call back in exactly one hour for further instructions.

He purposely did not call back.

He smiled, thinking the timing was perfect. He had plenty of time to plan Sergeant Delaney's kill and prepare a future meeting with his handler.

* * *

Micky, reading the personal ad, smiled. He had the assholes on the ropes.

* * *

After reading Cynthia's article, the informant figured he was in the clear. With the desk clerk gone, they would blame the shooting on a government conspiracy. He sat back in his chair with a smile. The killer was on the run. The chances were remote they could connect him to anything. But just in case, he adjusted his story to explain any problem away.

CHAPTER 53

"HI, MARGIE, IS everybody waitin'?"

She looked up and watched him walking toward her with a bounce in his step. She wondered if he knew how much trouble he was in.

"Hello, Jack. Yes, they're all inside."

She waved him closer to her desk, looking from side to side.

"Stay calm and be careful," she whispered.

Micky smiled, giving her a thumbs up.

After introductions, Micky was directed to a seat that just happened to be strategically placed for the best intimidation. He plopped down with a smile, giving them a brownie point for putting some thought into this.

"Sooo…, what's up?"

All four faces before him flushed, returning snarled grunts. The man with the fake name, representing his secret friend, started.

"Sergeant, we know you leaked the story to the Post. I don't know what you're trying to accomplish, but you're not gonna to get away with it."

Micky assumed his best-surprised look.

"Gee, guys, I thought it was a very positive article. Shows we're all on the same side."

The FBI agent almost came out of his chair.

"You admit it?"

"Admit what? That I read the article? Sure did. You know there was not one misspelled word?"

The other FBI guy, red-faced, blurted, "Look, asshole, you're flirtin' with an obstruction of justice rap."

"Damn, I knew the Post was a rag, but I didn't think reading it was against the law."

The agent smirked, sitting back.

"You shit, we're moving up our takeover of jurisdiction to tomorrow."

"You said you were coming in next Monday?"

"We changed our mind," he snapped back with a sneer.

"Well," Micky hesitated, pretending to consider a thought, "If you change your mind and interfere with my murder investigation, I guess it's only fair that I change mine."

No-Name guy shot back, "What! Is that some kinda threat?"

Micky, tenting his fingers, calmly held No Name's eyes.

"Unlike you, I don't threaten. I do exactly what I say."

"Why, you fucker."

The young FBI agent popped out of his seat toward Micky.

Micky sat, without a flinch, as the other fed pulled him back. Micky grinned, if that asshole took another step, he woulda felt Micky's right jab into his eye-height balls.

Micky glanced at the mayor's face, thinking he might have a stroke. Now that woulda been a nice way to end this meeting.

No Name studied Micky with new respect. The guy didn't rattle and we don't know what else he's got up his sleeve. He also knew he couldn't take the chance.

"Okay, sergeant, what do you want?"

"Simple, get off my ass and let me do my job."

The four sat quiet, staring.

"If this meeting's over, I'll be leaving." Micky stood, walked out, thinking he heard the "proverbial" pin drop.

He walked past Margie with a wink, "Thanks, doll."

Surprised, she silently smiled a few minutes later when the four left the mayor's office looking like they were run over by a ten-ton truck.

* * *

Micky and his brother stood silent before Shamy's grave. Father Mike asked if he could come along. Shamy was also like a brother to him and this was the first time he was able to pay his respects. As he silently prayed, he watched Micky go down on one knee to clean the weeds around the simple headstone.

"Shamy, old man, Father Mike came by with me to say "Hi"."

. . We finally got a new guy on the squad. Joseph O'Brien, a real smart-ass. Not as bad as you but almost. You'd like him."

Micky kneeled a moment before standing. Father Mike's eyes watered, never seeing his hard-ass brother show his soft side.

Micky slowly stood, making the sign of the cross.

"One other thing, partner, we're working a real humdinger series. Any help from upstairs would be appreciated."

CHAPTER 54

MICKY AND KATHY stepped back in a corner with a cold soda, catching their breath. The reception was in full swing with Cheeks and his new bride all smiles. Kathy felt especially good escorted by her man and his brother. Glancing around, she spotted Father Mike making the rounds, talking to old friends.

The wedding ceremony went off without a hitch to the surprise of Cheeks. He said he dreaded the part where the priest asked if anyone had any objections to the marriage, *speak now or forever hold your peace.* The moment of silence seemed like an eternity. He thought sure one of the guys would say something just to get a laugh. But they didn't and he sighed in relief.

What he didn't know was they planned to have Spook, being black, declare, claiming the bride was already married to him. The whole squad thought that would be a hoot, but Micky told them their ass would be his if they pulled that bullshit. They left, chastened like kids who lost their prize bull's eye agate.

The V.F.W hall was big and decorated with hundreds of balloons. A buffet stretched along the far wall and a one-step stage hosted a three-piece band with very loud speakers. A bunch of tables and chairs circled the edges with about two hundred guests having a good time dancing and cutting up.

"Oh, my god, I can't believe it!" Kathy exclaimed.

"What?" Micky said, following her eyes.

"Suzie, my friend at work. She's dating Tony."

Micky spotted the couple move to the dance floor.

"Hey, Dago . . . I mean Tony isn't that bad."

Kathy looked up at him.

"Yes, he is, but that's not the problem. I'm worried about him."

"Huh?"

"Suzie grew up with eight brothers. She knows every nasty, perverted fantasy a male ever thought of. He doesn't stand a chance."

"She looks kinda sweet and innocent."

"And what's worse, she's Irish."

"Damn, maybe I oughtta warn him," Micky grinned.

"Oh no, on second thought, this might be very interesting."

"Well, my money's on Tony," Micky said.

"Ten bucks says she spins him like a yo-yo."

"You're on," he said, suddenly thinking he'd been sandbagged.

"Remember when you were sitting on the examining table

and I dressed your wound by moving between your legs, brushing up against you?"

"Yeah."

"Well, Suzie calls that the wishbone. It's her creation. She guaranteed if I pulled it on you, you'd ask me for a date."

"You're kidding. That was on purpose?"

She returned a coy smile.

"Did she tell you about alllll-male fantasies?" he asked.

She looked up at him, a twinkle in her eye.

"No, I thought you'd teach me."

"Professor Delaney at your service. I must warn you it is a very long course requiring hours of show and tell. It's a lifelong study."

"I'm counting on it."

With that, he whisked her out to the dance floor, holding her tight as the band struck up his favorite Elvis song.

The evening wore on and it started raining. The pair teamed up with Father Mike and Micky left to get some drinks. When he got to the bar, he spotted Mabel talking to another female.

"Mabel, "Hi"! You havin' a good time?" he asked, his eyes scanning the immediate area. "Is . . ."

"You kidden', I wouldn't be seen in public with that storm-trooper. Anyway, it's over. He's been actin' weird."

"He's always weird," Micky said, noticing she was tipsy.

"Yeah, but this is a different weird, kinda nervous and jumpy. Anyway, spanking an ass is nice, but sometimes a girl needs more. You know what I mean?" she said, raising the same eyebrow.

With that, Micky scooted away, telling her to enjoy herself. He didn't want any details.

Heading back, he noticed teddy bear Kraut out on the dance floor with a ring of five kids dancing and giggling, having a grand old time. He remembered the only time he ever saw him crazy mad was when someone hurt a child. In that arena, there was no forgiveness.

Returning, he spotted Julie and Pop talking to Kathy and his brother. He was really happy for both of them. They looked like a good match remembering both asked him to drop by Billie's football practice with Pop. They wanted the kid to get used to Pop being around.

*   *   *

The Ghost waited, patient in the rain, falling steady, in what he judged to be a ten-mile per hour wind. He didn't like the conditions. The street was parked heavy from the crowd at the reception. He stood in the shadows between two buildings about seventy yards from the target area. It was the closest he could get without possible detection. It would be perfect without the rain, but now the visibility was not the best. Wiping his face, he glanced up at the slate sky, knowing the shower would last into the night.

He studied the sergeant's picture in the paper and located his car parked a half block away. That gave him a half block to pick his shot when the sergeant walked to his car. He preferred killing him coming out the front door in front of his friends, but if conditions were bad, he would kill him on the street.

* * *

Everyone joined in a rousing performance of the "Hokey pokey" and a few minutes later, Cheeks slipped the garter belt off the thigh of his new bride to the hoots and hollers of men with one beer too many. Micky laughed at Cheeks pale skin turning bright red around the shiner from Casey's bar.

Then, all the single ladies gathered on the dance floor for the traditional tossing of the bridal bouquet. Micky spotted a few young women looking like they would commit some real bodily damage to capture the rose-petaled omen.

"Aren't you going to try?" he whispered to Kathy.

"Why, I've got my man," she said, taking his arm and pushing into him. "And . . . I'm having his baby."

The band struck up some music, starting the count against the roll of the drums. When the cymbal was struck, the bride tossed it over her shoulder, and Micky watched it float almost in slow motion toward the band of women. The bouquet flew straight to young girl and as she reached for it, another hand stretched over her from nowhere, snagging it like a right field Stan Musial. As Micky admired the play, he noticed it was Suzie, pretending to be surprised it was thrown right to her.

"Man," Micky whispered, "she's good."

"Told you," Kathy answered.

Micky watched Suzie walk toward Dago with a look that would surely doom him.

"You know when you said she'd have him spinning like a YO-YO?"

"Yeah?"

"Was that a Duncan YO-YO?"

The evening ended and party guests started leaving in pairs and bunches. Micky and Kathy were saying their goodbyes when Father Mike came over.

"It's pouring. Give me your keys. I'll run to the car and bring it around."

Micky handed him the keys, turning to another as Father Mike slipped Micky's trench coat from his arm, heading for the door. In the foyer, he slipped the raincoat on, pulled up the collar, and ran out the door holding a newspaper over his head.

* * *

Even from this distance, Ghost spotted Micky leaving at a run. He swept his face, cursing the rain and raised the bow. He pulled the arrow full but held the shot. The sergeant was a fast-moving target at seventy-five yards with wind and rain. It was a ninety percent shot, not bad but not good enough. He wanted a hundred percent kill.

Father Mike continued his jog, the newspaper covering his head.

Ghost would take him when he stopped at the car door.

A fifty-yard shot. He couldn't miss.

Ghost, with animal patience, watched as Father Mike stopped at the driver's door, fumbling with the lock. Ghost raised his bow, smooth, sure, picturing the arrow piercing the side of his skull.

Suddenly, a car, driving by, blocked his shot.

Ghost cursed, holding his death kill full to the steel point, waiting for the car to pass. When it did, his fingers prepared to slip when he saw Father Mike already behind the wheel with the door closed. The raindrops on the glass blurred his view, plus the angle to the door window made the shot impossible.

Again, cursing, he watched the car make a U-turn and realized, because of the rain, he was bringing the car to the front to pick up his woman. He smiled, knowing the shot would be simple through the window at that distance.

* * *

Father Mike pulled to the curb in front of the hall and tooted the horn. He could see Micky and Kathy in the foyer saying their last goodbyes.

Darn, he thought. He forgot to say goodbye to Kraut. He decided to run back in as Micky and Kathy started toward the car.

* * *

Ghost smiled mean. It was a straight shot through the driver's door glass. Listening to the horn toot, he raised the bow, pulling the arrow to his chin. Just then, the driver's door opened and Father Mike hopped out of the car.

Perfect, Ghost thought, his fingers slipped free like a harp player to the soft twang of the bowstring.

The Death Whisper was on its mission.

* * *

Micky watched the arrow strike his brother in his right eye.

Time froze. He could actually see, in slow motion, the arrow piercing his brother's skull and push out by his ear.

Micky yelled, jumped forward and slipped, tumbling down the flight of steps. Staggering to his feet, he ran to his brother's side, sliding to the ground, slipping his arm under his shoulders.

His mind crazed, he stared at the arrow sticking in his brother's head.

He screamed, "Call an ambulance."

Listening to his brother's moans, he checked for a pulse as Shamy's death, months ago, flashed before his eyes.

The rest of the men, mostly cops, fanned out with side arms at the ready. The fucker killed one of their own and now it was personal. They moved out as one in an ever-widening semi-circle praying for one good shot, just one.

* * *

In the still air, Ghost heard the crack of the arrow entering Micky's skull and smiled.

Folding the bow, he slipped away in the growing shadows, returning to his lair, looking forward to a special bottle of wine, one his sister loved, to celebrate the kill.

* * *

Micky followed the ambulance while his men turned up the heat. Within a half-hour, every officer on duty was centered on the manhunt. In an hour, officers off duty reported and volunteered. Teams were assigned to check every hotel, rooming house, and boarding house for anyone checking in after the date of the Commodore hotel shooting. For those fleabags not civic-minded or too thick to get the message, officers leaned hard with appropriate threats of future inspections.

Within two hours, a team of city first-line supervisors were put in a room with maps of the storm drain system and told to identify by priority the most logical locations to search. Five-man search teams were formed with vests, gas masks, shotguns, and helmets borrowed by the local army reserve unit.

Dago called a few contacts in the mob and put the word out. The killer shot a priest. From that moment, every number's runner, trucker, deliveryman, hustler, gambler, and loan shark was watching. Dago didn't have to say it, but they knew their cooperation would be worth a huge future favor.

Every radio and television station was contacted and *diplomatically* asked to broadcast the description of the suspect hourly. The newspaper composite drawing and suggested it should appear on the front page.

Cinthia said she would personally handle it.

* * *

Kathy stood by Micky in the waiting room, her arm wrapped in his. They stood to the side. The room was packed. Father Mike, still alive but in surgery. No one spoke of the injury, but those witnessing it didn't hold much hope. Their thoughts were the same. even if he lives, the sure brain damage would be devastating.

Kathy was worried. Once Father Mike was loaded into the ambulance, Micky never said a word. His expression was flat, cold, unfeeling. She was afraid he was going into shock, shutting down. She tried talking to him, but he just stared ahead at the operating room. She wished she knew what he was thinking and how she could help.

Suddenly, he whispered low to no one, "The killer's arrow was meant for me."

Kathy looked at him suddenly frightened. The sound of his voice seemed not his own. It was flat, cold, unearthly. She gazed at his face staring toward the operating room, feeling a chill, knowing it was the voice of an executioner.

An hour later, he still did not move. He seemed in another world with thoughts foreign. Kathy stood there, holding on, hoping for the best.

A half-hour more slipped by and finally, the operating room door opened. Kathy felt Micky's arm tighten like steel as the surgeon removed his mask, walking toward them.

"Your brother's going to be fine."

Kathy felt Micky slump against her arm, buckling to his knees in tears. She stooped to hold him, hearing the doctor tell everyone Father Mike was a very lucky man.

The arrow entered at an angle through the eye, skull, and out below the ear. It didn't even touch his brain and the shaft sealed the wound, stopping any heavy bleeding. He lost sight in one eye and hearing in one ear, but he should be on his feet very soon.

Kathy hugged Micky, her tears matching her husbands in relief. The others gave them space, slowly leaving, wishing them the best.

After a while, with Kathy at his side, Micky rose, took a step and fell to his knee in pain. Kathy pulled up his pant leg and saw the swollen ankle. Helping him to a chair, she noticed his right hand and wrist were swollen.

Two hours later, she rolled him out to the curb from the emergency ward. He had a broken left ankle and a torn muscle in his right thumb. He told Kathy he felt a little something when he fell down the steps trying to get to his brother but didn't feel any pain until the doctor told him his brother was going to be okay.

Hugging him that night in bed, she couldn't imagine loving anyone deeper or more completely than this man.

The next day when they arrived at the hospital, they were surprised to find Father Mike could already have visitors.

Walking quietly into the room, Kathy noticed flowers all over and Father Mike propped up. Heavy dressings and bandages covered the right side of his face as he smiled his welcome.

She watched Micky walk to the side of the bed and take his hand.

"Damn, brother, don't you know how to duck?"

"Quack, quack," he answered weakly.

"You know, it's just not fair. I'm the one who always wanted to be a pirate, and now you get to wear an eye patch."

"Aargg," Mike answered, noticing Micky's limp and bandaged hand. "Why're you limping? Sympathy pains?"

"Well, I didn't want you to outdo me in the pirate game, so I'm having a peg leg and hook installed."

"That's carrying sibling rivalry a little far."

"Say, did you ever confess about sneaking my comics?"

"No. But if this is your idea of getting even, it sucks."

"I don't know, you read my classics."

"I'm going back to Arizona. Scorpions don't sting this hard."

Kathy watched, surprised at their bantering, realizing this was how men showed their love and caring. They never cry or hug in a crisis. They are males, required to stay strong, keep control, stay calm, and none more than a priest and a cop.

Just then a nurse poked her head in and said he needed his rest.

"See you later, brother," Micky said as Kathy watched him bend over and kiss him on the cheek.

Now it was her turn to cry.

CHAPTER 55

AFTER READING THE headlines, Ghost paced the rim of his narrow ledge. His lobo gait matched his growl of anger knowing he missed his kill. Mistaking the brother for the sergeant was understandable because of conditions, but his arrow should have killed him. Knowing the sergeant would suffer, as he, over the loss of his sister, would give him some satisfaction.

He paced at the very brink; not aware each step brushed the lip of the twelve-foot drop. Dusty light strained through the grates, pouring crooked shadows on his face and body as he tested the edge.

Finally, he stopped. He would change directions. They would expect him to try for the sergeant again or target the prosecutor and judge. He already scouted and discovered the heavy protection provided them and now, he knew, measures would be taken to protect the sergeant.

His next target would be the police informant listed on his brother's arrest report.

CHAPTER 56

THE DOOM TEAM, minus Cheeks, were sipping their coffee when Micky parked his crutch and slipped in the booth.

"Mornin', sarge, how's your brother?"

"Well, he told me I was full of shit so I figure he's good to go. Doc says they'll cut him loose in a week."

Julie coasted over and filled his cup. He looked up with a smile of thanks and caught the smile she gave Pop. His days were numbered.

Just then Cheeks ambled through the front door and started dodging marital digs.

"Yer walkin' bowlegged, boy."

"When ya fall off that filly, ya gotta get back in the saddle, use your horn."

"Looks a little peaked, don't he?"

"Hey, yer wife called. Ya hafta be home by five."

"Meow, meow, crack that whip, Mama."

Finally making it with a huff, he slipped next to Spook, signaling Julie for a cup.

What the hell you doin' here?" Pop asked. "Weren't you goin' to Bermuda for your HM?"

"Yeah, we were all packed and ready to go, but I wasn't looking forward to it with what's been goin' on. When I started carrying stuff to the car, she sat me down and said we had to stay until this was over. Then she kicked me out the door telling me to get that asshole."

"No shit! Now that's what I call a woman."

"Cheeks, you're a lucky man."

"Say, sarge. How ya gonna handle the shooter on the roof?"

Micky paused, thinking of Barnes and sighed.

"Everything points to him, but I want to be absolutely sure. Either a positive ID from the desk clerk, a witness or physical putting him on the roof."

Micky remembered Barnes was a deer hunter and owned several long guns with scopes. It didn't look good.

"Not to change the subject, but does anybody have any ideas on how to catch our psycho, Robin Hood?" he asked.

"You want to hear wild and crazy ones?"

"I'll take anything."

"Well, how about city crews spot weld all the drain covers and let the fucker starve."

"Next."

"We have every citizen turn on their hoses and have the fire department crack the hydrants and drown the rat."

"Next."

"We build up the levels of methane gas and light a match."

"Next."

"We dump a fifty-gallon barrel of Mabel's coffee. It's just like Drano. He'll fizzle."

"Next."

"We feed Kraut a pot of beans and hang his ass over the hole and gas him."

Micky grinned at that one.

"Now that we got the bullshit out of the way, give me something solid."

"Sarge, we've been kicking this around since Saturday. He's a rabbit in a hole. We can't get to him. We have to set a trap and lure him out."

"You're right, but how?" he asked.

Everyone just sat there.

Micky made cleanup assignments making sure everything to this date was organized and recorded properly to present to a district attorney or a grand jury. The paper trail marked every step from New Orleans to St. Louis and would stand up to any test.

"Sarge, it'd be a hell of a lot easier if we just killed the bastard."

"Yeah, you're talkin' a tenth of the paperwork."

Micky hobbled down the hall, said good morning to Mabel,

balancing the cup she handed him, and pushed through the door. He set the cup on the desk with a fleeting thought the fifty-gallon Mabel coffee idea down the storm drain might be a good idea.

Plopping in his chair with a huff, he read through the front-page coverage. Cynthia didn't kick him in the balls this time, just a few jabs in the chin.

Checking the classifieds, he found the same personal ad for the Ghost. He wondered what his special government friend was doing?

Mabel buzzed, "Mayor on line two."

"Tell him to get screwed."

"Okay."

Shit, she'd probably do it, he thought, setting the paper aside, glancing at the files on his desk.

He pulled the disposition and arrest reports from all eight starting with Marion's, concentrating on the top half listing the facts. By the time he finished the last one, certain similarities became obvious.

All were all young males and used old trucks with less than a half load of booze. They were pulled over on the same highway within a mile of each other, and all were handled by Attorney Brunner. Everyone was found guilty or pled guilty, sentenced to prison but were given the opportunity to enlist in the army. Marion was the exception because of his disability.

The dumb shits apparently didn't consider that problem.

Micky sat back, staring at the wall. They used a back road to slow the driver down plus they'd be easy to spot.

Why only half loads? Well, he knew, there definitely was a pattern pointing to an organized plan.

He decided to take a break thinking he could brave another cup of Mabel's paint.

* * *

The Ghost crawled out of his underground den and loaded his gear in the Plymouth. He looked forward to killing his enemy in his own backyard. While the police manhunt for him covered the whole city, he would violate their very home.

* * *

With a fresh cup, Micky sat back down, deciding he would wade through the narratives describing the circumstances of the arrests. When he picked up Marion's arrest report, Dago popped in the squad room, heading back to Micky's office.

"Sarge, got a minute? I need some advice."

"Sure, have a seat."

Micky noticed his serious look.

"Well, you know I've been datin' this chick, Suzie."

"Yeah?"

Damn, he thought, where's this goin'?

"Well, I'm striking out. I've tried all my smooth moves and nothin'. I can't even get to third base."

Micky looked at him with a blank face, thinking, *Sooo?*

"Anyway, I really like her. I think she's the one and thought you could tell me what I was doin' wrong."

Micky was speechless.

"You're asking me? The guy that thinks women are aliens?"

"Yeah, I know they're aliens, but that don't mean I don't want one."

"Good point . . . Jeees, Dago, what makes you think I have any answers?"

"Well, you're older and wiser."

"I'm only two years older than you, asshole."

"But you're a sergeant."

"True, I guess that does make me wise."

"And you landed Kathy."

On that one, he wasn't sure who landed who. However, he was now sure he lost ten bucks.

"Damn, Dago, the only thing I can suggest is just relax, be yourself, the real you, not that macho, cool, smart-ass you. The asshole you just works when you're with broads wantin' a good time. A serious woman wants a man, not a wimp, but they also want to know you love them and care for them. They want somebody they can depend on."

"You think so?"

"Hell, give it shot. You're not scoring with what you're doin'."

"Good point, sarge. I'll give it a try."

He watched Dago walk through the squad room, wondering if Kathy had change for a twenty.

* * *

The police informant decided he'd leave early today. It was a slow Monday and everything was moving along well. The FBI would be knocking on Delaney's door next Monday, and he'd be busted back. He dropped a hint to the mayor that a good assignment would be night shift vice, working weekends and holidays.

Teach him a lesson.

Once he was there, he knew this little spinner who would swear she gave Delaney a blow job in lieu of arrest.

That would cost him his badge.

Yeah, he thought, it was a beautiful day. He'd swing down and get the car washed, put the top down and take a cruise, showing off his new ride.

* * *

Micky picked up Marion's arrest report, continuing where he left off. Two minutes later, he spotted the name of the officer providing the information leading to his arrest.

He blinked. He couldn't believe it, but there it was. He grabbed the other reports and found the same name listed.

Fuck, he thought, I got him. This cinches it. He fell back against the back of his chair, excited and pumped, deciding he'd put more icing on the cake before slicing and dicing him in little pieces.

* * *

Finally, the Ghost's telephone call was transferred to the police informant's office and as he hoped, he found himself talking to his secretary.

"I'm sorry, sir, but he's out of the office."

"Shoot, we're supposed to meet up. We're old friends and I

just arrived in the city. I wanted to tell him I was goin' to be a little late. Say, have you been workin' for him long?"

"Yes, sir, three years."

"Is he still drivin' that clunker or is he finally driving somethin' respectable?"

"Oh, he just bought a brand-new Buick Roadmaster. It's beautiful."

"I bet it's red."

"No, canary yellow and it's a convertible."

"Well, if he comes back, tell him I called."

"I will."

She thought he sounded nice but when she hung up, she realized he didn't leave a name.

Ghost stepped out of the phone booth across from the precinct and drove around until he found the yellow Buick convertible parked in the police lot. Then, like Vietnam, he scouted the immediate area, checking for the best location for the kill.

In a few minutes, he found the perfect spot in the shade of a hundred-year-old oak tree. Pulling to the curb, he noted the rising slope of the street was about fifteen feet above the exit at the police lot.

"Perfect."

Ghost settled in for the wait hoping the officer was tall. He rechecked the street map for the fastest escape route and checked the storm drain schematic in case he needed an alternate escape.

*   *   *

Micky dialed the mayor's office.

"Hi, Margie, it's Jack, your favorite sergeant."

"Hi. How do I rate?"

She knew with some regret he just got engaged.

"I gotta' pick up that file that Lieutenant Sutton dropped off when he met with the mayor."

"When?" She couldn't remember any file.

"It was Tuesday, the day of the shooting at the hotel."

"Oh, that was terrible, wasn't it? Let's see . . . it couldn't have been Tuesday. The mayor was out until three. Are you sure? What file is it?"

"Gee, I'm sure that's what he told me. You didn't see him up there anytime that Tuesday?"

"No, and I was glued to the desk. What file do you need?"

"Well, I don't really know. I was just supposed to pick it up. Maybe I heard wrong. I'll check with him. thanks a bunch."

He hung up thinking another couple of nails would seal his coffin.

He buzzed Mabel and asked her to come to his office.

"Mabel, you were in SS's pad, weren't you?"

"Yep, why?"

"Did you notice any long guns with scopes?"

"Yep, he has three in a gun rack. Why?"

"Can't say right now. I noticed the new Buick he's drivin'. How long has he had it?"

"About two months. It's loaded, convert, leather, air, top of the line. Why?"

"Where'd he buy it?"

"Farrow's Buick on Taylor. Why?"

"Can't say right now, Mabel. This conversation's just between you and me."

"You ever goin' to tell me why?"

"Yep."

His next phone call was to Farrow's Buick.

"Hi, my name's tom Sims. A police officer friend of mine, Lt. Stan Sutton, bought a car from you guys about two months ago. I'm interested in getting one too, and he suggested I talk to the salesman he dealt with."

"One moment, please."

Micky, tapping his desk with his pencil, waited, thinking how sweet this was gonna' be.

"Happy Dan here."

"Hi, Tom Sims. I'm a police officer and work with Lt. Stan Sutton. I really like his new Roadmaster and he gave me your name. Said you'd treat me right."

"Happy you did. What are you lookin' for?"

"Well, I want the same car but red or blue."

"You're in luck. Gotta a spankin' new red one. It's a beaut," he said, wondering where cops were getting this kinda money.

"Great. Can you get me the same financing?"

"Financing? He paid cash."

"Cash. You mean he just plopped all that green on your desk?"

"Sure did."

"Well, I can't handle that."

"No problem. Come on in and we'll work somethin' out."

"Okay, but it'll have to be this weekend."

"Just ask for Happy."

Shit, Micky thought, I'm ready for Hollywood.

He dialed Sutton's extension and the secretary said he hadn't returned. He hung up, quickly dialing the central operator.

"This is Sergeant Delaney. Please page Lieutenant Sutton. It's an emergency."

At the same time, Sutton was walking down the hall, heading for the parking lot, when he heard Micky's page. He started to ignore it, but stopped, thinking the asshole never called him. He figured it must be connected with the series.

He grabbed a phone in the next office.

"Delaney, this is Lieutenant Sutton."

"Lieutenant, we got a break on the Ghost series. Can you come to my office?"

When Micky hung up, his blood flushed with a squirt of adrenaline, anticipating the snap of the trap. It felt good.

Five minutes later, Sutton came through the door and marched across the squad room toward his office. Micky fought the urge to stand and click his heels with a stiff arm "Heil Hitler".

"Thanks for comin', Lieutenant. Have a seat."

Micky went through the act of shuffling some papers.

"I'm tyin' up loose ends to present to the grand jury and you're the one that tipped the department on the illegal booze on all these cases," he said, holding up the files in a nice fan.

"How'd you get the information on the booze shipments?"

Sutton shifted, suddenly panicking.

"A confidential informant."

Micky eyes locked, straight into his.

"What's his name?"

"I said confidential, sergeant."

"You can't even tell a fellow officer?"

"No!"

Sutton felt sweat forming on his upper lip.

"Well, at least tell me if he's a criminal informant."

Sutton's mind spun. He'd better give the fucker somethin' to appear cooperative.

"Yes, he is."

"So, this guy just calls you up from New Orleans with a tip?"

"That's right."

"Whatta ya got on him?"

"What do you mean?"

Sutton's fingers clamped the armrests, forcing his eyes straight. His heart revved, doubling its beat.

"I mean what beef are you holdin' over his head in New Orleans causing him to call you with these tips?"

"Uhh, what?.. What the fuck you think you're Doin'?" Sutton blurted.

"I'm trying to understand, Lieutenant, so I can explain to the grand jury and a judge, why a criminal from New Orleans calls St. Louis and asks for you specifically to tattle on illegal booze shipments."

"I don't have to answer that."

Micky smiled.

"Lieutenant, it's now or later, but you will answer the question."

"Fuck you!"

Sutton bounded out of the chair, storming out of the office. Micky sat there, smiled, and gave him the one-finger salute.

"Damn, that felt good."

* * *

Sutton was pissed and frightened. He was in danger. That fuckin' Delaney. He had to go on the offensive. He needed something, but what?

Ah, he had it. Changing directions, he headed outside. He'd drop in on the mayor and mention he heard through the grapevine it was one of Micky's men on the roof that screwed up and shot the girl. the cop took the shot and Delaney was covering for him. Everyone knew the Doom team was thick and covered each other's ass.

Suddenly, feeling better, he trotted down the front steps, heading for the parking lot. The sun was full, so he took a minute, put the top down to make himself feel better. Two minutes later, he twisted the ignition, feeling the quiet power of the engine.

He loved this car.

* * *

Ghost checked everyone leaving the cop building with a trained eye and patience. There was a lot of foot traffic in and out of the front, but he concentrated on watching the Buick.

Suddenly, his body tensed. A man walked up to the car, opened the door, slide behind the wheel, and put the top down.

Seconds later, the car pulled from the parking space turning toward the exit. Ghost knew police informant Sutton would stop a moment at the dip in the curb line, making sure traffic was clear.

Ghost stepped from his car and nocked his arrow. In one smooth motion, timed to the car moving to the curb, he pulled it full length, holding steady.

A fifty-yard shot, clear, dry, perfect.

Ghost's mind clicked, feeling the death of his human game, and let his fingers slip from the catgut.

Death Whisper was in flight.

* * *

Lt. Sutton slowed at the street, looking both ways when the arrow shlunked down through his brow, through his brain, and out the base of his neck, pinning him to the hand-rubbed camel-leather headrest.

His beautiful canary yellow Buick Roadmaster convertible, with custom hubcaps, rolled slowly forward, stopping in the dip of the gutter, the engine purring like a kitten.

* * *

Ten minutes later, the Doom team surrounded the murder scene. The sun, just right, lit up the canary Buick like center stage. Micky could just imagine Cynthia's press picture on the front page. The whole area, like a circle jerk, with cops shocked, rushed around, thinking they were doing something important.

The press was raising hell as he pushed through to the Buick.

Micky thought the scene rivaled the time a monkey grinder's chimp went ballistic at the booking desk and started tearing the joint apart. He was running and jumping all over, shitting at the same time. He thought there's nothin'n worse than the smell of monkey crap.

Stopping at the hood, he stared at Sutton sitting upright, eyes wide open, with what Micky thought was a pleasant expression. He was pissed the Ghost stole his thunder, but was also unhappy Sutton died in such a manner.

Walking to the side, he leaned in close to Sutton's forehead, checking the back end of the arrow, finding the letter "A". Well, he thought, this gives us the correct number of letters to finish the killer's message assuming he rubs out the prosecutor and judge.

He made assignments and headed for city hall.

All was not lost. He could salvage part of the day and screw with the mayor, shake his ass up a little. After that, he would swing by the hospital and visit his brother.

He had some new jokes.

CHAPTER 57

THE DOOM TEAM sat quiet and serious with every brain cell centered. Micky, looking over from the podium, felt the energy of the pack. These men were the professors of the streets. Each held advanced degrees and served internships operating on the city's underbelly, digging in with both hands, bloody and dirty, cutting out the criminal tumors. Sure, they were raw, flip, and cocky. Sure, they were irreverent, smart-mouthed, and full of swagger. But that's what kept them sharp, quick, and king of the hill. Men like these formed a blue wall protecting the civilized and punishing the predators.

And when one fell, another filled the hole.

"What's our status?"

"Sarge, every cop's turnin' and burnin'," Grezer said.

"If this turkey is roamin' around above ground, he's ours.

Any place he could hide is being checked and rechecked. Even vagrants got the word about our reward."

"Reward?"

"Yeah, since we can't legally do it, it's on the QT. We talked to the association. They promised ten grand for his ass."

"I talked to my uncle Louie," Dago said. "He told me they got their end covered."

"The city guys got a list of four hundred most likely places he might hole up in. they listed the largest drains and connection boxes first and worked down to the smallest. We've got nine teams outfitted, doin' the searches. The problem is, he could be movin' around and go back to a hole after we check it."

"At least it'll make him nervous," Micky said.

Micky briefed them on SS and his involvement. He arranged to have the lieutenant's rifles brought to the lab, to do a ballistics check. They already determined one was recently fired. Micky was sure he was the shooter on the roof but was waiting for the final lab report before sticking it up the mayor's ass.

Micky dismissed the team telling them to keep all the balls in the air. He visited Mable, filled his coffee cup, and wandered back to his office to let the whole mess cook in his addled brain.

Twenty minutes later, Margie called from the mayor's office.

"Sergeant, I checked all over but couldn't find the file you were looking for."

Damn, Micky thought, *I didn't mean to cause her more work. Why's she whispering?*

"Margie, that's okay, forget it. What's this sergeant bit, it's Jack."

"Well, sergeant, it's just things have been hectic around here with all that's been happening, and now with Senator Todd calling the mayor telling him he's requesting a congressional investigation into the CIA and FBI on reported assassination squads, I haven't had much time.

The mayor's friends naturally want to keep everything hush-hush until they find the killer. But you and I both know that's hard to do."

"Thanks, Margie . . . for looking for the file."

He owed her big time.

Micky hung up and dialed Cynthia, giving her the scoop of the day.

Suddenly, a Cracker Jack idea bloomed. He dialed the *Post-Dispatch* again, asking for classifieds. After he hung up, he briefed Mabel, giving her three questions to ask any callers. You know, he thought, strolling away, sometimes he could be a real devious bastard.

That evening the *Post* headline in huge block letters read:

CIA AND FBI ASSASSINATION SQUADS

Also, the newspaper carried six ads in the personal's column with two separate messages in addition to the one placed by Stan Levy:

Ghost. Disregard other messages. It is a trap. Call S. L.
(347) 619-5345

Ghost. Remember Vietnam and evil men. Call S. L.
(347) 619-5345

That'll screw 'em up, he thought. He'd love to see his secret friend's face when he reads 'em. Tomorrow, he'd tell the guys his big plan to nail that fuckin' Ghost.

CHAPTER 58

STAN LEVY READ the paper in a controlled rage. He would not tolerate any more meddling from that flatfoot cop. How dare he interfere with the plans of the nation. Stan decided at that moment to eliminate this burr on his ass once and for all.

With that decision, his mind floated several ideas. Killing him was fairly simple but would cause a big hullabaloo which he didn't need right now.

As he mixed another martini with two olives, he decided on a plan he used several times before that never failed. He made this decision as any businessman would make on a purchase or an investment.

His telephone rang. He knew who it was before picking up the receiver. He listened quietly, but intently, for about five minutes.

He replied, "I'll handle it, sir."

Then, gently hanging up the phone, he threw his martini across the room, splattering against the wall, following it was the whole bottle of gin.

Sergeant Delaney will know the feeling of real fear, he thought, and if that did not work, the feeling of real sorrow over the sudden demise of his fiancée.

"You fuck with fuckers, you get fucked," he muttered to the empty room.

CHAPTER 59

THE MAYOR WAS pissed, the FBI was pissed, the CIA was pissed, and Micky was pretty damn sure his secret friend was pissed. It was hard to hide his smile, calling the team to the briefing.

Breed had the paper.

"What's goin' on, sarge?"

"Just a little one-up-man-ship."

"It looks heavy, secret government assassins, palace intrigue, and all that shit."

"Well, while they run around butt-fuckin' each other, we got work to do. How's the search goin'?"

"It's pluggin' along but nothin' yet. If I didn't know better, I'd think this guy was the invisible man or somethin'. We even got half the citizens in the city watchin' out for him."

"Well, like Kraut said, 'the guy's a rabbit in a hole.' We gotta lure him out with a carrot on a stick, trap him. Here's my idea."

Micky spent the next hour, behind closed doors, laying out his plan, discussing the pros and cons.

"Jeez, sarge, this is not a good idea. There's gotta be a better way," Grezer said.

The rest of the squad nodded, seconding Grezer's comment.

"It's my decision, it's goin' down Saturday at 10 AM."

"If the captain finds out, he'll have a fit."

"But he's not gonna find out, is he?" Micky finished, locking eyes.

Twenty minutes later, he was out the door to the hospital to run it by his brother. Even though Micky tried to soften him up with some jokes, Father Mike agreed with the team it was a stupid plan.

"Don't worry, it'll work. Just don't say anything to Kathy until I got a chance to sell it."

Micky made the phone call, settled in the same coffee shop and the booth with a high back, nursing a cup of coffee, waiting for Cynthia.

Sliding into the booth, she said, "You know, we make a hell of a team."

"I'm still engaged."

"You know, you're a real smart-ass."

"Ditto, that's why we get along so well."

She quieted, looking close, trying to figure the guy.

She finally gave up.

"Whatta ya got?"

"If you help me on this one, I'll give ya an inside personal exclusive."

"I'm listening."

She studied Micky close as he laid out the plan. She was amazed at his casual manner like it was as routine as going to a baseball game. She was an "Ace" figuring out hidden motives and discovering secrets but this guy threw nothing but curveballs.

"You sure about this?" she said.

"Yep."

She hesitated, thinking. She didn't know it but she had the same opinion his men did. It was a stupid idea. She could stop it right now, right here, by refusing to do what he asked. "I'm tempted to say no just to save your sorry ass. But knowing you, you'd come up with something even dumber."

"Is that a, 'yes'?"

"Yes, dammit."

Looking into his blue eyes, she saw the twinkle. For the first time, she regretted he was engaged.

CHAPTER 60

G HOST EASILY FIGURED out which ad in the newspaper was legitimate. He wondered why someone was creating a smokescreen, but figured it was for some other purpose.

He called the correct number, answered the three questions again, given a code number, and told to call back on the hour for further instruction. He told the operator when he called back, he would only speak to "S. L." and no one else. The woman at the other end said she would relay the message.

He called back at four o'clock sharp, repeated his code number and put on hold while his call was transferred. He did not worry about the call being traced because the phone booth he used sat on a high knoll with a three-hundred and sixty-degree view on all streets leading to his location. If anyone headed his way, he would disappear in the storm drain just to his right. But they would not be that foolish. They would plan carefully, prepare for all contingencies. They hated spontaneity because something always went wrong.

"Ghost! Thank you for calling," Stan Levy said. "It is good to hear from you, my friend. Are you well?"

"Yes, I am fine. I have two questions."

"Of course, but I would like to extend my sympathies for your sister. It was a terrible tragedy. Your mission has been difficult."

"Yes. Number one, if I come in, will Sergeant Delaney be eliminated?"

"Yes, I guarantee it."

"Number two, will the prosecutor and judge be eliminated?"

"Again, I guarantee it."

Ghost listened for the next ten minutes to the specific plans to bring him in. He hung up wondering about colleagues betraying one another. But there was one thing he was sure of. One that shows a false face has an evil mind.

He retired to his underground den thinking his brother and sister would be proud when he avenged them. He knew he would join them soon and looked forward to it.

CHAPTER 61

T HE MORNING HEADLINE
blasted:

PRIEST DIES FROM ARROW WOUND

A Catholic priest, Father Michael Delaney, died suddenly last night at 8:00 PM. Doctors were expecting a full recovery but stated that apparently a blood clot formed and caused a stroke.

Father Delaney was the fifteenth victim of the Ghost who kills with a bow and arro . . .

Senator Thompson has demanded a complete congressional investigation and . . .

Father Delaney is survived by his brother, Sgt. Jack Delaney, who is in charge of the manhunt for the killer . . .

The police have no motive and do not know why Father Delaney was targe . . .

Closed casket services will be held at St. Mary's Church this Saturday at 9:00 AM with interment at Resurrection Cemetery immediately aft . . .

Flowers and donations sho . . .

Kathy was furious and so frightened her whole body trembled. She cried, she reasoned, she screamed, she begged, she said she wouldn't marry him, but nothing worked. She called the guys in his squad and was told they tried everything to talk him out of it. As a last resort, she threatened to go to the press and expose it all.

That was when Micky sat her down and explained that if this killer wasn't stopped, he would kill others and still try to kill him. They would always be looking over their shoulder in fear not knowing when he was going to strike. Just as important, if she was with him, her life was in danger also. He couldn't live with that.

"Look, Kath, let me do this on my terms instead of letting him pick and choose. This way we'll be ready and end it once and for all."

That night, she cried again for a long time. She held him

close imagining she would never let go. She spooned him, laying her head against his back, listening to the strong beat of his heart. It was a good heart, a heart she loved.

Please, God, protect it for me.

CHAPTER 62

AT 9:00 AM, Stan Levy sipped his special blended coffee thinking of Cynthia Roberts's news article on the murder at the wedding reception and the officer at the police station. Setting the paper aside, he thought it a shame an innocent priest was killed. It was also a shame the sergeant didn't get the arrow. It would have solved his problem. He realized his thoughts sounded cold and hard, but the sergeant chose to play the game and he was subject to its rules.

You fuck with fuckers, you get fucked.

At ten, he held a briefing on bringing the Ghost in that afternoon. He carefully chose an open area in tower Grove Park. The closest tree line was a hundred yards in any direction.

A statue of a military hero in the center was ringed by park benches. The plan was simple. He had thirty agents disguised as families on picnics, park workers, a ten-man volleyball team to the side, an ice cream vendor, two guys throwing sticks for their dogs, and pairs of people strolling, enjoying the afternoon.

If Gabriel refused, for some reason, to accompany them willingly, each agent carried a hypodermic with knock-out drops or tranquilizer gun. Also, there were several capture nets hidden in strollers, just to be sure.

He ordered everyone to be in place two hours before the rendezvous.

He would man an observation post on a footbridge about a hundred yards from the target and direct any adjustment that might be necessary. Everyone was equipped with the new Motorola Handy-talkies recently issued to the secret service.

After dismissing the teams, he made arrangements for follow-up action. He would meet Gabriel at a safe house and make him feel welcome. He would be told arrangements were made to terminate the sergeant, judge, and prosecutor.

Knowing Gabriel's mind, he was prepared to convince him that although his team conducted the actual termination, it was at his request and therefore his act. Because of this, he could be comfortable with the fact it was his kill, which would satisfy his vow. He mentally reviewed the argument in his mind making sure he chose his words carefully.

He made arrangements for a private jet at St. Louis Lambert airport to whisk him away to Los Angeles where a military plane would take over and deposit him in Vietnam.

He made a last check of his appearance in the full-length mirror, complimenting himself on his ability to fashion the perfect plan. Yes, sir, proper planning wins the day. He straightened the handkerchief in his breast pocket before leaving with his two bodyguards.

* * *

Ghost was in position four hours before the meeting time. He watched the agents take their positions, irritated they thought he was so stupid. Their actions, to trap him, convinced him the article in the paper was correct. Stan Levy and the police were working together. This fact also sealed his belief Levy lied from the beginning so he would kill for them.

During his time in St. Louis, he read with interest the differing views regarding the Vietnam conflict. What was reported by the government did not match what he told.

He questioned whether those he killed were evil men. In retrospect, he doubted it.

Well, he thought, today would be a reckoning. It was time to balance of the scales.

He would set things right.

Looking over to the footbridge, he watched the three men take their position, pretending to lean on the rail, just enjoying the day. He noticed the shorter man in the middle held a pair of binoculars around his neck.

Ghost unzipped his canvass case and pulled out the collapsible bow. With a twist and a click, he was ready. Taking an arrow, he knocked it loose and checked the wind. The target was an easy one hundred yards.

He made the same kill shot dozens of times in the jungle with never a miss.

* * *

Stan Levy, flanked by his two bodyguards, looked over the rail of the bridge satisfied with his evolving plan. Everything appeared to be just a normal day in the park. He glanced at his watch. Five more minutes and they should see Gabriel enter from the south.

If Gabriel refused to cooperate, Levy's backup plan called for the contact person to take off his baseball cap, signaling the takedown.

The kid wouldn't know what hit him.

With a nervous calm. Levy looked at his watch again, glancing to his left, making sure the panel truck was in position to swoop in.

He smiled. It was.

Leaning his elbows on the rail, he lifted the binoculars to his eyes. They were ten-power and if you didn't brace your arms on something, the image jumped around with the slightest shake of the hand or arm. He adjusted the focus, congratulating himself for taking this contingency into account, making sure he had a firm surface to stabilize his arms.

Moving the binoculars up to the tree line, he swept the perimeter. Then, he swung to the south along the path expecting to see Gabriel any second. As he held steady, the slightest glint to the left of the lens almost caught his attention.

*   *   *

It was time.

Ghost lifted his bow as he did a thousand times, took a soothing breath, pulling the bowstring to the crease in his cheek. His mind clicked into that special place as his brain automatically computed wind and distance.

Instinct told him how the day's humidity and air pressure would influence the arrow's flight. Then, releasing his breath in a steady rhythm, he felt the hunter's spirit, the spirit of death.

His fingers straightened.

*   *   *

Levy saw a car come down the road. He saw the contact man fidget on the park bench. He saw the agents acting like couples. He moved the binoculars and saw the volleyball team, but he never saw the arrow slam into the right lens of his binoculars, piercing through his eye and stopping in his brain that manages man's logic. As he fell slowly back, before his brain died, it computed the message, *you fuck with fuckers, you get fucked.*

The two bodyguards, stunned, starred at their charge lying on his back, binoculars nailed to his face. With a glance to the other, they grabbed the body, ran to the panel truck, tossed it in the side door, and sped away.

The driver, grabbed the new Motorola walkie-talkie, yelling, "Abort, abort!"

CHAPTER 63

"ALL RIGHT, SETTLE down, let's get this show on the road," Micky announced.

The team grabbed a seat, balancing a fresh cup of Mabel's concoction. With eight cups wafting fumes to the ceiling, Micky couldn't resist a fast glance to check weather conditions. As he suspected, the tobacco clouds, swirling slow by the ceiling fan, darkened from sucking up the coffee mists. A tornado was imminent.

Delaney, my boy, he said to himself, you have a weird mind. Standing at the podium, he tapped for attention.

"I want to bring everyone up to date before the briefing on tomorrow's operation. First, we received a report a man was killed by an arrow in Tower Grove Park around 4:00 PM yesterday. The victim was hustled off in an unmarked panel truck, hauling ass. Nothing has officially been reported to us, yet."

Micky knew it was connected to his special government friend. He guessed they tried trapping the Ghost and it backfired.

"The reasons we're goin' forward with our operation are the following: Number one, we know the arrow my brother took was meant for me. It was raining, with poor visibility, and he was wearing my rain coat and drivin' my car.

Two, when Ghost's sister was killed, the newspapers gave me the credit with the rest of the press.

Three, the killer don't know we know I was the target. The press reported it as another senseless attack so he'll think he can try for me again.

Four, this guy's killed fourteen people he thinks are responsible for his brother's death. With his sister dead, we know damn well he'll try for me again."

Micky stopped and looked up. Nobody even coughed.

"Number five, we know he won't stop unless we stop him. So rather than wait, wonderin' when I'm gonna to get an arrow in my head, we're goin' to set a trap, using me as bait. We're gonna lure the rabbit out of his hole by creating an opportunity he can't resist and we'll be waiting."

"As you know, I started the ball rolling. the *Post-Dispatch* reported the sudden death of my brother listing the time and location of services plus the location of the burial site. Cynthia arranged to repeat the same info in all editions. Also, local radio and TV are cooperating."

"Father Mike is on his way back to Arizona and the hospital staff is onboard providing we correct the record when it's over."

Again, he looked up.

"Any questions so far?"

The room was still. The only sound, the click of the ceiling fan.

Micky turned the blackboard around with a map showing Resurrection Cemetery and connecting streets, including the River des Peres.

"I'll hand out smaller versions of this map after the briefing. This map shows the cemetery, interior access roads, burial plots, and tree lines. The dotted lines show the storm drainpipes."

Micky dragged his pointer along the dotted lines.

"Note, they converge here to a larger pipe that empties into des Peres. The distance from the target sight to des Peres is right at a quarter-mile."

"This is important because it'll probably be the killer's escape route. As you know, des Peres is a huge open ditch, and we'll have the high ground. If he manages to slip away at the gravesite, once he exits into des Peres, he's ours."

"I surveyed the cemetery and found the perfect place for the burial site. It's in a new section without any large trees. Everything's a sapling. Also, there aren't many graves, especially with tall gravestones. The closest tree line is a hundred and fifty yards away."

He picked up the pointer again.

"Notice this ridgeline here about fifty yards from the gravesite that drops off pretty steep. There're no graves between ours and the ridge line and that means the killer can only attack in this area, between the tree line and our grave-site."

"Since his bow range accuracy is about a hundred and twenty-five yards or less, it's ninety percent sure he'll stay within that range. So, in order to attack, he has to be within this area I marked."

Micky slid the pointer, tracing the open space.

"There are eleven gravestones, marked and numbered by these circles. We can assume he'll try to get as close as he can to avoid a miss . . . But he will also want to ensure his escape route so he would look for fast access to a storm drain, which can only be entered at these two gutter locations, here and here, on the access road.

"We'll have two sniper teams in the tree line here and here. The elevation is about twenty feet above the gravesite. I checked it out and it's perfect. You can clearly look down toward the grave where we will be standing and every gravestone he could hide behind. You also have a clear line of view from any gravestone to the two storm grates."

Micky turned to the group.

"Everybody with me so far?"

His eyes, like needles, scanned the group.

"Okay . . . This is the way it's goin' down. Me and the undercover police group of thirty, acting as mourners, will follow the coffin to the gravesite. Sniper teams will be in place two hours before. When the killer shows himself, the sniper team can take him out. If for some reason, they miss and he makes it to one of the storm drains, we have two officers ready to go down and flush him out. When he comes out the other end, we'll have a team of officers waiting at des Peres."

He turned back, with a smirk.

"Piece of cake . . . Any questions?"

"Who're the snipers?" Pop asked.

"We'll decide who does what right now. I want Kraut with a long gun because of his experience. Pop will be his spotter . . . They will be team one. Who else is a hunter? Breed, how about you?"

"Hunted bighorn sheep since a young brave," he said.

"Yeah, but with something other than bow and arrow?"

"Of course."

With that, Micky stepped to the side, unlocking a metal cabinet. He pulled out two 306 bolt action rifles mounted with Bausch and Lomb scopes and handed them to Kraut and Breed.

Breed took his with a confused look, grabbed it by the barrel, holding it up like a baseball bat.

"This sure is a funny-lookin' club." The whole room busted ·up, releasing the tension flowing through the room.

"Just funnin', sarge." He grinned. "I'm a crack shot."

"Well, to be sure, I want you two at the range this afternoon to practice. It's my ass, I mean my head, that's hangin' out here. . . Breed, Cheeks is your spotter. You're team two."

"Who's goin' down the hole?"

"Spook and Grezer already volunteered. They're shorter and skinnier. They'll be with me at the grave-site so they can move in either direction to the two drains."

"Spook's perfect. He'll be invisible down there," Kraut quipped.

"Yeah, if they need a light, all he's gotta do is open his eyes," Pop added.

"And if he smiles, we'll have high beams," Grezer piped in, giggling.

Spook shot back, "At least you can squirt through the tubes first and grease the way."

"Ho-ho, good one," they all chipped in.

"All right, pipe down. We still got a lot to cover."

"Sarge, are these the only drain openings the killer can use?"

"There's only one more but it's over the edge of the hill down on the access road about two hundred yards down. He can't get to it because his attack has to be from the opposite direction."

"Sarge, we want this guy as bad as you, but this plan sounds like a military operation and we know what happens with those. Something gets fucked up."

It can be a real FUBAR, Sarge.

A few of the others, nodding their agreement, knew Micky was going in harm's way and the killer, so far, had outsmarted them at every turn.

"It'll work, don't worry about it. I have twenty officers to take care of traffic and outer perimeter problems plus thirty officers volunteered to be in the mourning party. They'll be right next to me, armed to the teeth."

"Sarge, what about me?" Dago said.

"You're gonna handle the end of the drainpipe at des Peres.

I'm assigning six blues to help. This guy's so slippery, I think he just might make it to the drains . . . Spook, Grezer, I want you to scout the drain this afternoon so you're familiar with it. I was told it was five feet around and not much water."

Micky leaned forward, elbows on the lectern.

"Guys, if the rain is heavy tomorrow, we call the whole deal off."

With the meeting over, Micky and the team walked over to the patrol squad room and met with the uniformed officers and briefed them on their roles. That finished, he made arrangements to close the road into the cemetery after the procession entered to prevent civilians from wandering around. This also would prevent the killer from driving onto the grounds with a getaway car.

That evening, Micky and Kathy ate a quiet meal. Kathy was miserable, still not wanting him to go. She couldn't remember not wanting anything so much in her life. Even her son joining the navy wasn't this bad. But she kept quiet. She already voiced her opinion and he knew she was upset.

She sat there, playing with her food, knowing there was nothing else she could say as tears rolled down her cheeks.

Micky watched her sadness and took her in his arms. He didn't want to do it either, but this was the best option. He promised he would be careful because he had something important to live for, his wife and child.

They went to bed early and held each other. Finally, she dozed off. Her adrenaline finally drained leaving her exhausted with worry and dread.

Micky stared at the ceiling wondering if he was a fool.

CHAPTER 64

G HOST READ CYNTHIA'S
cover story on the sergeant's
brother several times, not believing his good fortune. He would
have another opportunity to avenge his sister and what better
place when the sergeant is standing at the gravesite of his
brother.

He rechecked the time. Tomorrow morning, he had a lot
to do.

Finishing his coffee, he crawled out of his hole and slipped
into a phone booth.

"Good morning, Resurrection Memorial Park, may I help
you?"

"Good morning. Yes, I need some information. I will be
attending the graveside services for Father Michael Delaney this
Saturday, but my flight will not arrive in time to be part of the

funeral procession. Would you give me your address and grave plot number so I won't get lost?"

"One moment, sir."

"Sir . . . the entrance is at Watson Road and Kenrick. The plot number is one, six, three, four. When you enter the park, you will see small signposts on the right side of the roadway to help guide you. You should have no trouble finding it because it's the only service we have scheduled that morning. Just look for the crowd."

A half-hour later, Ghost drove through the cemetery checking the site to design his plan of attack. After parking the car, he walked to marker 1634 and stared into the freshly dug grave. When his arrow struck, he thought, perhaps the sergeant's body will fall in the hole on top of his brother. Smiling with the thought, he turned slow, letting his eyes scan the entire area.

He immediately recognized a problem. The tree line was too far away to make a hundred percent accurate shot. He strolled over to several gravestones large enough to hide behind, checking distances to the target. Then, he walked over to the access road, locating the two storm drains. He finally picked a gravestone close to the road giving him a chance to escape.

He paced the distance from the gravestone to the target at seventy-five yards. A simple shot. He paced the distance from the gravestone to the closest storm drain at forty yards. It would take six seconds to cover the open ground and four seconds to get down the drain. The confusion after the arrow struck the sergeant in the head would easily spend the ten seconds.

Still, he didn't like the setup. He missed the cover of the jungle.

He stood, thinking, looking closer at the grave-site. The mound of dirt to the side was covered with a green grave blanket that looked like grass. Apparently, he figured, the blanket was used to disguise the mound of brown dirt making the area look clean and neat.

From there, he walked to the edge of the hill and looked down, noticing the other access road about two hundred yards down. Past the road it was another two hundred plus yards down to des Peres.

Glancing around, making sure there were no curious eyes, he strolled down the hill to the access road. As he suspected, there was a storm drain in the dip by the curb.

Climbing back to the top of the hill, he stood at the crest, looking toward the empty grave. He guessed the distance at fifty yards, twenty-five yards closer than the gravestone he decided on. Unfortunately, there were no large gravestones on the slope but there were a few smaller ones about two feet high and two feet wide.

Not high enough to hide behind but he had a plan to solve that problem.

Ghost walked slowly back to his car as a plan started taking root. He drove along the access road, circling down to where he found the storm drain, drove past the maintenance shack, and smiled.

He had the perfect plan and escape route.

CHAPTER 65

S ATURDAY MORNING, 7:00
AM, the Doom team and the
full contingent of officers involved in the operation reported
to a VFW hall for final instructions. Micky didn't want to meet
at the precinct, knowing some cop with a big mouth might slip
and reporters would show up.

Forty-five minutes later, the plan was laid out and each
assignment was reviewed.

"Guys and gals, this is it. please be careful. Do not take any
chances."

"What about you?" someone quipped from the back.

"Hell, I'm not takin' any chances," Micky shot back. "I got
damn near fifty cops watching my ass."

"You mean head," another shouted from the back.

"Maybe he's got it stuck up his ass?"

The whole room whooped.

"I'm just glad I'm not standin' next to him," another added.

Micky knew that copper would be front and center throughout the whole operation.

"Okay, okay. Let's hit it. I want everyone in position by zero eight thirty."

With that, the room emptied. Everyone looking forward to the hunt.

* * *

Earlier, at two AM, that same Saturday, under a bright moon, Ghost parked on Kenrick Road just outside the cemetery. He hopped over the short decorative stone wall, heading for the maintenance shack. A second later, the padlock was snapped off and he was inside grabbing a couple grass blankets. By the door, he found tent stakes, a spade, a small hatchet, and threw them in a small canvass bag.

Twenty minutes later, he stood at the ridge of the hill, looking at the serene view. The cemetery lawn, green and lush, glowed against a full September moon, a hunter's moon. Except for small gravestones here and there, the sloping hill stretched clear and barren all the way to River des Peres. He guessed the total distance to be a quarter-mile, no more. He also verified the distance of the access road to be about two hundred yards, in the middle between the ridge where he stood and the river.

He stilled a moment, listening to the night silence as a few clouds hung around in the windless sky.

"Today will be a beautiful day for a death," he whispered low.

Ghost blew a breath, grabbed the spade, and went to work. Turning, he faced the priest's gravesite and backed down the hill until his waist was even with the level ground of the target site. Then, he started digging in front of a two-foot gravestone. The night was cool and the earth soft. The work felt good as he shoveled, calming him, reviewing his plans for the kill.

A half-hour later, he had a hole two feet deep, six feet long, and three feet wide. He carefully placed the shovels of dirt around the edges, giving him a raised berm of about six inches. Standing in the hole, he turned to face the target. His head was now level with the crest of the hill. Anyone standing at the grave-site looking in his direction would only see a small two-foot-high gravestone.

Gabriel, the Ghost, would be invisible to anyone standing at the priest's grave-site.

His field of fire would be perfect. He could almost make the shot blindfolded.

That done, he walked down the hill to the road and pried up the cast iron grate to the storm drain, making sure it was free. Lifting the edge, he twisted it over a half inch, catching it on the lip of the road so he could quickly slide it aside to disappear down the drain.

Walking back up the hill to his hole, he placed one edge of the grave blanket along the lip and pinned it down to the ground with the tent stakes. Then, he stretched it over the hole, staking it tight on the opposite side.

Finished, he stood back, checking it in the moon light and smiled. It looked like a freshly filled grave.

Placing the spade and hatchet inside his hole, he grabbed the second grave blanket and walked down the hill about a hundred yards in a straight line toward the storm drain.

He stopped at another gravestone, looked back up the hill, gauging the distance from his hole to where he was standing. He double-checked, making sure the gravestone was centered between the hole he dug and the storm drain.

Satisfied, he unrolled the grave blanket and spread it out, covering the grave in front of the gravestone.

He checked the time. It was 4:00 AM.

Walking back up to his hole, he grabbed his jacket, deciding to take a break. Sitting on the gravestone, he pulled a sandwich and a small carton of orange juice from his jacket pocket. As he ate, he felt the night silence and some peace, sitting alone, surrounded by the spirits of death. These were the souls the archangel Gabriel would call forth when announcing the end of the world for God's final judgment.

He sighed, bringing his thoughts back to his dear sister Angel. He missed her deeply. He wanted to be with her. He knew he would join her soon and welcomed that time.

Suddenly tired, he stepped down into his shallow hole to catch a few hours' sleep. Laying on his back, he stretched the grave blanket over the hole and hooked it over the tent stakes. By his side, his binoculars, bow and arrows, stood ready.

At 5:00 AM, a light drizzle fell and water trickled into his hole, getting him muddy and soggy. It was irritating and chilled him, but not a problem.

He suffered much worse in Vietnam and the bayou.

CHAPTER 66

THE DAY BROKE dreary, unusual this time of year. The early drizzle left a murky mist of foreboding that would shiver the superstitious. But the police team stood, excited, at the command post like hounds at a foxhunt, waiting for the blast of the bugle.

The fake funeral services at St. Mary's went off without a hitch. The thirty officers, mostly men with a scattering of female detectives, played their roles perfectly. All were appropriately dressed in dark suits hiding a variety of weapons, ready for war.

As planned, the hearse loaded the empty casket in a covered alcove providing no opportunity for an ambush. The drive to the cemetery in the hearse with dark tinted windows again offered a stalking killer nothing to target. And, at the cemetery, everyone huddled around Micky, providing a human shield, escorting the casket to the brother's grave-site.

Micky limped along, the sod wet and gushy, his single crutch sinking in the ground. His eyes roamed the area, nervous, checking every gravestone, expecting the killer to pop up like a "Jack-in-the-box". Glancing to the tree line, he knew he could not see the sniper teams so he lowered his head, keeping his eyes lifted, sweeping the area.

There was nothing ahead but the peaceful setting.

A few birds complained while morning rabbits hopped away in the lazy mist hiding in the hollows from the early sun. Limping along, his eyes settled on his brother's grave-site just ahead, where he agreed to be a bull's-eye target.

He took a deep breath. Well, he thought, so far so good.

* * *

In the tree line, a hundred and fifty yards away, team one, Kraut and Pop, were in position. They spread the tarp and laid prone, facing the target grave-site. They exchanged grins, knowing they held the high ground with an excellent field of view.

Pop, the spotter, lay, resting on his elbows, kept sweeping the area with his ten-by-fifty binoculars with a three-hundred-and-fifty-foot field of view. He had to admit they were in a great location, elevated above the grave-site. Looking down on the whole area, he saw the backside of every large gravestone, including the two storm drains.

* * *

Seventy-five yards away, to the left, along the curve of the tree line, Breed and Cheeks, team two, enjoyed the same luxury.

If that asshole showed, he was a dead man.

* * *

Dago led his team to the ditch, River des Peres, assigning positions to snatch the killer if he came out the drain.

Everyone there hoped he would.

* * *

Spook and Grezer walked along with Micky. They wore long dark coats to cover the jumpsuits underneath if they went down the storm drains. Both saddled a GI web belt strapped with a sidearm, knife, gas mask, flashlight, and a tear gas grenade.

The group of mourners, reaching the grave-site, spread out, formed a half-moon shield around Micky in front of the grave, facing the ridge of the hill.

Pallbearers placed the coffin on the rollers and pushed it over the rectangular dug grave.

The priest, a friend of Father Mike's, started the service. Mourners, heads turned down, eyes lifted, scanning and searching.

Micky could feel their energy waiting to explode.

* * *

Laying in his hole, Ghost was mud-soaked from the drizzle.

The grave blanket created a sauna as he heard the group approaching the gravesite. He forced himself to wait for the priest to recite some prayers before pushing the grave blanket aside, raising like a dead man, seeking is kill.

Lifting his eyes to ground level, he smirked, reaching for his binoculars to make absolutely sure. With everyone in dark clothing, at this distance, he wanted to be certain there was no mistake. He knew from the newspaper, the sergeant injured his hand and leg when the brother was shot, but he didn't know how bad.

With a quick scan of the group, Sergeant Delaney's face filled the lens, with a crutch and a bandaged right hand, his head turned down in prayer.

An easy kill.

Ghost felt a rush of pleasure as the hunter spirit flowed through his veins. The man that killed his sister would now die.

It was a perfect time.

* * *

The four members of the sniper teams continually scanned their area of responsibility. With the target gravesite as home plate, the semi-circle view of the hundred and fifty-yard space in front of them was as good as a center field seat at Busch stadium. The four cops swept the area with their binoculars and riflescopes. If a field mouse twitched, they'd spot it.

But the area was barren, not even a bird.

Frustrated, Pop swept his glass up to the grave-site and the backs of the cops hunched around the Micky. He wondered if this was going to be a big waste of time.

Just then, a speck of glare caught the upper edge of his lens. Lifting his binoculars, a tad, his heart jumped to his throat.

The killer was in front of the grave just over the ridge of the hill, looking at the sarge with binoculars.

"Jesus! Kraut, the fucker's in front, over the hill!"

Kraut swung his rifle up, trying to pick him up.

"Where? I don't see him!"

"Fuck, ya got him. Shit, move your scope up to the ridge. He's right in front of the gravesite at the ridge line," Kraut cursed, knowing a rifle scope had a very narrow field of view making a target difficult to locate. that's why a spotter was necessary.

"Shit, Kraut, ya got him?"

"Fuck, gimme a better reference point," Kraut said.

"Shit, he's gone. He's by the small gravestone on the ridge of the hill. Pick up the sarge and lift up a notch about fifty yards out . . . Ya got him?"

*　　*　　*

At the same time, Ghost disappeared, lowering to his hole to grab his bow and arrow. Still stooped, he nocked the arrow in the catgut and stood, slow and sure.

No one at the grave-site noticed the mud-smeared face seemingly rise from the earth. They also would not see the upper end of the camouflaged bow and the man-killer needle-arrow.

Ghost, pulled the bowstring back, slow, deliberate, focusing all his training, all his ability, all his concentration. He felt the tickle of the turkey fletching against his cheek and smiled, letting his curled fingers unfold.

* * *

"I got 'em, I got 'em," Kraut yelled, watching the killer rise, cocking his bow.

"Shit."

Kraut, seeing the killer ready to release, squeezed off a shot before he was ready. He didn't get the split second to set up. Yanking the bolt, he jammed another round in the chamber, centering the scope.

"This time the fucker gets one between the eyes."

* * *

Kraut's first steel jacketed round slammed into the gravestone a split second before the bowstring left Ghost's fingers. The exploding rock chips caused the arrow to miss its target, burying into the empty coffin.

The top of the gravestone exploded like a grenade, splattering rock slivers like needles into Ghost's face, stabbing him in a dozen places. The tiny barbs stuck like arrowheads and one, like a dagger, pierced deep in his left eye. His left hand, the one closest to the gravestone, was mangled by the stone barbs causing him to drop his bow to the ground.

He cursed, jerking back in pain, hearing the yell of the police mob. Spinning around, he dove out of his hole as another round from Kraut's rifle whizzed past his head. Stumbling to his feet, Ghost ran, bent over, down the slope toward the storm drain, wiping the blood from his eye with his good hand. The slivers held like fishhooks; the gravestone was just steps ahead.

In five strides, he ran around it, ducked down, and disappeared.

* * *

When the arrow hit the coffin, Grezer and Spook charged forward to the ridge. Spook got to the crest of the hill first and spotted Ghost dodge around a gravestone heading for the storm drain. With a yell, he plunged over the side in hot pursuit, the others close behind.

In seconds, they circled the manhole resting on its lip. Without a word, Spook jerked off his coat, slid the grate back and scrambled down the iron ladder with Grezer close behind.

* * *

Left alone at the grave-site, Micky stood with his crutch and hobbled over to the ridge to see the gang huddled around the storm drain. He looked down at the hole the Ghost dug, spotting the spade and hatchet. On the other side, lay the empty carton, a paper bag, binoculars, and two arrows. By the hole, to the side, lay Ghost's bow peppered with blood.

Just then, the two sniper teams, running full out, pulled up at Micky's side.

"What the fuck's happenin'?" Cheeks asked.

"The rabbit's on the run. Grezer and Spook went underground to flush him out." Micky said.

"Fuck, I missed him," Kraut said.

"Shit, you saved my ass. The guy was right under our nose, right where we didn't expect," Micky said, his mind working.

"Kraut, Pop, you go to the right and work your way to des Peres. He might be able to give Dago the slip by coming out somewhere else. Breed, Cheeks, you take the left. On your way down, tell those guys at the river to spread out. The more eyes we got lookin', the better our odds."

"What about you, sarge?"

"Shit, I'm okay. I got a grandstand seat."

The four hustled down the slope and few minutes later, Micky was alone on the hill, now dead quiet, hoping for the best.

* * *

Under the grave skirt in front of the gravestone, Ghost laid flat, still as the alligators in the bayou. Listening close for the slightest sound, he hugged the wet ground allowing himself the smallest smile, knowing the diversion worked.

Last night he intended to escape down the storm drain, but when he pried the cover-up, he realized it was too obvious. The newspaper reported his escape in the dead-end alley when he killed the stockbroker, and although they did not say how he disappeared, he knew they figured it out. Sergeant Delaney would assume he would escape the same way.

So, when he rounded the gravestone, he slipped under the grave blanket he laid out, and they ran right past him to the storm drain.

Ghost forced himself to lay still a bit longer. His face sticky wet with blood. Every touch of the rock splinters pulled and yanked at his flesh. Finally, there were no sounds, no voices.

Time to go.

* * *

From the ridge line, Micky watched from the high ground as the officers became smaller and smaller moving toward Des Peres. He'd give anything to be down there with them. He hated to miss the chase. As he watched, a movement by a grave down the hill caught his eye. The lump slowly started rising from the earth like an evil spirit.

"Shit, what the hell's that?"

The lump grew larger.

An eerie feeling crawled up his back with thoughts of the undead rising. The lump rose higher, tall as a man. He stared, transfixed. Real fear shook him as he stared at the grave blanket cloak, covering the unknown.

Thoughts of the underworld shook Micky.

"Damn, it's the Grim Reaper."

Then, he watched the earth cape slip off the figure that slowly turned and faced him.

A chill raised Delaney's neck hair, staring at the wet, muddy hulk with blood dripping from its face. He froze, unbelieving, as the zombie, caked in blood and mud, started climbing the hill toward him.

Micky watched the blood-caked face locked on with a snarl and passion for the kill. The glint of the skinning knife, clenched high in his hand, readied for the fatal slash.

"Shit, the fuckers got me cold," he said, fumbling for his two-inch colt with his left hand.

* * *

Ghost slowly stood, wrapped in the cloak of the grave blanket, watching the officers run toward River de Peres.

He smiled knowing he fooled them all. He would leave and try again.

Turning around slow, squinting against the early sun, his breath stopped, spotting the man figure standing alone at the crest. He wiped his blood-smeared face with his good hand, realizing it was him, Sergeant Delaney, his sister's killer, the prey he hunted. He dropped the grave blanket cape to the ground.

Blood rage surged through his body in a rush of pleasure as his nose, flared, sniffing the air. He felt no pain from the barb in his eye or cut ligaments on his hand. He was numb to all except the rapture of the kill. Without thinking, his good hand moved to the skinning knife, the knife of his father, gripping it high like a coveted jewel. Ghost felt his saliva flow in hunger as his scrotum pulled tight between his legs.

His body, mind, and spirit demanded the kill.

He moved forward to his destiny.

* * *

Micky's mind jumbled. He couldn't outrun the fucker. He never shot with his left hand. Micky's eyes locked on the knife. Stooping to one knee, he braced his arm on top of the gravestone, cocked his two-inch Colt and squeezed off his first shot.

He knew he pulled the shot. Fuck, maybe I can scare the shit out of him. He fired again.

Ghost stepped to his left.

Damn, he knows I'm pulling my shots. Calm down, ya dumb shit. You just need one good one.

Micky aimed a little right of the killer, compensating for the finger pull, and fired again.

Again, Ghost dodged left, moving ever closer.

"Shit!"

Micky could see he was hurt, watching him trudge slow but sure up the hill. He saw blood dripping from his face and saw him wipe it from his eye. Micky panicked, steadied his arm on the headstone, pumping the last three rounds at the killer.

He felt a rush of relief watching the Ghost spin around and go down. But then, fear shot back, watching the bloody, muddy body slowly rise, continuing toward him.

* * *

When Spook and Grezer exited the storm drain at the river, Micky's first shot twisted all the officers around to the distant hill. The next shot sent a chill, realizing the killer was at the gravesite, and Micky was alone. They started running back thinking about his bum foot and hand. Spook and Breed judged the distance about a quarter-mile, all uphill. If they were lucky, they could make it in a minute and a half, two at the most.

They took off, running the race of their lives, leaving the rest to follow as best they could. Their feet sunk into the rain soaked sod with each stride, making it feel like running in wet concrete.

Already huffing, they thought the same. Hold him off, sarge, just give us two minutes.

*   *   *

Micky threw his gun down, looking around for some kind of weapon and spotted the hatchet in the hole. He dropped his crutch, went to his knees, reached down, and snatched it. Damn, he thought, no way I can go man to man with this guy with a bad foot and flipper.

Micky watched his executioner moving ever closer, dragging his leg, his face twisted in a snarl of rage. Wet and plastered with bloody mud, he was like something from hell. The stone splinter, like a small arrow, sticking out his eye, made him look like a dead thing possessed by the devil. His one black eye locked on Micky, his mouth muttering in madness.

Micky grabbed his crutch and scrambled back. He had no plan. He didn't know what to do, gnawing fear gripped his guts.

He couldn't think.

He hobbled to the other side of the coffin, still resting on rollers over the empty grave. He needed something to hold the fucker off until help came. He saw the guys running back up the hill. He needed to hold him off like a lion tamer with a chair or something.

Peeking around the corner of the coffin, Micky watched the ghoul stop at the top of the hill, his one good eye, searching.

The blue sky circled behind the killer. Micky believed he truly looked like the messenger of death.

* * *

Plodding up the hill, Gabriel, the Ghost, smelled Micky's fear and felt pleasure. When the bullet punctured his thigh, it spun him around, knocking him to the ground. But his body, like a dead thing, felt no pain and he rose again, limping, climbing ever forward, Reaching the crest, he stopped, scanning the area. The sergeant was gone. Spitting a glob of blood, he caught movement by the corner of the coffin.

He smiled, raising his knife.

* * *

Hiding behind the casket, Micky gripped the hatchet in his left hand, reaching for the crutch to get to his feet. At least he would face the asshole, making a last stand.

Trying to get up, pulling the crutch, he suddenly, had an idea.

Reaching down, he twisted the rubber cushion off the bottom of the crutch and started chopping the end like sharpening a pencil. In four swings, he had a good point. This might keep the asshole at bay until help arrived. He pushed backward to get more space, trying to get to his feet. At the same time, he wondered which end of the coffin the fucker would come around.

Scooting back on his butt, he heard an animal snarl of hate.

The Ghost, smelling his prey, jumped to the top of the coffin and crouched, staring into Micky's eyes.

Micky, backpedaled in a panic, watched the figure loom above him like the demon from hell.

Possessed with the fury of a wounded animal, Ghost, throwing his head back, howled his hate and in the next instant, eyes crazed, he leaped through the air like a rabid wolf, arms wide, his blade curved like a giant claw.

Micky yelled, yanking the crutch, point up, braced against the ground, to hold him off. The Ghost, dropping with his full weight, hit the point of the crutch just under his breastbone, piercing through his gullet into his lung.

Ghost's scream of rage and pain echoed through the graveyard.

Micky rolled to the side, scrambling to his feet. The Ghost, squirming on the ground, growling, pulled at the crutch as Micky slipped the curved top under his armpit, and leaned down with all his weight, twisting it deeper, pushing with all his strength. Ghost bowed, arching back, thrashing, gaffed to the ground like a landed shark.

Flailing, he jerked against the crutch, mouth frothing, bubbling blood.

Ghost's screams of rage filled the air.

Micky held on, hammering down with all his weight, like staking a vampire.

Spook and Breed reached the top of the hill, hearing the Ghost's eerie wail. With a glance to the other, they charged forward, rounding the coffin, heaving for breath, hand guns at the ready.

They froze.

Ghost's body, twitched in spasms of death, his mouth gushing blood like a fountain.

Finally, with a last snarl of hate, his body shuddered its last, relaxing, surrendering its soul to hell.

Micky leaned on the crutch, slamming down with all his weight, unaware they were there.

"Die, fucker, die!"

Spook put his hand on Micky's shoulder.

"It's done, sarge. He's dead."

Micky, turned with bright eyes, noticing them for the first time. With a relieved breath, he let his arms drop from the crutch and slumped to the ground, sucking gulps of air.

He felt sick, fighting back dry heaves.

Finally, his mind grasped it was over.

The fear for this invisible killer he harbored but denied, flowed from his body like a poison. Suddenly, for the first time since his brother's attack, he felt free and safe.

"Shit, sarge, ya speared him with your crutch!"

Micky, looked up from the ground into Spook's face, and for the first time in a long time, he didn't have a smart-ass comeback.

Shit, he thought, I must be getting old.

CHAPTER 67

A S THE CROWD of officers poured around the scene, the Doom squad took control. They allowed everyone to pass and see the killer pinned on his back by the crutch. There wasn't one that didn't shudder or wince at the bloody body still holding a snarl of hate, looking like it may come alive at any moment.

The tales would be long and tall tomorrow.

EPILOGUE

"HI, ARE YOU Margie?"

Margie looked up at a smiling hulk of a guy.

"Yes?"

He handed her a large sealed envelope and said, "Sgt. Delaney asked me to deliver this file to you personally."

"Oh? Well . . . thank you."

She wondered if this was the famous missing file he was asking about. She glanced up. He was still standing there.

"The sarge told me to stick around until you reviewed it to make sure it was the right one."

"Oh, okay, why don't you have a seat. Can I get you a cup of coffee?"

"No thanks," he said, moving to the chairs along the wall.

Margie tore open the envelope full of curiosity. She pulled out the brown file folder, opened it, and read the following:

> Margie, just a little note to say thanks. I survived because of you. Thought you might like to know that the big lug delivering this package is a teddy bear. He's also lonely and shy.
>
> He loves children more than anything else, and he's one of the best men I know. Take another look at that mug sitting there, and if you're interested, turn the page.

Margie put her hand up to her mouth to hide her smile, looking over at Kraut. He was shuffling through magazines, but looked up, returning her smile.

Margie turned the page.

> I knew you were a wise woman. His name is Karl Shultz. Notice it's almost lunchtime. The next step is to thank him for bringing the file and ask him if he would do you a favor. When he says yes, you tell him you were just going to lunch, but there was a scary guy that had been following you and you'd really appreciate it if he would walk with you to the restaurant. At this point, he will turn beet red and probably start stammering because he won't believe his luck. If you're still on board, turn the page.

Margie had a hard time holding her giggles, feeling a nervous flush suddenly flow through her body.

Quickly, she turned the page.

> Lass, your good sense and brilliance amazes me. Go to lunch at Riley's. It's just two extra blocks. They are expecting you and have a surprise. When you're walking over there, ask Karl if he saw the article in the paper about the little girl that was hurt falling from the cliff. I predict that is when you will start to fall in love.
>
> Good luck. Your friend, Jack.

Margie placed the file back in the envelope, looked up at Karl and smiled.

"Is it okay?" he asked.

"Very much so. Officer, I wonder if you would do me a favor?"

On the way to Riley's, she asked him about the little girl that was injured, and sure enough, she started falling in love.

Riley greeted them personally, ushering them to quiet booth in the back.

"Ahh, and what a lovely couple you are. How long have you two lovebirds been married?"

Kraut turned as red as Riley's neon sign and Margie giggled.

When they explained they weren't married, he said, "Well, surely, you're engaged. I can see it in your eyes."

"Not yet," Margie said, also turning red but feeling brave.

When lunch was over, Riley did his usual, the same he

did for Micky. He brought over a small cake with one Candle, placed it on the table and said, "To celebrate the first of many anniversaries. Enjoy."

Micky watched Kraut cross the squad room to his office walking two feet off the floor. Handing Micky the file, his smile was so wide, Micky knew it must hurt. When he opened the file folder, there was a note from Margie saying, "Thanks."

He couldn't take all the credit. Kathy helped him with the plot, and he couldn't wait to tell her how clever and devious she was.

He thought Suzie might be a bad influence on her.

*　*　*

Dago was hooked. Micky paid Kathy the ten bucks.

*　*　*

Pop, Julie, and her son, Billy, were quickly becoming a family.

*　*　*

When Kathy was taking a shower, Micky jumped up on the bed, unscrewed the globe on the light fixture, and quickly wrapped the thin rope around the bracket. then he jumped down under the covers, trying mightily not to giggle.

Kathy came out of the bathroom starring in shock at the trapeze hanging over the bed as Micky peeked from the covers.

"Thought we'd start with lesson number one of my male fantasies," he said with a shit-eating grin.

Kathy started giggling as Micky reached over and pulled her into bed and made love the old-fashioned way. Later, resting on their backs, Kathy studied the trapeze, considering the possibilities.

"Do you think we could?" she asked.

"Jeese, woman, you're worse than me." he laughed.

"Well, if this is lesson number one, I can't wait for the final exam."

Micky realized he'd met his match.

Kathy and Micky moved the wedding date up for obvious reasons, and five months later little Micky came into the world. Micky thought he was a handsome lad, like his father, and carried a fistful of pictures to prove it.

Life was good.

*   *   *

Micky, sitting in his office, looked out toward the squad room, watching his guys doing cop stuff. It was eight months since the Ghost series and things were back to the normal routine.

He sighed, gathering his papers and started to take a sip of Mabel's coffee, but it sounded like it was fizzing. He decided to take it with him and wait until one of the guys took the first swallow.

His phone rang.

"Sergeant Delaney."

He listened without comment as Captain Barnes briefed him.

"Okay, we can be there in fifteen."

Micky went into the squad room and knocked on a desk to get their attention. His men turned, sensing the hunt.

"We got a hot one at . . ."

THE END

Join the *Doom* team as they hunt a female murderer that kills in a special way in.

"Die, Mother Goose, Die"

jimmalloy-author.com

CPSIA information can be obtained
at www.ICGtesting.com
Printed in the USA
BVHW080024180223
658738BV00013B/1023/J